THE
ACTOR?

THE ACTOR?

A Thriller and Love Story at the Height of the Cold War

LEE WELLING

www.bookstandpublishing.com

Published by
BOOKSTAND PUBLISHING
Morgan Hill, CA 95037

4434_4

Copyright © 2016 by Lee Welling

All rights reserved. No part of this publication may be reproduced or transmitted in any form or by any means, electronic or mechanical, including photocopy, recording, or any information storage and retrieval system, without permission in writing from the copyright owner.

Cover images Copyright © Shutterstock, Copyright © Can Stock Photo Inc./Perysty, and Copyright © Can Stock Photo Inc./rup.

ISBN 978-1-63498-363-1

Library of Congress Control Number: 2016943769

Printed in the United States of America

July 2016

To SUSAN,

who, when told that I was starting my writing career in my seventies, never said, "Are you crazy?"

And

For anyone who has ridden the ups and downs of a career and/or family relationship rollercoaster—from success to failure and then back to success again—this book is for you.

Lee Welling
New York
Cape Cod, Massachusetts
2016

Preface

The decade of the 1950s was the beginning of the Cold War with Russia. Words like "red scare", "the bomb", "duck", "roll-and-cover", and "backyard air raid shelters" entered the American vocabulary.

American spies, such as Judith Coplon and Ethel and Julius Rosenberg, were arrested, tried—and in the Rosenbergs' case—put to death.

In 1959, Fidel Castro led a *coup d'état* and became the leader of the Cuban government. With Cuba only 90 miles from the United States' mainland, Cuba became a puppet government of the Soviet Union and a major concern of the U.S. administration.

1962 brought U2 spy planes flying high over Cuba and jets flying low over Cuba to take pictures of missile silos and underground bunkers storing nuclear warheads.

So began "The Thirteen Days in October." President John F. Kennedy gave an ultimatum to Russian Premier Nikita Khrushchev to remove the missiles from Cuba. It was a tense time for both countries, and the world came close to a nuclear war.

The one question never answered was: *What was the initial information that prompted the United States to send U2 spy planes and low flying jet aircraft over Cuban territory?*

That reason has never been known—until now.

THE ACTOR?

CHAPTER 1

THE CRUISE SHIP

This place is a dump. I have been sailing around the Caribbean performing watered-down Broadway shows on a cruise ship called *The Regal Fantasy*. Some kind of name. It isn't regal, and I can't believe anyone would call it a fantasy. Not much has been done to fix her up since she left the shipyard and started sailing to Caribbean ports twenty years ago. What a way to end up. I had an acting career spanning many years and affording me all the finest things in life. No matter how horrible it is now, I will never give up fighting to get back on top again. The question is, will anyone still be listening to me?

For twelve months in 1979—and approximately six years previously—I had been entertaining 1,200 passengers three nights a week, two shows each night. It is hard to believe that 20 years ago, I, George L. Toomey, was the biggest star on Broadway, commanding the highest salary of any performer. I was once told that Ethel Merman's agent made sure her salary would never be lower than mine. That says it all about my ability to command a top salary.

I guess I should be happy. Considering what I went through and how I ruined my career, I should be thankful I have a job. Besides my performances, I am also required to be on the entertainment staff of the ship. Every Saturday, I must say goodbye and/or meet and greet all of the passengers getting on and off the boat each and every week. After all these years, I should be using the correct vocabulary. Let me start again. I say goodbye and/or meet and greet all passengers (not getting on and off) but *embarking* and *disembarking* from the *ship*.

Can you imagine—when I was the star of shows playing at the Shubert, Majestic, Imperial and the St. James Theatres in New York— if I had to stand out front and meet and greet the audience, point the way to seats, and, of course, answer the most frequently asked question of theatergoers: "Which way to the bathrooms?"

That's about all the interaction I get with the passengers each week. I eat in the crew dining room, and, to relax, I swim in the pool reserved for the crew and entertainers. I do get all my meals for free, and my room—excuse me, my cabin—is cleaned every day. Each Saturday gives me the chance to socialize with others who don't work and live on the ship.

I guess I'm being a little negative. After all, it isn't *that* bad. Many a Saturday, women who were sailing with their families liked talking with me. While mundane, given the circumstances that forced me from Broadway to a boat—sorry, ship—these conversations were great for my ego. All actors have big egos, and sometimes these egos can ruin many a thing. Ego caused many of the problems in my life.

George L. Toomey is my real name, not some phony stage name that was created to fit on a marquee. Actually, I am George L. Toomey II, but I dropped the second and my middle initial "L" when I first came to New York. I have been using the name George Thompson aboard ships all these years. I will explain the need to use two last names later.

When talking with some of the female passengers on embarkation day who had other ideas in mind, quite frankly, I was a willing participant. In just a few minutes of talking with these female passengers, the conversation would turn to a more professional topic. Since they knew I was an actor appearing in the ship's shows, they believed I could help them. They were quick to tell me their daughter or son was the star in their college shows. They had no idea of my

Broadway background, nor that the advice I would be giving them wouldn't be worth a damn.

"Would you be able to give me some advice on how to break into show business and how they can get started as an actor in New York? Any advice you can give me, I will be indebted to you," was the common refrain.

By then, they had my attention, but the next was the kicker: "Anything you want from me just ask. I will pay you anything. In fact, if you can spare some time out of your busy daily schedule, I would meet you in your cabin to get the advice from you personally."

My busy schedule. What a laugh. All day, I sit around the pool eating and drinking. I've gained 20 pounds in the past six months. With the exception of Saturdays, I don't work until nighttime, so I have a lot of time to give out advice.

In the past, I slept with many of my leading ladies, and I always loved talking with them about acting and giving them advice on their careers. For the mothers aboard the ship, I'd say, "If I can help a young person with their career, it gives me pleasure. To give advice to their mothers—it also gives me pleasure."

The knocks on my cabin door sometimes came fast on Saturdays. Many times, I had just returned from my meet-and-greet responsibilities and had no time to change my clothes, nor to straighten up my very small cabin. I guess the visitors didn't care much about the size of my cabin, nor if it needed straightening.

Then, I met Ingrid, the nurse on board, and everything changed. She is a wonderful and a lovely lady. She is nice to everyone, even when no one is looking. I care for her very much. The last thing I wanted to do was ruin this relationship, like I have done with so many other relationships in my life in the past. If the clock could only be turned back, many of my relationships would have been different or would have never happened at all.

THE NURSE

I think I may be a hypochondriac. If I have a gas pain in my chest, I think I am having a heart attack. If I get lightheaded, it *must* be an irregular heartbeat, causing me to think I will faint. If I have pains in my legs, it *must* be a tumor. If I feel sick, it *must* be a serious illness. For the past two days, I have felt lightheaded, and I wonder if I am going to faint or something worse. This time, I am not going to tell Ingrid of my newest complaint. I think she has heard enough complaining from me.

Let me tell you more about Ingrid Jameson, the Norwegian nurse aboard the *Regal Fantasy*. She has become important to me, and, in time, I'm sure she'll become important to you as well. She comes from a small town called Alesund, north of Bergen, Norway. She always tells me that if one wants to hide out where no one can find you, Alesund is the place.

Ingrid had a very tough life. When she was a teen in Norway, the Nazis took over the country. Her father and several of his friends belonged to the Underground. Living near Bergen, many were commercial fishermen. Three days a week, they would transport Jews by boat from Bergen and then out of the country. They made regular runs to England, based on the phases of the moon, in the pitch black of night.

All the fishermen knew that if they were caught, it meant certain death to them and severe punishment for their families. They did it anyway. One early morning, around three, the S.S. broke into Ingrid's house and took away her father. The putrid smell of cologne permeated the leather of the S.S. uniforms these sub-humans wore. The stink of those soldiers—who hadn't bathed in days—will probably remain with her a lifetime.

It took years for Ingrid to forget the cries of her mother, who was taken to the bedroom down the hall and raped repeatedly while Ingrid's father was dragged out of the house and into the waiting cars of the S.S. Ingrid never saw her father again. Ingrid, her mother, and her younger brother left Alesund and spent the next years on-the-run and in hiding. Friends throughout Norway took them in, without any questions asked, nor showing any concern for the danger. She learned about evil, and she learned about goodness in those dark days. Both have made her who she is: a healer who steals people from the jaws of death. Even on this ship, she sometimes sees more than a sunburn, skinned knee, or seasickness.

With so much death and cruelty in Norway during the Occupation, Ingrid was devoid of feelings. It was very hard for her to think of love or develop any close relationships with anyone. Although she had no training, she helped nurse many of the wounded back to health. When the War was over, Ingrid realized she wanted to enroll in school in Oslo and make nursing her career.

For many years, she worked in Oslo's finest hospitals. Then, it was time, as she likes to say; she was ready for a change in her life. With all of her nursing experience, she felt she could find something different in her field. Reading about the growth of the cruise industry in the decades after the War and the need for medical staff on all of the new ships, she thought it would be an exciting experience. Never in the same place on any day and the ability to travel all over the world sounded interesting. Being a nurse on board a ship seemed to be just right for Ingrid at this stage in her life.

Although I was on the *Regal Fantasy* for a year, I started seeing Ingrid about ten months ago. She treats passengers every morning in the ship's hospital for their pains and ailments. She is also on-call if there is any medical emergency during the day. She spends the rest of the day with me. She brings me seasickness pills, and, if I put out my back, she brings me muscle relaxants. She is just what the doctor ordered: a perfect girlfriend for my existence. It is like having my own private nurse to take care of all of my aches and pains.

There is not much to do every day on this damn ship. There is plenty of time for wonderful lovemaking. I'm not sure if I have anything to do with it, but Ingrid is very much at ease taking off her clothes and seeing me naked. I guess it is all those years of nursing school and being at ease treating patients who are completely undressed.

I love looking at her beautiful blonde hair. I can honestly say she is one of the first women in my life who really cares for me. It is difficult for me to say, but I think I am falling in love. Throughout the last six months, our relationship has steadily grown.

We don't have much time before my contract is up. I am returning to New York in three days. I must make a big decision. Will I tell her about my past? How I ruined my career, the reason my wife threw me out, and how I lost my relationship with my daughters? Then, there is the explanation of what actually happened on my government-sponsored cultural exchange tour nineteen years ago to end my Broadway career.

I even wonder if Ingrid has heard about all the women visiting my cabin before she came aboard the ship. Once, it wouldn't have mattered if anyone knew anything about my multiple affairs and sexual encounters, but, now, it does. I care for her, and I don't want to hurt her.

The ship will spend two months of the summer in New York but sailing to Bermuda every Saturday. When we finally dock in New York, I will leave the ship for the very last time. Although I am ready to leave, I really want Ingrid to come with me. I realize it is impossible, because her contract runs through the summer. She doesn't want our relationship to end, but I can't see how it can continue. She is at sea every day, and I will not be aboard. When she has her next leave from the ship, she plans to visit Norway. She wants me to come and meet her surviving family. I can't force myself to tell her I can't afford to buy a ticket to Norway. For someone who has flown first class all over the world for business and pleasure, not being able to even buy a ticket in coach now is hard to take.

Maybe we can make it work. I could see her on Saturdays when the ship docks in New York. After two months, if I can get some commercial work, I could scrape together enough money to buy a plane ticket to Norway. I keep asking myself, why ruin this beautiful relationship?

Thinking about all of this makes me feel sick again. It could be the waves. The seas have been a bit choppier than usual this week, but I'm sure it is really just nerves. I used to feel those nerves before a big show. Of course, there was excitement mixed with that too. In this case, however, it is only nerves.

I have always lived in the theatre fantasy and world of make-believe. When I was a boy in the early thirties, I would stand in front of a mirror in my room and sing songs from current hit Broadway musicals, imagining myself as that character. Now, when I have to make a tough decision, I put myself in a character from one of my shows and think how I would solve a particular problem. I've been getting lost in too many shows lately, and, at times, I have no idea what I should do. Life isn't Broadway, although Broadway is still my life.

The trip back to reality must begin now. Ingrid and I might have to settle for the memories of our beautiful relationship. I will be with her until I leave the ship, except for a couple of hours a night on stage. No matter what happens, I must concentrate on what I have right now, tonight, and the three remaining days we have together. But can I?

It is eight decks up to the theatre. Since I don't get much daily exercise, I like to walk the stairs. The walk is good for my heart. The first show went well, although it is quite depressing to perform for the audiences on this ship. They are tired and have had too much to drink or too much sun during the day. Many of them end up dozing off and sleeping through most of the performance. Of course, without much reaction from the audience, the show moves along at a quick pace, leaving me more time to be with Ingrid.

As I am taking my bows at the end of the second show, the feeling came over me. You know what I have told you: irregular heart beat and the feeling that at any moment I am going to faint. I am fighting it, fighting it, but it is getting worse.

Right in the middle of the curtain call, I feel I am falling through space. The spotlights are blinding me.

I BLACKED OUT.

CHAPTER 2

CURTAIN CALLS

20 YEARS EARLIER

They are screaming, yelling, and cheering from all over the theatre. The spotlights are blinding me, so I can't see all the faces in the back rows. I am certain many are out there, including standing-room, but I have no idea the size of the audience. The show has been sold out for years, and today, I assume, sold out again. I received three curtain calls, not bad for a Wednesday matinee, but not the eight curtain calls I received on opening night.

Each performance, when the curtain comes down at the end of the show, I like to stand behind it for a few minutes and listen to the orchestra's exit music. This is the way I unwind after a show. However, today, I am in a rush. I'll have to hurry back to see a visitor in my dressing room, and then on to an early dinner at Sardis with my agent. Matinee days are always such a rush.

It is seven blocks to Sardis. I wish my theatre were closer, like the St. James Theatre, practically next door, and then there wouldn't be such tension running back and forth all the time.

I have made sure my dressing room is filled with memorabilia from almost every show I have ever performed in, including pictures of my first shows in high school. On the coffee table is the latest issue of *Variety*. On the front page is an article of how Kermit Bloomgarden, the producer of *The Music Man*, has tried to get me to perform the title role of Harold Hill for more than four years.

In it, the reporter recounts the tale of Kermit Bloomgarden offering me the original role of Harold Hill in *Music Man*. I had told him the show would never play well in New York. All of the sophisticated theatre goers would never accept, nor be interested in, a story about Iowa farmers and townsfolk all up in arms over forming a kid's band. It would seem I didn't know as much as I thought, because it won the Tony, beating out *West Side Story*. Mr. Bloomgarden has also talked to me about starring in the national company of *Music Man*. When it tours, I'd get to perform before thousands of people who would otherwise never know my name. He says Hollywood would come calling, because I would be building up my fan base. It would be an impetus for Hollywood producers to think twice about finally offering me the roles I created on Broadway.

That is what Bloomgarden says, but, really, what do any of us know about much of anything in our subjective industry? Right now, I know I'm enjoying wild success, the company of most of my leading ladies, and a wonderful apartment with a view. I understand, too, that just as putting me in front of people across the U.S. would expose them to me, it would also take me away from the New York scene. I've learned that a leading man is easily forgotten, and an audience can be fickle. If I were to disappear for a year—or even more if I got in the movies—how could I ever get back on Broadway? Just the same, I'll take the time to meet him.

I prepare to quickly jump into the shower, but, first, I must send a message to the stage doorman to let Kermit Bloomgarden know I will see him in just a few minutes. I make the call, get in the shower, washing as quickly as I can, and then get out just as quickly. Very little is leisurely in my life right now, and I'm fine with that. I am wrapped in a towel and drying off after my shower when my co-star, Jenny, also wrapped in a towel, barges into my dressing room.

"George, let's stay here between shows? I would love you to see what is under my towel." Her hair is still twisted on her head, and her towel is provocatively low. She follows my gaze and then smiles up at me, letting her towel teasingly slide down another inch. "I have two big surprises for you."

Jenny has two of the biggest breasts on Broadway. Although I wouldn't mind enjoying what lies beneath the towel, I can't take the time today.

"I have to meet David, my agent from William Morris, for an early dinner and then rush back for the evening show," I explain.

"Why?" she whines. "I haven't been alone with you for a while, and I need you. Can we please plan to be together at the end of the evening performance?"

"We'll see, Jenny," is my quickest answer. She rewraps her towel, momentarily flashing me as she tightens it and lifts it higher. She is incredibly beautiful, but also incredibly spoiled. Her pout is like that of a three-year-old, rather than that of a grown woman. It is her least attractive quality and, thankfully, helps me forget her offer and prepare to meet my guest.

I put on my slacks and am buttoning my shirt when I pick up the intercom to tell them to send Mr. Bloomgarden back.

"He's already on his way, sir."

"Okay, thank you," I say, and then hang up the phone. I'm tying my shoes when I hear a tap at my door.

"George," Kermit Bloomgarden says, "It is so great to see you."

"And you too, Kermit," I say.

We talk about the show and its current run, but, being a business man, he quickly shifts to the reason for his visit. "George, if you will agree to play Harold Hill on my national tour, I will suggest to the film producers that they offer you the screen role in *Music Man*."

I didn't want to be rude to one of the biggest and most important producers on Broadway, but there was no way his offer would really help me or my career. "I made one film in Hollywood, and the critics hated me," I started. He sat up straighter, clearly surprised by my revelation. "I came back to New York with my tail between my legs."

"When was this?" he asks, scooting forward in his chair.

"It was a while ago. I like it here, but, more importantly, there is no way the powers in Hollywood wouldn't offer the role to Robert Preston." This meeting is over as far as I'm concerned, but I have to let him be the one to close it. He hasn't moved from the edge of the chair, holding a pose that reminds me of that statue "The Thinker." The more he thinks, the more I feel time tapping its second hand at me, like a nervous man does his toe.

"Well, okay then," he says, standing.

I see my opportunity. "I have to run for an early dinner meeting, so I really want to thank you for the offer—but let's say I promise to star in your next Broadway musical."

"Of course you will, George." He smiles. Kermit says goodbye, and I finish dressing for my meeting at Sardis.

Table #1 at Sardis is always reserved for me. Above the table is my framed autographed caricature. I love all caricatures of me, especially the ones drawn by the famous artist Al Hirschfeld. I was quite proud of having five Toomey drawings appearing in the theatre section of the *New York Times*. David was already seated, and I couldn't wait to hear about the matter that was so important that there was no way we could discuss it on the phone—and we had to meet on one of the busiest days of my week.

"George, how was the matinee?"

"Good show. Had three curtain calls."

"That's damn good for a matinee," he says. He's paid a percentage of my salary and a percentage of the gross I receive. So, more curtain calls for me adds up to more money for him when he negotiates my next role. I realize he is more excited for himself than he is for me, but it doesn't offend me.

"David, you wouldn't believe who I met with just before I came. Bloomgarden came back stage today to ask me again to take the *Music Man* out on tour."

He looks at me, but doesn't seem that interested. What he has must be *really* big if Kermit Bloomgarden didn't get a reaction.

"Didn't he read this week's *Variety*?" David asks, coming out of his momentary trance.

"He has a new offer. If I agree to the tour, he would ask the powers-that-be to offer me the role for the film." David and I laugh simultaneously, but David is the first to speak.

"George, you are good, but Preston has it in the bag."

"That's almost exactly what I told him," I say. I sip my drink and lean back. As if on cue, David begins to speak about the reason for the meeting today.

"Mr. Toomey?" interrupts a woman, who looks to be about twenty, standing beside me with a pen and small notebook in hand. "Could I please—?"

Before she can finish talking I take the notebook, scribble my autograph and say, "What is your name, young lady?"

"Ava," she says, smiling.

I write *To Ava* above my signature and hand her the notepad. She thanks me and walks back to her table.

"Okay. I got a call from Alan J. yesterday. Lerner and Loewe are writing a new musical about the Knights of the Round Table. They would like you to read the script and hear the music when it is finished. It is another year or so before it will hit the boards. I told them we would be very interested in getting the script and hearing the score."

Okay, that is good, but it doesn't explain this sudden meeting. "Send them to me when you get them," I say, hoping he'll take the cue and tell me why I am really here.

"There were a couple of other offers, but I don't want to waste your time today."

"Okay, then don't." I force a smile, but I am losing my patience. I could have had food delivered to my dressing room, enjoyed two great surprises—compliments of my leading lady—and still had time for a nap in the time it has taken David to tell me about a manuscript that is getting sent to him.

"George, I need to talk to you about something else."

"I had hoped." My tone is a bit sharper than I'd intended, but David doesn't seem to notice, so I don't mention it.

"I've been contacted about an offer you will love."

"Then let's get to it," I say, looking at my watch to remind him of the time. It really isn't like David to give so many introductions and explanations about a single project. He is building it up to be something that I'm sure can't measure up to the hype he is creating.

"We have talked so many times about how Broadway stars are hardly ever offered their Broadway roles for the Hollywood film. The list is long. Julie Andrews in *My Fair Lady*, Ethel Merman in *Annie Get Your Gun*, Alfred Drake in *Oklahoma* and *Kiss Me Kate*, just to name a few. I have solved the problem for you. Never again will you be turned down for a role you have created on Broadway."

"Are you kidding?" I respond. "How?"

"I had a call from the State Department. They are well-aware that Broadway musicals are an American art form, not able to be recreated anywhere else in the world. *Pajama Game*, *Damn Yankees*, *West Side Story*, *The Most Happy Fella*, *The Music Man*, *South Pacific*, *Carousel* and *The King and I*—all created by Broadway composers and writers," David says, pushing his plate to the side.

"Why is the State Department interested in Broadway?" I ask. This conversation is now taking a very odd turn.

"They want you to star in a Broadway musical revue tour. You would visit England, Russia, and other European cities. Stopping in Russia would be a great step in advancing relations with Russia and the United States." He looked at me expectantly. I am not entirely sure what he expects, so I make no reaction, and he keeps talking. "With things heating up between the two countries, this would be a great diplomatic coup. Under the heading of an artistic exchange program, you would be the toast of Europe and Russia."

I don't object in principle with the idea of being an international celebrity, but I still haven't caught David's enthusiasm. How is going overseas any better than what I'd been offered in my dressing room an hour ago? The same concern is still there: out of sight, out of mind.

David continues on, clearly not distracted by my lack of enthusiasm. "The tour would last for six months, and, when you get back, we won't have any problem getting you a new Broadway show."

"I'm not clear how that all works," I say. "What about touring in Europe guarantees I'll be on Broadway and in Hollywood?"

"The way it was explained to me, the government is having a very difficult time getting important information out of Russia. You, being a big American Broadway star, would be able to receive and take out documents important to the government. You would be in no danger; it would be simple maneuvers," David says.

"That doesn't answer my question." Then, what he says starts to sink in deeper, and I really hear what he's saying. "Although it does create a few more questions in my mind."

"Now for the exciting part. I was told, in strict confidence, that if you agree to go on the tour, the Secretary of State would arrange quietly to finance the Hollywood films of your shows."

The government will finance the films? It wouldn't be about my talent, but, instead, it would be about my backers. The idea only momentarily offends me, because the truth is that much of success is a combination of talent, hard work, luck, and funding.

"You know what this means, George?" David's voice pulls me back to the present and our conversation. "You would star in films. For participating, your future acting career in Hollywood is all but assured. You won't need Kermit or the studio heads or anyone. The studios need funding. You'll have the bosses of the studios in your back pocket." His voice rose slightly with excitement, "It is the dream we have both talked about for years. You have nothing to lose."

"David, the offer seems too good to be true—and you know what they say, 'if it is too good to be true—'"

"'—it isn't,'" David cuts me off. "It *is* true, George. It *is* true"

"So, how would this work," I ask, slightly more interested, but still not entirely convinced.

"Once I give the green light, sometime next week, a representative from the Government, a Franco Livingston, will visit you backstage to discuss your role in more detail. You know, cross the T's and dot the I's." It sounded very simple, which is why I wondered how my level-headed agent had been so duped.

"David, I guess it is hard for me to understand why the government would make such an offer," I began.

"George, our government works in strange ways. Let Franco explain in more detail at your meeting next week. You will be as excited as I am," David assures me. "George, this is a great opportunity to star in future Hollywood musicals."

I nod and stab a piece of meat with my fork. "So, David, how is your family? The kids okay?"

He has been my agent long enough to understand that I need to get back to the theatre. He begins to answer, his eyes focused on his plate, but, before he has completely answered my question about his family, I cut in and say, "I need to finish dinner and hurry back to the theatre."

It is going to be very hard to finish dinner with all of the fans coming over to the table to ask for an autograph. On matinee day, they are all in Sardis: Hal Prince, Bobby Griffith, Leland Hayward, George Abbott, and Jerry Robbins. Then, there is always David Merrick. His office is a couple of doors down the street. He is always in Sardis. I try to avoid him—he hates actors. However, if he wants me to star in one of his musicals and meets my salary demands, I will learn to like him.

David and I eat quickly, neither of us talking. I am interrupted only four more times by autograph-seekers. The State Department offer continues to confuse me, but it is growing on me, too. I know there are no guarantees in life, but, with me as a front acting in films and the State backing films and dictating terms, no one in Hollywood would turn me down.

I finish eating and have them wrap up the little bit that remains. I will eat it later if I'm hungry before the evening show. I must head back to the theatre. The walk always slows me down with people stopping and asking to pose for a picture. On the seven-block walk back to the theatre, I will have time to contemplate the offer from the State Department. Would it be good for me to get out of New York? Would it be a good career move?

It is difficult to forget David's words.

The toast of Europe. Creating a new fan base that has never seen me perform. Having financing for a future Hollywood projects in my back pocket. Doing something good for my country.

And as a Lucky Strike Extra, I would get a breather from the continual pressures of having to perform sexually with my leading ladies. All in all, it seems to be a good move. Even though I begin the mental preparation for the evening's performance, I think about the offer. Kermit was going to put in a good word to Hollywood—one they'd ignore. David is offering me a guarantee; something unheard of in this difficult industry. More importantly, it will solve a problem that has dogged me all these years. So I guess David was right, I have nothing to lose.

CHAPTER 3

FRANCO AND GINA

TWO WEEKS LATER

I was cautiously optimistic waiting for the pending visit from Franco Livingston, but it was impossible to hide my excitement. I had so many questions to ask about this program and why they were doing it. The government had made a very generous offer, which caused me some serious concerns. Why was I getting myself involved?

Outside my dressing room, cast members chatted, and the stagehands put away all of the scenery and props. At any moment, someone could knock on my door, because I was constantly in-demand. It is nice to feel like people want you around and value your opinion. Some people got obsessed with the attention. I'd seen it destroy them because their ego made them impossible to work with or, even more tragically, it became an addiction to them, and, during the periodic wanes of attention they turned to overspending or drinking to give them the feelings they craved. They destroyed their voices, ruined their health and, ultimately, their careers.

My mind turned back to the offer, and I mulled over how valuable it truly was. I love the stage, and I love the comfort with my familiarity here. However, the idea of finally being able to star in a film of my show was an offer I couldn't refuse.

The next two weeks were uneventful. I did sixteen shows in those two weeks, so when I say that they were uneventful, what I mean is that nothing new happened. My life is rarely, if ever, without some form of activity. It keeps me away from home a great deal, but I try to make it up to my daughters on the days when I don't have a performance. I also bring gifts home with me and leave them on the kitchen table when I get home late at night. It feels good to be able to provide the girls with a good life.

I will certainly be leaving the stage for the movies on a high note. Each of those sixteen shows was a sellout. As always, I brought down the house at every performance, which is always a good feeling. The work can be tiring, but the exhilaration of the applause at the end helps me push through.

When I was new to the theatre, I sometimes got tired at the end of a show—but I don't let these long runs wear me out like I used to. I've built up endurance, like anyone else who gets used to a demanding job. Except for a bad cold that affected my singing for a couple of days, my performance was as strong as ever. I had another reason to be on my top game. I wanted to be sure that if anyone from the government program was watching, they'd be impressed. After each night's show, I wondered if it would be the night Franco would show up. But, night after night, I went backstage, and there was no one waiting.

Tonight was no different. Saturday performances require more endurance, because there is a matinee and an evening show. I followed my usual routine of lunch and a break between shows, but Franco didn't show up between the two. After the Saturday evening performance, I went back to my dressing room and shut off my intercom to the stage door man's cubicle. This run would be over soon, and I still hadn't heard from this Franco guy who was supposed to meet with me. I tried not to let it worry me, but, since I was waiting on him, I didn't have my next project lined up yet. I had other offers in the wings, and, for a moment, I considered calling my agent to have him put together a contingency plan, but I knew that this was the best offer I'd get.

I rested on my couch, trying to motivate myself to go home. Lately, I'd seen less and less of my family. We all ran in different worlds. When the girls were younger, they were excited to see me on the weekends before I left for the theatre and on the occasions when I'd had an afternoon off, but, now, their lives were getting busier. They were old enough to catch cabs, ride the subway, and go visit with friends. When I came home, the place was often as empty as this dressing room. We were still happy to see each other, but sitting here today, I realize that it has been more than nine days since I saw them for more than a couple of minutes in passing, when someone was coming or going.

There is a knock on my dressing room door. I get up and open the door. When I open the door, a very tall, good-looking man stands in the doorway. He smiles broadly at me. "George," he says, extending his hand immediately, "I am Franco Livingston."

"Hello, Mr. Livingston," I reply, thrilled to finally have him here and get my mind on a new show.

"Please, call me Franco," he insists. I step to the side and allow him to come into the room.

"Please, sit." I say, gesturing to the sitting area in my dressing room.

"Sorry I didn't tell you I was visiting tonight," he apologizes, walking to the area, but not yet sitting. "I just flew in from London and didn't have the time to call you in advance. I hope you will forgive me?"

"Of course," I assure him. "There is nothing to forgive. I'm just thrilled to have you here. Can I get you a drink?" I walk to the bar in my dressing room and make a drink for myself.

"I will have whatever you're having," Franco says, watching me. "Are we able to talk in private?"

I look around, confused. Then, I see my dresser organizing my costumes. I am so accustomed to him being there I hadn't even noticed. I'm not sure if that makes me a jerk or not, but it is the truth. I ask my dresser to leave us alone, and I prepare Franco's drink and carry both of our drinks to the sitting area.

Franco takes the drink from me and begins to talk. "You already know that I'm from the government." He sips his drink. "I am responsible for organizing and setting up everything on the tour. Your agent at William Morris has told the State Department that you are willing to star in our Broadway revue tour."

"Yes, it sounds like a great opportunity and a way to create an entirely new fan base."

"Can I give you a bit of advice before this tour?" Franco asks. He doesn't have the slightest bit of ego, which is a nice change from most of the theatre people you get used to working with on a daily basis.

"Certainly. I have learned that one true key to success is to always listen to the director and respect them for their expertise."

It was something my early theatre instructors told me, and it has served me well over the years. I watch some of the newer actors come to Broadway assuming that it is talent alone that will make them great. It is an important piece. Without talent, there is no point. But you also have to make the others feel valued—even if you're acting when you do it—or they won't advocate on your behalf. The key is to make people like you by making *them* feel liked.

"This tour will be a very rewarding experience for you, both personally and professionally." He looks around my room at the various mementos, awards, and letters. I wonder for a moment if he is impressed or just curious. Before I have a chance to ask him, he begins to speak again. "In Europe, you will have exposure to an audience you have never had before, and most have never seen you."

"That is a definite benefit to the trip." I think about the European ladies who might be interested in meeting an American actor. I also consider the rumors I've heard about European women—particularly the French and Italian women—and I hope that we'll be offered time to explore on this tour.

"Russia will be a little trickier," Franco says, breaking into my thoughts briefly. "Although the U.S.S.R. has agreed to sponsor this cultural exchange tour, relations with our two countries are at a low point." He leans forward, his eyes quite intense, and I am glad that this man is helping my career and not interrogating me. "Now, with Castro taking over Cuba, there is a lot of tension between our CIA and their KGB. The Ministry of Culture, secretly backed by KGB, is setting up this cultural tour, and, since they have just started working with Castro in setting up security and forming a new Government in Cuba, the relationship between the KGB and CIA is, to say the least, a delicate situation."

"I don't care much about who was in power in Cuba or what the government in Russia thinks," I reply.

"If I had my choice, I would rather have had Batista still in power, but it is too late. Maybe Castro won't be there long, and we won't have to worry about a threat ninety miles off the Florida shore. But the future of Cuba will have to be decided on by more senior officials than me." Franco's smile was broad, but something in the depths of his eyes tells me clearly that this is certainly a point of contention for him. Franco has clear passions and opinions about this topic.

"As long as the audiences in Russia love me—that is all I care about," I say, trying to lighten the mood a bit. "Of course, it wouldn't hurt if the ladies in Russia loved me, too."

Franco smiles at my remark. "Yes. That really is all that matters in our case, isn't it?"

We are both quiet for a moment, and I realize that I don't know much of the world outside of the theatre. I guess that also makes me a good candidate, because I don't have a long string of political speeches or pet causes that could make me a potential threat to either side. I'm really not interested in all of the political stuff that goes on. Theatre, food, wine, and ladies are my passions. Leave the governments to others.

"I know you will probably have quite a few questions," Franco says, reaching down in to a leather briefcase and pulling out a notepad. "But let me answer a few questions I'll assume you have first, and then you can ask me anything else. Is that fair?"

"Absolutely," I reply, again pleased that he is so well-organized and knowledgeable.

"I am sure you're wondering three things. Why you? Why in these countries? Why now?"

In fact, I hadn't wondered these things at all. I was more concerned with storyline, production schedule, and my level of input on the production, itself, but Franco seemed focused on these other points, and I realize that I should be, too.

"George, we need your help." He unfolds a small map of Europe and the western portion of the Soviet Union. I looked down at the various borders and capitals. "As you travel on the tour—especially in Russia—I need you to handle messages and documents in the form of microfilm given to you."

"Why me? Why do you want me, of all people, to receive messages?" The idea was a bit intimidating, but it was also a little exhilarating. What was it about me that made me the right candidate to help them in spy work? I suppressed a smile.

"You see, as a famous American actor, you will be able to move around Russia more easily than anyone else from our country," Franco began. To be honest, this was the direction I hoped the answer would take. "No one will be watching you closely, and you will be able to pick up the microfilm and give it to my liaison traveling on the tour. It is the same type of atmosphere we experienced with the Bob Hope tour to Russia."

He loses me there. Bob Hope is an amazing entertainer, but also a very wholesome one. I guess I thought my image was a little more on the daring side than the trusting side. This time, I *do* smile a little, but more at my own thoughts than at what Franco is asking.

Franco smiles back. "Mr. Hope did not help or receive messages for the government, but, on many of his visits to the Soviet Union, he was able to move around freely and visit many areas in Russia that are off limits to most foreigners."

"I wondered," I say. "I hardly think of myself as being of the caliber of Bob Hope."

"I will always look out for you and take care of you," Franco assures, completely ignoring my comment. I really like this man. He has a way about him that really intrigues me.

We sit quietly for a few moments, letting his last statement hang in the air. Franco's face is completely unreadable—I mean completely. It isn't serene. It isn't reflective. It is as if he is sitting there with nothing to think of. I wonder if I ever look that way to people. His non-expression is quite unsettling to me, because of what he has said. I would like to know why I would need him to look out for me.

"When you say you'll look out for me, do you mean you'll be one of my handlers?" I ask, assuming that he will, most likely, deflect my concerns. "Do you mean you will take care of all arrangements—because you come across as a man who is far more than a simple lackey who follows actors around."

"Perceptive," he says, smiling. "I am CIA."

"I thought so!" I am thrilled not only by his status, but also by what that status means for *my* status. I am much more than simply an actor. I am a *spy*.

"I approve covert acts and the dissemination of information," Franco begins, and, as he speaks, I already I feel myself being pulled in his inner circle. "My whole career has been spent in undercover and furtive activities."

"That must be very exciting," I say, realizing that I sound a bit like an enamored woman.

"The same is said of what you do, George." And he's right.

"It is wonderful, but there is a routine and monotony that sets in after a while," I confess.

"And the same is true for me," he says. "In the Second World War, I was in the OSS stationed in Italy. In 1947, when the OSS closed down and they opened the CIA, I moved to the CIA and worked my way up to the number two man on the ground in Europe and Russia."

"So you are far more than a secretary for a group of actors," I say.

"Well, yes and no," he answers. He has a warm personality, and I genuinely like this man. "While my title is very impressive, the reality is that because of that title, there are times when I am assigned to help with the itinerary of a group of actors. Working intelligence is more about moving paper than it is shooting bad guys."

"I am still very impressed and glad to be a part," I respond quite sincerely. Inside me is the same sensation I felt when I landed my first Broadway role. It is a wonderful mix of vibrations in my chest and tightening in my gut.

"Well, it is quite late," Franco concludes, "and my body is telling me it is six hours later than it is."

"I appreciate you stopping by."

"Certainly. Thank you for the drink," he says, setting his glass on a coaster on my table. "I will be back with all the plans for the tour. The liaison for the tour will be in New York shortly and will visit you after one of your performances."

"Do you know which one?" I ask, not wanting to spend another week or more waiting for a knock on my dressing room.

"Her name is Gina Marie."

"A woman," I say. I know that women are moving into more jobs that have traditionally been held by men, but I am still surprised that we are being coordinated by a woman.

"Yes. She is a very capable agent." Franco's admiration is apparent. "Oh, a few more things."

Franco lists a few more details, handing me sheets of paper one-by-one. I am a bit surprised, but I didn't have more questions. It all seemed fairly clear.

"Everyone associated with the tour is looking forward to working with you," he says, extending his hand. "I'm pleased the government will make an investment in helping you to further your Broadway-to-Hollywood career."

"Thank you. That means a lot."

"I hope I will be invited to see your next show and the premiere of your Hollywood film."

His last statement sealed the deal. If I had had any doubts about this tour or staying with it to the end, I now knew I would complete it all. This trip is going to change everything for me.

Gina Marie

Gina Marie spent several days sightseeing and shopping when she arrived in New York. Franco set her up in a very nice place and authorized a very large expense account. She loved New York for many of the same reasons she likes Firenze. New York has the excitement of a large city, the convergence of different cultures, and a variety of architectural styles.

However, New York also has a singular modernity that she hadn't seen in Europe, where youth is defined in centuries or millennia, rather than decades. It has only been two days since she arrived, but she has experienced so many of the sights and sounds of the wonderful town. The only one she hasn't done yet is Broadway, which is where she is headed to now. Her prime reason in coming here is not sightseeing, but to meet George Toomey and discuss various aspects of the cultural exchange tour.

Hopefully, he will be as nice as the characters he portrays and not the egotistical stuffed shirts she has encountered at other times. She will be spending a great deal of time with *The Actor*, as she refers to him, and if this mission goes well, Franco will have much more in store for them both. It was Franco's love of Toomey that led to his being selected for the cultural exchange.

She walks to the "Will Call" window. A perky woman with platinum blonde hair sits behind the glass, flashing a bright red smile that is as fake as anything else in New York.

"There is a ticket waiting for me for tonight's performance," Gina tells the blonde.

"Certainly. Your name, ma'am?" Somehow, she manages to speak without losing her smile.

"Gina Marie."

The woman moves to a shelf a few feet from the window and looks through files. She turns back with a smile and a small white envelope. "Here you are, Ms. Marie."

"Thank you," Gina says, taking the ticket and putting it in her purse.

There is a poster to the left of the window, and she notices again how good-looking George is. It is no surprise that he is a big star on Broadway, nor that he has a reputation with the ladies.

Gina goes back to her hotel, eats dinner, and dresses before taking a cab to the show. When she enters the theater, she thinks about how many times over the next couple of months she will sit in an audience and watch George.

The lights go dark, the overture begins, and the curtain rises. She watches Toomey deliver a brilliant performance. At the end, she stands with the entire audience to cheer and yell "bravo" at the stage. Looking around the theater, Gina cannot recall seeing such universal admiration for a performance or a performer, even at the dozens of operas and plays she has attended since childhood. Franco had been absolutely right. Toomey is an undiscovered gem who will dazzle Europe and the Soviet Empire. This man is *exactly* what they need for the mission to be successful.

As the audience starts to file out, she walks to the front.

"Hi," she says to a man who seems to be guarding the pass through door. "My name is Gina Marie. Mr. Toomey is expecting me."

The man looks her over and smiles. She doesn't like what his look implies. If this man's reaction to her is any indication, the rumors of Toomey's womanizing are true. He looks away long enough to glance at a clipboard.

"He certainly is, Miss Marie," he says, opening a door. "William, show Miss Marie back to George Toomey's dressing room, would'ya?"

William's expression is similar to the expression of the man with the clipboard. While a fine actor, Gina thought, they certainly would have their work cut out for them to be sure that his hormones don't jeopardize the mission.

She is shown back through a group of people and around a corner. The door to his dressing room is open, so she taps on the doorframe and announces herself.

"Hello, I am Gina Marie."

***

At first, I can only stare. She is the most gorgeous Italian female I have ever seen. She is wearing a low-cut sweater that is so tight I am able to make out each curve and ripple of her delicious shape. The hem of her skirt is inches above her knee, and I'm certain when she sits down that I'll be able to see almost her full leg. Her lips are full and beautiful, with only the slightest pout, but it is her eyes that hold me. They are at once seductive and intelligent. She is beautiful; she clearly knows it and understands the power that comes with beauty. It is a mystery how she could make it through the streets of New York in such an outfit without being accosted. I'm also not entirely sure she'll make it out of my dressing room without me at least *trying* to see what is underneath.

"George Toomey? It is wonderful to meet you."

She speaks my name in perfect English, laced with the ripples and rolls of her native Italian. It sounds like music on her tongue. I cannot recall when I've wanted someone or something as bad as I want Gina Marie at this moment.

"And likewise, you, Gina Marie." I step back and motion her to my couch. She, however, walks past it, opting for the chair on the other side. When she sits, as I had suspected, the skirt slides even higher, and I struggle to suppress the groan of desire that threatens to erupt from my throat.

"I loved your show," she says, sitting now with her hands neatly folded in her lap. "It was wonderful. I am thrilled that you are part of this mission."

Every muscle of my face is pulled tight in a smile, and, try as I might, I can't wipe the expression off of my face. She is radiant, and she loved my show. It was as if I'd won a Tony. "I am so glad you liked it."

We begin talking about the show and the theatre in general. She wasn't brought on for her looks, as I had initially supposed. Gina is quite knowledgeable about theatre past and present, American and European. I could have been talking shop with any producer or leading lady.

"Now, we need to discuss a bit more about the mission." She pauses and raises her hand to her lips. "The tour."

That's right. She isn't a leading lady or any producer. She is an agent sent here to talk to me about exchanging intelligence and other spy things.

"We will all meet in London, rehearse several weeks, and preview the show in the West End," she began, removing a small notebook from her purse. "In London, you will meet with Franco and several friends, who will explain his plans in more detail. Then, it is on to Russia, where we will be spending four weeks in Leningrad."

"That sounds great." I am genuinely happy that I'll have the opportunity to work with Franco throughout this tour.

"I am looking forward to working with you," she says.

"Likewise," I reply, leaning back.

There is no question: I am looking forward to working with Gina. In fact, I couldn't wait to start. Looking at her, I now know that no matter what Franco wanted me to do on this tour, I am a willing participant.

"So, Gina," I begin, ready to move to the next level with her. "Will you be in New York for a while? We should have dinner?"

"I will be in New York a short while." Her emphasis on the word "short" didn't dissuade me. Not all women fling themselves at me. "And, then, I go back to my home in Firenze, Italy, but I don't think it would be a good idea to meet for dinner."

"Gina, we both have to eat, so why not dine with me and tell me more about the tour?"

"Sorry, not now." She puts her notebook back in her purse and zips it shut, before looking at me firmly. "If it is any consolation, we will have plenty of time for dinner during the next six months of the tour."

"True." Yes, she clearly knows the power she has over men and is an expert at using that power. She leaves just enough hope to make me follow. This makes me want her even more.

"I will be in touch with you soon to give you your script, documents, and further instructions," Gina concludes, leaning over and kissing me quickly on both cheeks, like Italians do when greeting and saying goodbye. I definitely wanted a better kiss—and not on the cheeks, but the brief contact is like a jolt of electricity, just the same. It looks like I'm not going to have as easy a time with Gina sexually, but that doesn't mean I'll quit trying. I have six months to win her over.

CHAPTER 4

WAITING

I spent so much of my early career waiting: waiting to get into acting school, waiting in line to audition, and, of course, waiting hundreds of times to see if I got the part in a project. Now, I was at the end of my latest Broadway show, and I would have to wait a month before I would leave for London to begin the tour. Waiting wasn't anything I enjoyed, and these days, I rarely had to do it. Since I had to wait, and I'd be gone from home for months, I planned to make the most of this downtime to catch up with my family and all the other things I'd always promised myself I would do but that I never got around to doing.

The highest thing on my list was spending time with my wife and two daughters. For all these years, I have been appearing in shows— eight performances weekly with rehearsals, acting, singing and dancing lessons in between— and giving interviews with the press, as well as having clandestine meetings with my costars, which took nearly all of my time. I barely had free time for anyone, let alone free time to spend with my family.

As my career grew, having time for my family on Sundays became a problem, too. Sundays were the days other shows on Broadway had performances for those less fortunate in the Industry— the Actors Fund performance. I attended these Sunday shows, leaving my family and meeting up with other performers for drinks, dinner, and after-show parties. As I think about the last few years, I begin to realize how little time I'd spent with any member of my family. Even less of that time was spent together as a family. Even our Cape Cod house on the beach that once served as our family escape was now more of a place where my wife and kids went to escape the City or where I went to entertain producers and costars. It really wasn't a family retreat at all anymore.

I determined that all of that was about to change this month. I am ready to make up for lost time and devote every spare moment to my wife, Carol, and our two girls, Missy and Jody. They really are the loves of my life. Theatre is my career and my passion, but those three ladies are my love. I'm excited about making this month special. We will go out to dinner in the evenings; I will take the girls to movies and, maybe, take Carol as well to spend some time together. We can do a few weekend excursions, and then, the last weekend of the month, we will go to the Cape Cod house as a family, like we did when the girls were little.

I called and made dinner reservations and told the doorman to be ready with a cab at 6:15. Then I waited for everyone to get home. So waiting began again for me; waiting for the girls to come home from school. At 4:30, Carol got home, but the girls still weren't here.

"I have a reservation at seven," I say, when Carol says she is going out.

"Well, you should have told me, and I would have told you that it would be impossible tonight," she responds, without the least bit of sympathy. "Jody has sports after school, and Missy has study group. They aren't usually home on Tuesdays until at least 6:30."

I guess I didn't think to check their calendar first. I stay calm, but some of my excitement is waning. "Should I make the reservations later?"

"Of course not," she snaps. "They have to be up for school in the morning, so they need to be in bed at 9 PM."

"Then what will they eat?"

"Whatever I bring home," Carol responds, the matter clearly settled in her mind. She walks out of the bedroom and down the hall. I follow her, irritated by her brush-off.

"What about tomorrow? I could—"

"No." Carol cuts me off before I can say anything. "Just look at the calendar." She points to it hanging on the wall. "I have to go, or I'll be late. I will see you later."

I walk to the calendar, which is covered in sporting activities, trips with friends, and more activities. It looks like I have direct competition. My kids are just too busy for me. We won't have time to do a single thing on my list unless they wanted to cancel some plans to make time for me.

While I had hoped for family time, I understand that kids need to have a life, so try not to take it too hard. Instead, Carol and I can spend some time together, getting reacquainted over the next month. I look at her activities, and she is even busier than the girls. She has card games, charity events, luncheons with her girlfriends, and meetings at night.

I hadn't noticed they were gone when I was in the theatre. I had slept in late while the kids were getting ready for school. Then, I had performances in the afternoons or evenings. It didn't seem strange to come home and not see anyone. Now, I looked at what we were, and I realized we were four people who lived in a common residence, but were we really a family? I changed the reservation to an earlier time, called the doorman, and asked him to hail a cab.

While I ate at Sardis, I thought about our schedules. I was going to be gone for half of a year. Didn't they want to spend any time with me before I left? It hurt a bit more than I'd like to mention. Picking at my food, I came to a conclusion. I would need to talk to Carol about my concerns.

After that was settled, it was a bit easier to eat. I was watching the various other people in the restaurant. Three women recognized me and asked for my autograph. I happily signed their books—and one napkin—and left the table to return home.

I waited for Carol, but, when she got home, she was so tired that she didn't want to talk and went straight to bed. The same thing the next night. The third night, the kids were home early, but they went straight to their rooms. It looks like the entire family feels I am just in the way. I gave them everything to make their lives comfortable, and now I am an albatross around their necks.

So, again I wait. Only this time, it is waiting at home to leave for Europe. It isn't horrible, and certainly no one would feel sorry for me, being stuck in my apartment. I live in a beautiful duplex penthouse at Seventy-Ninth Street and Park. I've always loved the apartment, and, most of the time, I have the penthouse all to myself. The weather is still pleasant, and I spend my time walking around all 12 rooms, watching the newest color television sets, playing with the new TV gadget called "the clicker" to change the stations, and preparing a snack on the latest appliances in our kitchen. The only people I was able to talk to during the day were the maid, the cook, or the building's maintenance staff. They didn't make me wait for conversation.

A couple of times, I've wandered in to Jody's room or Missy's room. I look at the pictures on their walls and scan their books and trinkets. These things really don't tell me too much about my girls that I don't already know. I also flip through old photo albums, but many of the albums are filled with memories I don't share. They are people that Carol and the girls know from various functions I never attended or groups I'm not a member of.

I try to distract myself with the long list of tasks I need to do before I leave the country. My residence is near all of my doctors, and I'm quite certain I will need certain shots to leave the country. I look at the paper that came with my travel visa from the various embassies and make appointments with my doctor. I don't think I need any special tests, but if I do, my hospital, Lenox Hill, is only two blocks away. That is good, because it is convenient; bad, because it won't help me kill very much time.

My family doctor had offices on the ground floor of my building. I spent many hours downstairs having physicals and receiving shots for my trip overseas. With little else to do, I busied myself with those appointments, too. One perk of being a Broadway star is that I don't have to wait to be seen by the doctor.

I tried calling a few Broadway friends, and we met occasionally for lunch, but all of them were working on new projects or auditioning for others. They don't have any more time for me than I'd had for the family when I was auditioning.

Today has been especially hard for me, because I'm half way through this month off, and it occurs to me that not only am I starting to run out of things to do, I still haven't gotten to spend any time at all with my family. I have to face some hard truths, since there is nothing left to distract me from them. Did I expect my family to wait around for years, so someday I may have four weeks to spend with them? Quite obviously, they didn't. I also realize that when the family was all together, I felt everyone was very distant. Not just the kids, but my wife, too. She walks past me and hardly says a word. This isn't the kind of reception I expected.

On the Friday evening at the end of the second week, the girls were at a sleepover at their girlfriends' houses. I walked out on the balcony of our apartment and looked over the City I'd called home for so long. In fifteen days, I'd leave this place and two seasons would pass without me seeing this view.

"I want to talk to you." I turn and see Carol standing behind me in the doorway.

"Sure," I say, glad to have the company.

"Inside, please?" She turns and takes a drink from the bar. "Do you want one?"

"Sure, thank you." She pours my drink and the two of us walk into the study to talk.

"George, we have grown apart, and I want a divorce." I stand, stunned. Her face holds no sadness or anger. She is simply unreadable.

It reminds me of that first meeting with Franco. The loss of over a decade together only warranted a deadpan expression from her.

"Haven't I given you and the kids all the comforts of life?" She nods but says nothing. "Why haven't you said anything about this before? Can we do something to save the marriage?" She takes a sip of her drink, but continues to remain completely silent. It occurs to me that I have a drink in my hand and sip from it, trying to calm my nerves.

"I thought at one time we could save this marriage," she says, stepping from the bar and walking to the window. "I never said anything sooner, because you were never around."

"Yes, earning a living for you."

She turns to face me, her expression cold. "On you giving the family all the comforts of life," she begins, her voice matching her expression. "They are only financial comforts. They aren't love comforts, they aren't physical comforts, and they certainly aren't companionship comforts."

She puts her drink down hard and some of the amber-colored liquid splashes on to the table. She leaves it there. Something I'd never seen her do before. Her eyes bore into me.

"I know about your affair with Jenny," she hisses. "I know all about the many affairs with your other leading ladies."

I say nothing in response. What could I say? There was no denying them, but those were all physical relationships. They didn't change the way I felt for Carol and the girls. I considered saying this, but that certainly wouldn't make my situation any better.

"This tour?" she continues. "How many affairs are you going to have across Europe?"

"Did you want to come with me?" For the first time, I consider that maybe she is upset that she and the girls haven't been invited. That might be arranged. I would certainly keep them far from me when we had exchanges of the microfilm, but, if she wanted to go with me, I would make it happen.

"No, I don't want to trail along behind you across Europe," she says. "The size of your ego is simply impossible to measure." She is nearly shouting now as she runs through a long list of abuses I have thrust on my family, including the embarrassment she has felt having all of her friends knowing about my continual affairs and philandering.

"There is something else I have to tell you," she adds.

What more could she say? I feel eviscerated, naked, exposed. "I have met with my lawyer. When you come back from your tour, the girls and I will have left the penthouse and moved back with my parents in Chicago."

"You don't have to do that," I say. I worked so hard to give them this place and the life I'd always dreamed of.

"No, I want to. We don't care much for Broadway and living on Park Avenue isn't important to us."

"Okay," I manage to squeak out. I feel like I'm no longer a man. She couldn't hurt me more if she were wielding a knife to physically stab me. I hurt all over, and anger is slowly smoldering and burning the places where my hurt was.

"In regards to the Cape house, you can have it. I always wanted to tell you— I hate the sand."

"If that's what you want, I won't stop you." Carol finishes her drink, leaves the study, and goes down the hall. After a while, I hear the sound of drawers opening and closing. I go down to our bedroom and realize that she has moved her things over to the guestroom. How had I not noticed that gradually the dresser and closets were clearing out? I guess I assumed that she was donating her old clothes. I stand alone in our—now *my*—bedroom and feel the emptiness weigh down on me. She comes in and walks around to her side of the bed, picks up her pillow, and pulls the blankets back up. She walks into her room and closes the door.

I want to get out of the house. The sense of urgency is nearly overwhelming. I close my bedroom door, suddenly feeling it improper that Carol should see me undressed, and put on a nice outfit. Then, I call down to the doorman to hail me a cab. I don't tell Carol I am leaving. I don't leave a note. I simply walk out of our apartment, take the elevator down, and go to the ground floor.

I sit in the back seat of the cab and look out the window at all the buildings on Park Avenue going by. Now, with the emotions out of things, I can think about all she said. I was surprised by Carol's remarks, but not shocked. In retrospect, I wish I would have said, "I understand your position, but, after all these years at our beautiful ocean side Cape home, you really *don't* like the sand?"

Well, I like sand. I'll keep the Cape home.

The cab heads across town to Sardis on Forty-Fourth Street, between Broadway and Eighth Avenue. I can taste the stiff drink I am going to order when I make my entrance into Sardis. I look down at my watch. Hopefully, I will be able to spend some time with my pals from the theatre. They are always hanging out at the bar. Maybe I will have more than one drink.

As the cab draws closer to my destination, I realize that no one has told anyone at Sardis I would be coming in tonight. Will table #1 be available for me? The last thing I want to happen this night is to have to wait to be seated. I have waited long enough these past couple of weeks.

CHAPTER 5

THE *QUEEN MARY*

Finally, my waiting was over. I was very happy to use my persuasive personality to convince the State Department to allow the cast and crew and me to sail to England on the *Queen Mary*. At first, the State Department fought the idea. They claimed it was too expensive. Trans-Atlantic jet flights started a couple of years ago. They claimed it was more economical to move everyone by air. But I pointed out that the cast could rehearse during the crossing, and the government would save money on hotels, meals, and rehearsal expense in London by sailing. I got my way, and everyone on the tour is going to be happy to spend six days sailing to Southampton, England.

Of the 2,139 passengers sailing, only 700 are first-class. Of course, I demanded and received the best first-class suite. I also made sure that I had reservations at the best *à la carte* first-class Verandah Grille on board. I also made sure there were preparations being made to welcome me to London.

Next, there was the matter of the *bon voyage* party in my suite. The *Queen Mary* sailed on a weekday, and, since the sailing was not on a matinee day, I planned a gigantic sendoff party. Invitations for everyone and anyone who was important on Broadway: directors, composers, actors, designers—all were invited. I invited my two daughters, as well, but they declined. They had other plans. When the

State Department found out they were paying for the party, heads turned, but, once again, if I wanted it, I got it. I'm looking forward to the party, but I wouldn't want to be around when Cunard Line presents the final bill to the State Department.

The day to leave has finally arrived. I look around my apartment, realizing that it will look and feel quite different when I return. There is no one here, and there is nothing to hold me here. I climb in my cab, and, soon, my two cabs pull up to the piers on the West Side of Manhattan. One taxi for me, and a second for all the steamer trunks and luggage for my six-month tour. The porters line up to take care of me. They can smell when a celebrity arrives at the port, and are accustomed to many celebrities sailing transatlantic from New York. They are the really great actors who know how to give the extra service to guarantee a generous tip.

"Right this way, Mr. Toomey," a man from the Cunard Line in a cutaway jacket at the first-class entrance bows and gestures for me to follow.

"Thank you," I reply. Turning to one of the porters and handing them some money, I say, "See to it that this is divided equally."

I follow the man in the cutaway to a room where I go through immigration quickly. Everyone is quite polite, and, more and more, I find that I am looking forward to this trip. After the last page is stamped and the last photograph taken, I am personally escorted to my suite on the ship.

"This is perfect," I say when I open the door. The butlers and the stewards have already set up my suite to accommodate the 65 guests I invited. There will be unlimited liquor and enough champagne to offer as many toasts as we need for my send-off.

"We're glad you like it, Mr. Toomey."

"It is exactly what I'd hoped for," I say. "I mean that sincerely."

The butler follows me as I walk around the suite inspecting things.

"One concern," I say.

"What is that?" he asks, a second steward coming at his silent summons.

"How can we be sure all of my guests disembark before the ship sets sail?"

He waves the second steward off. "Don't worry, sir," he says. "All guests will be jolly off at least thirty minutes before departure."

"Very good then," I reply.

The stewards started to unpack my luggage while I wait for the first guests to arrive. Again, I am waiting, but this isn't too bad. I feel as though I am already on my adventure.

"You made it, George." I look up and see Franco and Gina walk in.

"What a wonderful surprise!" I exclaim. "I thought I wouldn't see you until London." I look from Gina to Franco, and, then, I let my eyes linger again on Gina.

"George," Franco interrupts, and I reluctantly break my stare. "Don't be surprised. I always show up when you least expect me."

"Good to know, my friend," I reply, smiling.

"Gina and I will be sailing with you to England on the *Queen Mary*," Franco continues.

"Wonderful." I smile at both of them, but my smile is a little broader for Gina. "Can I offer you a drink?"

They accept, and, while the bartender is mixing, more guests begin to arrive. Soon, the place is full of people, and my once-spacious suite feels rather cramped. I'm sure this must be the largest *bon voyage* party ever thrown on a Cunard White Star Line ship.

I move around the room, telling the same stories over and over and hearing the same promises of great roles and rendezvous when I return from my tour. We are all having a wonderful time, and I have no idea how many bottles of wine and champagne are consumed by the end of the night. About forty-five minutes before departure, the steward comes in.

"We need all unticketed guests to disembark. Those of you who are ticketed, please present your tickets, so we may escort you to your staterooms to prepare for departure."

All at once, guests swarm me to shake my hand and kiss my cheek. True to their word, all party guests are escorted to the pier in time for departure. Some, however, have consumed large amounts of liquor, and the stewards have to place them in wheelchairs and roll them down to the gangways. I watched them go and feel the excitement of this new adventure build. Three horn blasts later and the *Queen Mary* has left her berth to begin her crossing to Southampton.

I invite Franco and Gina to stay in my suite to watch as the ship sails past the Statue of Liberty. It took about forty-five minutes to reach the Lady in the Harbor. We spent the time toasting the success of our tour. As we sailed closer to the statue, everyone was quite moved at the sight. Sailing out of New York Harbor is the only way one can properly witness the complete thrill of seeing the Lady in the Harbor in all her splendor.

"Well, I think I'm going to take a nap for a bit, so I'm ready and awake for dinner," I say. I consider asking Gina if she'd like to stay, but, with Franco there, I decide to wait. She'd shot me down once. I didn't want to risk it a second time in front of him.

"You do that," Franco says. "We will have lots of time to get to know each other over the course of this tour."

"I will see you both later on then." I walk them to the door and close it quietly behind them. The room is quiet now, but not lonely. I am done with waiting. I am now sailing to destiny.

***

"Gina, may I get you a drink?" Franco asks.

"No, thank you. I think I've had enough." The two sit in a pub at the stern of the ship. The view is beautiful. It is far slower than flying, but she had to agree with George that it was a wonderful way to travel.

"So what has you so worried about the upcoming stop in Leningrad?" Franco asks, turning serious. He had an unnerving way of seeing past her words and directly to her meaning. When she'd asked him to meet in the pub to talk, she'd been certain that her voice, words, and body language were light. It would seem she'd failed.

"He is not a team player. He's only out for himself," she replies. There is no point moving into it slowly if Franco already knew she was worried. "Will he follow directions, or cause the mission to fail by something stupid he may do or say?"

"We have to trust him. The agency wanted to make the deal, and the top officers feel confident in its success." Franco pats her hand. She looks at him, and he quickly withdraws. "We will have to make this mission work, and I am sure we can," Franco continues with his focus now on the glass of water in front of him. "Nothing more to be said. We know our orders."

Gina nods. It is true. They know their orders, and there is nothing to say beyond that.

***

Rehearsals began the next morning, the first full day at sea. The sea was calm, so all dancers were told to show up for rehearsals at 10 AM. The actors had the day off, but had to be ready to start on the second day. All was going well. For now, the apprehension that had bugged Gina yesterday was either gone or waiting for a better time to assault her. Her job required her to prepare for all contingencies and expect the worst case scenarios, but, so far, things were actually working better than she'd expected.

Around noon, just as everyone was preparing to break for lunch, the seas became rough, and the director decided to cancel the rest of the day of rehearsals.

"Enjoy the ship, but be careful," the director called. "The last thing anyone wants is for someone to break a leg or sprain an ankle because of the conditions of the sea."

The rest of that day was choppy off and on. By dinnertime, Gina had to go to the on-board hospital for motion sickness pills.

The seas finally calmed down that night about 8 PM, and, for the next several days, rehearsals went on without any cancellations. The creative staff was pleased with the progress of the show; however, no one would be totally satisfied until we were in London, where they could see the show on its feet in a theatre, with scenery, lights, a full orchestra, and a live audience responding.

***

"During the rehearsal process, actors work on their performances, their process, and the development of the show. No one works full out in rehearsals; they are in the learning stages and want to work up to a full-out performance. This full-out performance can only be given with a live audience." Franco pauses in his lecture, and Gina waits. She's seen Franco like this before. "But George gives all he has, always. He has an incredible work ethic."

"Yes, he does give everything he has," Gina agrees. "But his rehearsal performance fits George's personality pattern. He wants everyone to love him immediately. He thinks by working at one-hundred-percent all the time, everyone will, indeed, love him and think he is the best. George is only thinking about himself and not the good of the show."

"You really aren't impressed with him at all, are you?" Franco asks.

"It's not that," Gina sighs. "He's an impressive actor, and I agree that he has a strong work ethic, but what I'm most concerned about is his motivation."

"You don't think he's a team player."

"No, I think he is just out for himself."

"So, Gina, have you had any more problems with George wanting to spend the night with you?" She laughs. He is never subtle when he wants to change the subject. That is what their superiors like most about him.

"Only every day, Franco. I think he is finally getting the hint that I am not interested."

"I guess he thinks if you spend the night with him, you will be receiving the greatest performance of his life."

"He gave his greatest performance today at rehearsal." They both laugh.

"Would you like to walk for a bit?" Franco asks. "We can leave the rehearsals to 'The Actor' and enjoy our last full day on the ship."

Gina follows Franco out to the promenade deck on the ship, where they stroll slowly and talk about past missions, America vs. Europe, and anything else that comes to mind.

***

I watched Franco and Gina leave just as rehearsal was breaking up. She is absolutely beautiful, and I think she is finally starting to warm up to me. The *Queen Mary* will be landing in Southampton in about a day, and this is our final rehearsal at sea. Most of the cast and crew are looking forward to finally arriving in London and starting the tour.

All rehearsals are cancelled on the last day of the voyage. The director wants the entire company to enjoy the ship, get plenty of rest, pack, and read about the disembarkation, customs and immigration regulations for arrival in Southampton. The stage manager has arranged a private car on the boat train for everyone to travel to London. The trip to central London takes about two-and-a-half hours, and, after check-in at the hotels, the night will be free to explore London's nightlife. But we have been strictly warned that rehearsals start again at the Drury Lane Theatre in London the morning after arrival at 10 AM, sharp.

The crossing has flown by, but that really isn't a huge surprise. The years on stage have flown past me, too. All of the staff and performers on the tour are getting excited.

The final day at sea, I tried to soak in the little bit of calm before the storm of London rehearsals. The problem with trying to enjoy the free time to the best of your ability is that you end up jamming your free time full of activities. I went to bed early and joined the other passengers on the top deck early the next morning.

Already, we've reached our destination, and the new chapter of my life is a reality. As the ship speed slows, I can see land off the starboard side of the ship. Shortly, we all see a large sign hanging from the entire side of the pier's facade. It was put up to welcome all travelers to Southampton.

WELCOME TO ENGLAND
WE HAVE ALL SURVIVED

The younger members of the cast start asking, "What does it mean: WE HAVE ALL SURVIVED?" The older passengers all murmur and share memories.

One speaks out above the others, "It means England survived the Second World War."

CHAPTER 6

LONDON

Although the entire cast and crew are staying at various hotels throughout London, I require a suite at the Ritz. It is the favorite of royalty, celebrities, and major Hollywood stars in the early fifties, so it makes sense that I would stay there. It also makes sense that they are preparing for my arrival. They have had to cope with some pretty crazy behavior from their VIP guests. There are so many stories. One goes that Tallulah Bankhead drank champagne out of her slipper each night in the formal dining room. I guess we can now say that I've arrived in Europe in a couple of different ways. Certainly I made it across the ocean to the shore, but I've also achieved celebrity status here as well.

I love London. I came here many years ago—long before my career success—and I experienced a very different London then. Today, I look forward to all the amenities and perks offered by the Ritz and my notoriety.

"Sir, we'd like to welcome you to our hotel," the hotel's general manager says as he begins to show me around the hotel and my suite. Bellhops flutter in with my steam trunks while housekeeping—or some other women, I'm not sure—all go about putting things away, and I focus on the GM's list of amenities.

"We would like to invite you, as our guest, to high tea daily."

"That is very kind of you," I say, noticing a lovely young lady in a knee-length cleaning uniform.

"It is held in our Palm Court," he adds, hands folded as he speaks.

"And where is that?" I ask, and, then, I think differently of it. "I'll just have someone show me down."

"Very good, Mr. Toomey," the GM replies.

Of course, over the next two weeks, rehearsals will take up most of my time, so I'm not certain I'll ever make it to high tea, but it is nice to be invited to such a lavish affair.

In truth, I may have liked a more casual hotel. I love the beautiful things of life, but I also despise having rules dictated to me. At the Ritz, any man in the lobby after 5 PM is required to wear a coat and tie. On holidays, more formal attire is requested. The idea of having to keep such clothing in my dressing room or hurrying back from rehearsal to get appropriately dressed grates on me. However, the Ritz is the place to be and to be seen. It will only be a short five-minute drive to the theatre for rehearsals, and this makes it very convenient for me.

"Is there anything we can do for you right now?" the GM asks, handing me his card. "Our concierge is available to you 24 hours a day."

I wait, a pregnant pause that brings all motion in the room to a halt, as, one-by-one, the staff begin to turn my direction.

"I need more time unpacking," I say, trying to sound both reflective and nonchalant. I look around, seeing past the lovely young lady a time or two, before returning. "Could you help me?" I ask.

"Of course," the GM says, not making eye contact. The others shuffle from the room, and the young lady folds her hands in front of her. I'm not sure what England is like, but I know how American women respond to a Broadway star. Here, I'm much more. I'm an international celebrity.

"Let's start in the bedroom, shall we?" I say, turning in that direction. "All of the trunks are in here."

She follows me in and begins to unpack. Two hours later, she leaves my hotel suite, having taken care of everything I needed, even serving me tea before she left. I then relax in the living room of my suite in order to look over the production notes from the last rehearsal.

***

Rehearsals began in earnest the next day, and, for two weeks, they have worked us hard. At night, I am so exhausted that I have dinner delivered to my suite. I am not required to wear a coat and tie to dine in my room, and I rather like having them wheel the trays in and serving me. Most nights, I come back slowly, sometimes taking half an hour to come back to the hotel. London is a wonderful place. So many of the buildings are quite old, but I also notice the scars from the war. It has been fifteen years since the bombings ended, and, yet, the damage is still quite evident. There is a sign on the building that says forty children were killed here by a bombing raid.

I would have thought that Europe would be back together by now. America has certainly recovered from everything and is now booming with industry and growth. Today, I take a new side street to unwind. It was a tough rehearsal, because we're getting closer, and the director is a touch uptight. Finally, I'd had enough of their ridiculous demands, and I fought back. We had quite a screaming match.

In the end, the star won out, but I'm still miffed that we had to waste so much time and make such a spectacle of ourselves in the process. When I turned down this street, the buildings were far more broken than others I'd noticed. Down near the end of the road were craters from German rocket landings and bullet damage from aircraft attacks on the side of buildings and trees. I walked slowly, almost reverently, to the edge of one crater and looked inside. They'd filled it in, so it was no longer dangerous, but it was quite clear what it had been.

A child—no more than three or four—plays with a stick and a hoop on the edge of the road, running right past the craters and damaged buildings, like any American child running down the street of their neighborhood. That such destruction earned no more attention than any common puddle shocks me.

I slowly turn around. For the first time, I realize the full magnitude of what happened here. The buildings I'd looked at one-by-one and the trees that were wounded formed a single picture. One night, bombs were dropped right here, just inches from where I stood. Only fifteen years ago—a decade before that child was born—people huddled in subways and basements and bomb shelters, hoping to survive the night.

I am not sure if it is because I have learned to visualize a scene to perform a character or if it was really the ghosts of this town, but, suddenly, I am certain that I can hear their screams—those who died. I begin to walk to a building, and there is a plaque. On it is a list of names of people killed in this area of the City. I remember I saw some of these on my other walks, but I never stopped to read them, assuming they were directions. I am here as a star, yes, but they brought me here to bring entertainment to these people. I will give everything I have to this performance and bring joy to London.

Then, I think about the second part of my mission—the part in the U.S.S.R.—and I get excited thinking about the role I am going to be able to play for my country. I turn around, looking one last time at this beautiful neighborhood and walk quickly back to the hotel.

The walk back isn't as peaceful as it normally is. There is a gnawing inside of me. When I reached the lobby, I realize I am underdressed, but I immediately go to the concierge to inquire about any museums or sites I could visit to learn more about the War.

"I am particularly interested in learning the way in which Londoners survived," I say. The concierge, a refined man who is certainly in his early fifties if he is a day, points to several racks of materials in the lobby next to the front desk with brochures are of important sightseeing attractions.

"Thank you," I say over my shoulder. "This is exactly what I was looking for." I take up one of each brochure, as well as reading material regarding the Second World War.

Back at the suite, I lay the materials all over my bed. I quickly read about the Imperial War Museum and other material about the war. I organize them by topic. Some focus on the way people survived during the War. Other attractions talk about the politics and the rebuilding. All of it has me captivated. I am hungry for more details and information about the 1940s war period. It was one thing to hear about it on the radio at night and see the various pictures in the papers, but, now, it is so real to me.

***

Night after night, I continue to read in detail how Londoners lived and survived through the War years. I find myself beginning to wonder how my life would have been different if I had been born in London and had to live through the nightly bombings. How would I have coped with living all night in air raid shelters in the Underground? How would I have handled the horrors the citizens of London endured?

There must be more that I can do. I am going to ask Franco to let me do more. I wasn't able to be a part of the war fifteen years ago when they needed soldiers—a sad bit of fate made me ineligible—but that doesn't mean I have nothing to give.

As the days and number of walks and reading increase, I think about the war years back in the United States. In fact, I was only twenty years old when the Second World War began. I never had to serve in the United States Military. I was deferred from the Army—not for some major medical problem, but because of my psoriasis. I did try to help in the war effort—in fact, I once got into trouble for trying—but they still didn't take me. I saw the soldiers go away with their beloveds waiting here, pining for them. I saw the beautiful girls who would wait outside the dance halls to dance with the soldiers. I wanted to be a hero, like them. I hated to be thought a coward. So many of the boys were overseas that a twenty-year-old man who clearly wasn't in college but who also wasn't overseas was quite noticeable. It was like history was being made without me.

Maybe this is my chance to make up for that. Fate has given me another chance.

This renewed sense of purpose makes it even more exciting to go to the theatre each day, and I throw myself into my character and role.

***

In the Mayfair section of London, Franco and Gina meet to have dinner at their hotel.

"Sir," the maître d' `says, coming to the table, "we have a telephone call for you."

Franco wipes his mouth and leaves the table to take the call. Gina looks around at the people. One of the great perks of her job is seeing all of the different countries and the different people.

She also finds it wonderful to work with Franco. He is an absolute professional and a wealth of information. When he is working a project, he knows that there will always be absolute professionalism and very few surprises.

"I am glad you are sitting." She looks up to see Franco wearing a broad smile. "That was George on the phone, and you won't believe why he called."

"With him, I can only imagine what it might be," she says, taking a sip from her water glass, in order to suppress a rude comment. Franco didn't tolerate too much infighting. It is easy to see a mission go wrong through a lack of trust or reliability. He has worked with her too long, however, and he gives her a look that immediately silences all further jabs at Toomey's character.

"It would seem," Franco reports, now beginning to relax slightly, "that George has been greatly impacted by seeing the results of the War on London."

"He should see the Continent," Gina quips. "I didn't mean that the way it sounded," she says, in response to Franco's chastising stare. "I only meant that the Continent fared far worse than London."

"I know that as well as you do," Franco's voice is unusually kind, given her harsh comments, "but this is more than just interest. He simply wouldn't stop talking about how much he admires the British people and how they carried on during the War."

"Clearly, it has done something to him, since he called, knowing we were eating."

"True," Franco continues. "He goes on and on about how he feels guilty, because he never did anything to help the outcome of the War back in the States."

And there it is. Gina has tried to give the man the benefit of the doubt, but everything seems to always come back to him and something he wants or needs. Coming to London, he now feels he needs absolution for being a coward during the War.

"He then asked," Franco continues, either unaware or uninterested in the fact that Gina had been in her own thoughts, "if I could please arrange a tour of the Imperial British War Museum, and any other museums I might suggest."

"You are a CIA agent, not a tour guide." Gina is now irritated. How dare this show-off now expect that they should add to their great list of tasks—including keeping him alive—tour guide.

"He says he must learn more about the War, and what was done to win the conflict," Franco relays.

The waiter brings out their meals, and, for a few moments, neither of them speaks. They'd met over a meal, because there was so much to do it was simply impossible to allow themselves even a moment to eat in peace. This mission was going to take absolute diligence around-the-clock to keep everyone where they needed to be, under the radar, and out of danger. Now, Toomey was adding tour guide to their long list of responsibilities. It angered her that George had asked Franco to do these things. That took nerve. What irritated her even more, however, was that she was certain Franco would eventually hand the task off to her.

"I will call the director of the tour to inform him that George will not be at rehearsal tomorrow, and, then, I will call the Secret Intelligence Service. He will love that!"

Gina doesn't look up from her food. The SIS in England was the British counterpart of the CIA and would probably really enjoy having a Broadway star visit—particularly if Franco had coordinated any part of their mission with any of them.

"The head of the agency is an old friend of mine from the beginning of the war in 1940," Franco continues. "I will ask my friend to arrange, and put on the agenda, a visit to Winston Churchill's underground war room under the streets of London. It's not open to the public."

"That is lovely," Gina replies, no longer hiding the frustration in her voice. "I'm sure it will be a fun outing for our star."

"When I get through with his personal sightseeing tour," Franco takes command of the conversation again, his voice stern, "George will see firsthand how intelligence and undercover activities work. He will also be shown how people must work together for success. By showing George all the teamwork that went into defeating the Nazis, maybe he will realize our Russian mission will take teamwork and strict adherence to all instructions given."

"Or he could feel that his whims are above the needs of the group—like replacing a rehearsal for sightseeing—and this will just reinforce the idea that he is above the team," Gina retorts.

"I'm going to make a couple of calls right now," Franco announces. "Are you going to be here, or should I pay the bill on my way out?"

"I'll be here, I hope," she says. "There were actual matters of the mission we needed to discuss."

"And we will." Franco leaves the table to make the calls, and Gina continues to fume. It would be great if she could command the same amount of attention from Franco that it seemed everyone else in the world could get from him. She had asked for nothing more than an hour of his time to go over a few points of the next phase of the mission. These were critical to her role in moving everyone around when Franco was gone for a week. Unfortunately, George's newfound love of history was far more important than her needs on this mission.

Gina finishes eating. The waiter brings a dessert menu, and she decides to order bread pudding and a cup of tea. If she has to wait, she might as well enjoy it.

Almost twenty minutes later, Franco returns and gives her a kiss on the forehead. "All the arrangements have been made." Franco leans forward and looks at her intently, "Now what is it you needed my help with?"

***

The next morning, I am standing outside the hotel early, when a beautiful, chauffeured silver Rolls Royce pull up to the front entrance of The Ritz. Franco and Gina are sitting in the backseat, engaged in conversation.

"Good morning, George," Franco greets me, stepping out of the Rolls. He turns and takes Gina's hand.

"No need to get out," I say. "I can slide in beside you."

"I will be sitting in the front." Her voice is kind, but firm, and she slides out beside him.

"Very well." I nod to her.

"Please, get in," Franco urges. "We have a wonderful day planned."

Franco opens the front door and helps Gina in. I slide in, and Franco comes in beside me. I am tremendously excited about the itinerary Franco has arranged for me. I feel like a young boy whose parents have invited him to a special outing. I wore a very nice jacket, though I did worry a bit that they'd feel me presumptuous. I needn't have worry about my clothing, if this was the way I was to be transported.

The first stop is the Imperial British War Museum. When we arrive, it takes a great deal of willpower not to push the car door open and go in myself. I wait for the chauffeur to get out and open my door properly, but, once the door is open, I rush out of the car to enter the museum as quickly as I can.

I walk into the world that shows me bits of what I'd researched the night before. There are photographs of bombed-out buildings and pieces of the rubble; the smell of death clings to the various artifacts. It is as if the spirits of the lives and the innocence lost in these horrible raids haunts my every step.

I walk to a picture of the London Underground filled with thousands upon thousands of human beings sleeping under ground. No doubt, there wasn't much sleeping going on as people huddled together while the German Luftwaffe was flying bombing raids over the city.

I am simultaneously awed and horrified while I walk for more than an hour. It takes hours to simply look at a summary of the devastation.

I spend another hour looking at exhibits. Children and women were living through this. Certainly, the bombs didn't discriminate against a person with a skin condition. No, here the war was very real. It wasn't about tea dances and Rosie the Riveter. This world was survival and devastation.

"Franco?" I ask, my eyes never leaving the photograph in front of me.

"Yes, George?"

"Why didn't anybody do anything to stop the madness?"

"They did, George. They did."

"It doesn't look like it," I say, almost too overcome to take in any more pictures, stories, pieces of history, or guilt.

"In fact," Franco continues, "let's go to our next stop and visit Churchill's war room, located deep beneath the streets of the city. You will see how the War was run and hear about how strategy was developed to defeat Germany."

At Churchill's war room, I read and absorb the documents, including the plan for the Battle of Britain. As if studying for a character, I put myself in Churchill's place. I see where Churchill slept, how he communicated with his military, and how he galvanized the citizens to fight on. While our president held fireside chats from the safety of the White House, Churchill had galvanized a nation while under constant bombardment in a deep bunker.

In one of the rooms, a news article hanging on the wall briefly mentions a place called Bletchley Park, an undercover and intelligence operation based in a countryside location.

"Franco, I am curious. Why wasn't there much material on the intelligence aspect of the war in the two museums we visited?"

"Well, George, that is because it is highly classified," Franco begins, looking at the exhibit. "Many of the techniques learned in World War II serve as the foundation for our current intelligence-gathering operations. If we were to share that with everyone, our enemies would have a leg up on us."

"I can understand that," I say. "I'm disappointed. I had truly hoped that by learning some of this would help me do a better job on my mission."

"Your mission is to be a great actor," Gina says. Her voice carries the same friendly, yet chastising, tone my mother's carried when I was a naughty child. I turn to face her, and she is smiling broadly, although her smile fails to make it all the way to her eyes.

"I'm already a great actor, but you know you're asking me to do far more," I say, not willing to be brushed off that easily.

"George, I have arranged a private tour of Bletchley Park," Franco says, stepping in between the two of us. "Bletchley Park is where the War was won and all intelligence operations were planned and executed."

"Really?" I ask eagerly. This isn't acting; I am genuinely excited.

"It is off limits to the general public. I am sure someday there will be a museum out there, but today, the activities are still secret," Franco continues. "Our activities towards the Soviet Union can be compared to the activities planned and executed at Bletchley Park. Undercover work helped win the hot war. Our activities now will help win the Cold War."

"That is what I want," I say, hoping I don't sound like a spoiled child. "I want to do my part to win this portion of the war."

"I have an old friend who runs Bletchley Park. He has agreed to invite you out there. It is most important—what you see and hear is secret, and you can't tell, nor mention, your visit to anyone."

"You can trust me," I say at once. Then, turning to Gina, I repeat, "You can trust me."

We leave the museum and get in the car. It heads out to Buckinghamshire to a collection of nondescript buildings. There are several armed guards at the gate to stop anyone from entering. This makes it even more thrilling.

"Papers?" a guard inquires. Franco hands him a stack of what appear to be identification cards and a letter.

"George. Give me some ID." I give it to him, and he, in turn, gives it to the guard.

The man sifts through the pile, looks at a list in his guard shack, and inspects our papers again. He looks each one of us—including the driver—in the eye, presumably comparing us to our photographs.

He reaches in and gives everything back to Franco. "The Colonel is waiting for you. Drive up the road and enter the second door on the right, after the parking lot."

A gate opens in front of us, and we pull through. It is an absolute wonder to me. I'm going to find out what actual spies do on actual missions. I will even get to meet some spies—other than Franco and Gina—who are living this adventure each day. I am simply overcome with excitement. We park and enter the building.

A man I presume to be the Colonel greets Franco warmly.

THE ACTOR?

"Sir, I'd like you to meet my colleague, Gina."

While they exchange pleasantries, I look around. It is remarkable to be here.

"And this is George Toomey, the Actor," Franco says. I turn from admiring the room and face the distinguished gentleman with white hair and a very refined British accent.

"It is wonderful to meet you, sir," I greet him, extending my hand and shaking his enthusiastically.

"And you as well, Mr. Toomey." He smiles and steps back after we shake hands. "It is not often that I have the opportunity to meet an international celebrity." He exchanges a glance with Franco. "I will be giving you the tour of our facility."

I manage to simply nod, but inside, I am jumping up and down with excitement. We start down a corridor, and people look at me first, then the Colonel. They are, undoubtedly, wondering who it is that can turn such an important man into a tour guide. I'm certain that it is Franco's importance, more than mine, that got the tour…but I'm equally sure that my fame helped.

"This building's activities were responsible for crushing the German war machine, ending the war and saving tens of thousands of lives," he began. For the next hour, he lays out the stories of the war from the inside. The Colonel tells me of what actually happened on the grounds. The British put together the top scientists, intelligence officers, and even chess masters and puzzle champions to work at Bletchley Park—first developing, and, then, building, a machine that could break the codes of the German military. In fact, teams in the buildings were called the code breakers.

"The biggest accomplishment was breaking the codes of the German Navy's Enigma machines," the Colonel says, pride still evident in his expression as he talks about how they broke the code.

"Once we broke that code, Bletchley Park could read all of Hitler's orders sent to the U-boat commanders prowling in the Atlantic, as well as all orders to generals in the field."

"That was certainly very exciting," I say. Franco smiles and Gina does a bit too. Maybe I am a bit childish in my wonder, but I am truly beginning to understand that with this tour, I'll be able to do even more in a year than I could have ever done in three years as a soldier. The idea thrills me, and I want to understand more.

"The Allies knew all the moves of the German Army, Luftwaffe, and Navy, before they even took place," the Colonel continues.

"Can we see the machine?" I ask.

"I'm sorry, you cannot. After the War, Churchill had ordered all equipment and records be destroyed, so as not to get into Russian hands."

I am heartsick. All of that wonderful history—gone.

"Colonel, don't torture the poor boy," Franco says.

"I'm sorry, Mr. Toomey, it is just me having a bit of fun at your expense," the Colonel says, smiling warmly. "I disobeyed the order, and, now, the record of what actually happened there will live on for generations to come."

I see so many more wonderful things on the tour, but the thing that stays with me the most is that the tour and the conversation with The Colonel serves to reinforce a previous conversation I had with Franco in New York.

"Intelligence, spying and undercover work is the only way to stop and rid the world of war-loving countries, dictators and evil regimes. Whether it was the First World War, The Second World War, the Korean War, or the Cold War, these clandestine activities must take place," he'd soliloquized then. Now, looking around at what was accomplished, I understand why he loves being a spy so much. I somehow think his conversation was geared to me and to the activities in store for me in Russia. This tour was Franco's way of sealing the deal. Well, he'd succeeded. I'm in this all the way.

I approach Franco who is standing to the side, listening to the Colonel. "Since the KGB won't be watching me that closely, I want to help you more," I begin. Immediately, I can read on his face that this isn't really what he thinks best, but I've never been a man to let a door slamming in my face stop me from something I really want. Acting is all about doors being slammed in your face. I continue, "I could work undercover and even try to obtain classified information."

"I thank you for wanting to help and want to remind you again of the conversation we had back in New York. There is one way for you to help us. We have agents inside Russia; the biggest problem is getting their reports out of the country."

I'm frustrated, because I know what is coming next. Franco continues, "You will only receive our agent's reports on microfilm, hide the film in the lining of the special suitcases being supplied to you, and turn everything over to me to decipher."

"That is hardly helping," I respond, disappointed.

"Under no circumstance are you to do anything else," Gina interjects. I look up at her, and I see something that very nearly resembles anger. I'm not sure why she has such hostility. I understand that she isn't interested in me, but it also seems that the harder I work on the mission, the more she dislikes me.

"Your only responsibility is as a *courier*," Franco emphasizes. "Other than transportation of the microfilm, your job is to make sure your tour is the most successful artistic exchange program between the two countries ever. Any other involvement would cause an international incident and would expose our intelligence activities to the KGB."

I look around the room wistfully before we all say goodbye to the Colonel and enter the Rolls waiting at the door. The ride back to central London is in complete silence. I'm certain Franco and Gina are thinking about my desire to help them on their mission. Maybe, if they warmed to me and realized how much I could offer, they'd change their minds. I don't think anyone had any idea of what was going through my mind, which was exactly the way I liked it.

Chapter 7

FLORENCE, ITALY

As we drove back to London, one thought pounded in my mind with each beat of my heart: *this is my chance. This is my chance to help more with the Cold War effort. This is my chance to be absolved from the guilt of not being able to fight for my country in the 1940s. This is my chance to have an impact on history.* A door had opened, and I planned to go through.

With ten days to go before the tour leaves for Russia, the director has called a meeting to be held immediately after the rehearsal. During rehearsal, I think about how close I am to beginning my new mission. The excitement has given me new energy, and I breeze through rehearsals.

"Great job tonight, everyone," the director says as we all file in to the sitting area. I never really paid much attention to the crew on my productions unless I needed a prop, but, tonight, I see something new. They are invisible people who move things around and manipulate their environment. They are like spies.

"This won't take long at all," the director promises. I turn my attention back to him, eager to finish this business and get back to my hotel and my plans.

"I'm giving everyone in the company a three-day vacation to enjoy themselves," he says.

It is like the fates, or God, or some higher power has smiled down on my mission. It *must* be some sort of sign. "Go sleep for three days, sightsee around London, or travel in Europe," he continues. "You are doing really well, and everyone has been working hard. We all deserve a break."

There are a few murmurs and exchanged smiles.

"I want you to enjoy yourselves, *BUT*..." Now, the director is nearly shouting. I look at my fellow cast members. No one is moving or speaking. "You will all be back in three days, sober and ready to start a week of paid performances at the Drury Lane Theatre. Anyone late will be sent back to the States."

I'm completely agreeable to those terms, and it seems that so is everyone else. We file out of the theater, and I go to my hotel straightaway.

***

"That was a wonderful surprise," Gina says when I tell her and Franco about the vacation.

"You mean you didn't know?" I ask. I had assumed that Franco and Gina would have been the ones to approve this decision.

"No," Franco says. "We really don't have much to do with the actual production schedule. We are working on the intelligence end only."

"Well, I've been trying to decide how to spend my newly won break. I've thought about more tours, maybe even tours to France to see how the War impacted the Continent," I say. I had spent the whole walk home considering what I could do with my time.

"I think he should go to Firenze with us," Gina proposes.

"I hadn't thought of that, but it is a great idea," Franco agrees, and I can tell he is genuinely excited by the prospect.

"It absolutely is," Gina continues. "Not only to get away from the heavy rehearsal schedule, but he can also meet the Russian Three."

"Who are the Russian Three?" I finally say, partially to find out information and partially to remind them I am actually in the room.

"They are the three CIA agents working undercover in Russia," Franco says, still looking at Gina. I cannot help but think there is something telepathic passing between them. Maybe this vacation wasn't as much of a surprise as they let on?

"It will be most important for everyone to hear about each person's role when the tour reaches Russia," Franco continues.

As they start to talk about the arrangements and meetings to set up, the fullness of what is happening settles on me. This is my chance, and I somehow must find some time in Florence to get an agent alone to talk with me. This is the beginning of executing my plan to help the United States in a very real way.

"How soon can we leave?" I didn't want to delay a moment.

"Well, we have to get you a room first, since it is an excursion that isn't a CIA expense," Gina says. "Would you like us to find you a safe house?"

"No" I reply. "Book me at the Excelsior Hotel for the three-day stay."

"How did I know that he'd pick one of the best hotels in all of Firenze?" Gina asks—and her sarcastic tone isn't lost on me.

"Glad I'm so predictable," I say, thinking about how shocked they'd be to know what I was actually planning.

"I will arrange for tickets to fly tomorrow. It is better if we don't travel together, so we will have a travel agent bring the tickets to your hotel," Franco instructs.

"That will be fine," I say. We talk for another twenty minutes before we all retire to our hotels.

∗∗∗

The next morning, I got up and flew to Florence. I was in a beautiful suite overlooking the River Arno. It is a perfect present to me for all the hard work I have undertaken. Gazing out the window, I can already see many places to explore. After unpacking, it is time for lunch, so I eat something quickly and begin a walking tour on my way to the Ponte Vecchio to buy some leather gloves for my girls. I got each girl two pairs and had the merchants ship them. I realize that I have no idea where they might be, so I send them to my Park Avenue address. The post office will certainly forward them for me.

I walk around the city a little longer, but, by five o'clock, I'm getting a little tired and hungry. I get back to the hotel, and there is a note waiting for me at the front desk. Franco and Gina have set up meeting for the following day in a conference room at the Excelsior. With the rest of the day to myself, I decide to rest up and prepare for the meeting.

***

"I want everyone to get along well at this the first—and probably only—meeting everyone will ever have," Franco addresses Gina and me. "We have to trust each other and do our parts if this is going to work out."

"We will be fine," I assure him. "I'm very excited to do my part."

Although Franco seems relieved by my response, Gina eyes me warily. I have never seen a woman who was so upset about a man finding her attractive. She seems to do little more than tolerate me on this mission. If anyone is going to mess things up, I am quite certain it will be her. If trust is the key, I wonder if Gina will ever trust me.

Frederick, Natasha, and Vladimir arrive early to the meeting. I recognized them immediately. They look like they just came from central casting at a film studio. Their facial features are quite severe, and their clothing is refined, but unremarkable. It is hard to articulate, but there is a recognizable manner about them. It is the same with the Europeans. They have a style of dress that separates them from the typical American style of dress. They likely recognize that in us, although they probably assume that we all dress like John Wayne or something.

I realize that I am smiling and force myself to put on a friendly, rather than amused, expression.

"Vladimir, Natasha, Frederick," Franco gestures to each one as he says their name. "I'd like you to meet George Toomey."

"Good to meet you," Vladimir says, reaching out to shake my hand.

"Spasibo. I vy takzhe." The three Russians smile and nod.

"You have learned some Russian," Natasha says.

"Ochen' malo," I say. "That is how you say 'a little', right?"

"Actually," Gina says, "it means 'very little', but close enough."

"What else aren't you telling us, George?" Franco asks, his smile a bit strained.

"Nothing," I reply, and it is almost completely honest. "I tried to learn how to say a more appropriate greeting, but I couldn't master anything other than to say 'Thank you. And you also' and 'very little'."

"Well, those are useful phrases," Frederick says.

"OH," I say. "And 'actor', but that is really the same word in English."

With that cleared up, Gina and Franco both seem to calm considerably, and we all get along pretty well. Considering the three are not used to trusting anyone, they warm up quickly to me.

Vladimir, who is in charge of the Russian Three, sounds a warning. "It seems something very big is about to happen." Then, he appears to remember that I'm in the room.

"He's okay," Franco assures him. "Continue."

"My sources are not sure, but they feel it is something to do with Russian armament movement."

Franco becomes quite animated. He always seems so calm that I'm concerned to see him this way. "I need to know more," he insists.

"There is information from a middle source in the KGB," Vladimir continues, "confirming an increase in manufacturing of missiles and long-range rockets. Friends of the Three working on the docks also reported many additional merchant ships arriving in port."

"Finding out what is taking place must take the highest level of priority," Franco says. "I will try to get to a higher level source at the KGB."

I'm concerned about this dangerous potential, but it is exciting to be included in their conversation. I can see now why it is so critical that I do all that I can to make this mission a success. There are constant threats against our nation, and I'm uniquely positioned to really take the lead on gathering intelligence. No one would suspect someone as visible and famous as me of being a spy—which is exactly why the CIA wanted me—and it would be wrong for me to do so little when I can do so much.

"We also need to make this our last trip out of Russia for the foreseeable future," Vladimir says. The other two are talking with Gina on the other side of the room. I try to listen, but since I can't make out what they're saying, I decide to focus my attention where it is welcomed.

"Why is that?" Franco asks. "Are they on to you?"

"No," Vladimir says, "not us, specifically, but our leaders are paranoid men." He pauses, as if considering his thoughts carefully. "They have determined that there are secrets moving out of the country, and they don't have time to figure out how."

"They are paranoid, as well as inefficient," Frederick says.

"Yes," Vladimir agrees. The smile seems a bit too broad, and I wonder if there is some kind of inside joke about this.

Natasha steps in. "There has been a major crackdown on all exit visas, except for official government business," she says. She steps up and walks to the window, and I wonder for a moment if she wouldn't like to run from Russia and stay in the West. "All other visas will be extremely hard to come by, and, shortly, non-existent."

"Maybe we should focus on the tour?" Gina suggests, pulling us all back to the present. Franco immediately steps up and takes over.

"Gina will be listed on the papers given to the Russians as the associate producer. At no time will she have any contact with the

Russian Three. She will be able to talk with George and be available to manage any issues that may arise," Franco begins.

Although Franco is normally fairly friendly, he is now direct and to-the-point, calling each person out by name and giving specific and detailed assignments. He puts up some of the promotional material and items pertaining specifically to the show on the board, but other than that, we are told to memorize our instructions and only take encrypted notes.

"You could be a VP of sales conducting a seminar," I say at a particularly light moment.

"I am the VP of this show." He winks at me, and I consider how much a spy is actually an actor. They live a life and a character that is completely different from their actual life. I never stopped to consider whether the Franco, Gina, Vladimir, Natasha, or Frederick I met were the real ones, or the personas they wanted me to know.

"George, I need you to listen closely to this part, because it is critical to the success of our secondary mission," Franco says.

"You have my full attention," I respond, feeling like a young soldier heading to the battle lines.

"These are the three—and only three—places where microfilm will be exchanged." Franco points to the map of the area behind him. "The hotel, the theatre, and the Hermitage Museum."

"Can I write down those places?" I ask, not wanting to break his rules.

"Yes, those are benign, which is why they are exchange venues. It is reasonable you would visit these," Franco reassures me.

Then, they give out code names, and Franco gives me my suitcase with the special fitted removable lining to hide all the microfilm. "Okay, those are the specs for the operation codenamed THE ACTOR."

I smile at the name used for the mission. Quite ironic, I think.

"I thought you might like that," Franco says, and everyone laughs.

"Now remember, your only job is to receive the microfilm, make sure it gets placed in the special suitcase, and then safely transport it to Franco," Gina emphasizes.

"Yes," Franco steps in. "Again, under no circumstance should you be involved with anything else that may jeopardize the mission."

"I understand," I say, but I don't agree. It isn't a lie, because I did understand.

The next hour, they give me a basic training session in Russian language, as well as other customs and nuances of visiting Russia. They hand out maps of Leningrad, so I can learn how to move around the city easily.

"In most cities in the world, one can figure out street names or find their way around. However, in Russia, it is almost impossible to figure out street names and be able to follow directions," Franco says. "Of course, if you speak Russian, it is not a problem. However, you do not."

"Yes," I agree. "And guidebooks are useless, since I don't know their alphabetic order."

"Exactly," Natasha agrees. "You're a quick learner."

We take a break for lunch, and Franco and Gina leave to make a phone call and a quick stop at the apartment they use in Florence.

"Vladimir, can we take a short walk along the river to get some fresh air?" I ask.

"Certainly," he answers.

The other two decided to go to the hotel restaurant, and the two of us walk out of the hotel and head towards the River Arno. My insides are tenser than when I face a new production, an interview with hostile press, or even a night when all of the critics come in a single shot. I face horrible rejection and the possibility he will go to Franco or Gina with what I'm about to say—but I must at least try.

We sit on a bench overlooking the river, and I start telling him about my career, my role in the tour, and my need to help with the cause all of us are fighting.

"I want to help the Russian Three, even if Franco is against any activity on my part," I blurt out.

"Ahhh," he says. "I thought there was more to you than acting. I will see if my bosses in Russia would want my help in any areas where Franco is not knowledgeable."

That is it. He said yes. I feel relief wash over me, and I take out my handkerchief to wipe a bit of perspiration from my hairline. Vladimir stands and shakes my hand. I realize I now have another ally when I reach Russia.

Although relieved, I am still nervous on our way back to the hotel for lunch. If Franco learns of my meeting, he will want details, but, when we return, I am happy Franco and Gina haven't come back to the hotel. They will know nothing about my clandestine walk with Vladimir.

The afternoon activities at the meeting move fast, and, in no time, the meeting comes to an end.

"Thank you all for coming. And you three get back safe," Franco says. Then we all exchange pleasantries around the room. As we start leaving the meeting room, I give a thumbs up, a handshake and a smile to Vladimir. They leave the hotel for their journey back to Russia, and the three of us remain. I sense Franco and Gina want to talk to me. I am waiting to see if Franco had any inkling of my walk and conversation with Vladimir, but, as soon as they're gone, Franco suggests that we all eat at his favorite restaurant in Florence and then meet back up in London in two days.

I spend one more day in Florence while Franco and Gina have meetings and preparations to take care of for the tour. I don't see them, and the last day passes comfortably. I pack, do some more sightseeing, and make a few stops to buy gifts. I stop into some fine leather shops along the river and purchase several warm leather coats I will need on the tour. While I had been focused primarily on the play and my role as a spy, my mind is now totally engrossed in the Russian tour. Even with that, I know I must first concern myself with the eight shows in

London before a paying audience. I have confidence the show will do well. However, as I have learned so many times before with shows, one must wait until performances start before getting too excited. If I mess this up, it will blow the whole mission. My first role as a spy is to be a great actor.

The plane begins to taxi for takeoff on the flight back to London. I close my eyes for a much-needed nap. After all the years of Broadway shows and performances of all kinds, I am now playing the biggest role of my entire life at the request of the United States government. I plan to make my country proud of me

CHAPTER 8

WELCOME TO LENINGRAD

You would have thought I was the tour director when the entire cast and crew checked in at the Grand Hotel of Europe in Leningrad. I made sure everyone was checked in properly and obtained the best rooms available.

"This is a wonderful place," I remark to a member of the chorus, a young man of twenty I always called Tim, but am fairly certain I always got his name wrong. "It is so conveniently located. Only a short walk to the Hermitage Museum and the Mikhailovsky Theatre, where the show will be performing."

"Thank you, Mr. Toomey," he says to me, and then walks off.

"Mr. George Toomey," I say to the man at the front desk.

"Certainly, sir." He looks down at a ledger and pulls a key off of the hook. "This is your key, sir. And your invitation to the evening's welcoming party."

"Thank you," I respond, reading the invitation. The invitation says that it is for the cast, crew, and Russian dignitaries and will be thrown by the manager of cultural affairs for the USSR, Alexander Kapersky.

I go up to my room, followed by the bellhops carrying in my trunks. In a short while, I will meet with Gina. She has been a bit friendlier since Florence, but I still get the sense she is always watching me suspiciously. She wants to meet, because she has an errand for me to run. Until my meeting, I want to get the lay of the land.

Everyone has left for their hotel room now, so it seems a good time to go for a walk. Outside, it is a bit cool, but not as cold as I had expected it to be here. I walk along the sidewalk, following the map I'd memorized on the trip. I let my thoughts meander from the performances in London to the meetings in Florence. Leningrad has a stoic beauty to it. There is a feel of history, but I also feel like I'm always being watched. That feeling could be caused by the fact that I'm a spy now.

I walk to the theatre and plan to return through the square in front of the Hermitage. That will allow me to get familiar with all of the paths I'll need to take during my stay.

As I approach the magnificent theatre, I am overcome. It is so beautiful. I am going to take the place of the ballets, operas, and symphonies that are normally performed here. The theatre will be transformed to accommodate our musical show.

As I approach the front doors, I am blocked.

"I am George Toomey. I will be performing here," I announce, loudly and slowly. The man looks at me uncomprehendingly.

"An actor," I say. "Ac-tor."

"Da. Ak-tor," the man replies.

Wonderful, communication. Again, I reach for the door handle.

"Nyet!" The man's voice is firm.

"English?" I implore, frustrated that the place we will perform doesn't know I am coming, doesn't know my name, and is barring my entrance.

The man replies in a string of Russian, at the end of which I hear something resembling the word "ing-gli-ski."

"Ing-gli-ski," I ask again.

The man indicates I should wait by pointing at the spot where I'm standing; then, he disappears inside. I feel like a child being told to stand still and not make a mess. I should have arranged the visit in advance, but I had assumed that they would know I was coming.

"Pri-vyet, my name Igor."

I turn to see an older man standing beside the first man—the one who told me to stay.

"I am George Toomey. The actor." I start to pantomime, and I realize I'm nearly yelling again. "For the show here."

The man pauses a moment.

"The actor for show."

"Yes," I say, trying to decide if I should give up and schedule a tour or if I should keep trying. "We are from America, and we are doing a show here. Musical."

Suddenly, recognition lights up in his eyes, and he turns to the first man, giving a string of orders in Russian. The one who barred me entrance waves me behind him to follow, smiling broadly.

Once they know who I am, I am welcomed warmly and given a VIP tour of my dressing room, the stage, the wings, orchestra pit, and, finally, a complete backstage tour. While I couldn't understand much of what was said, between the broken English and the similarity of theatres, I was able to figure my way out. The theatre was even more beautiful inside than out. It was regal and made me think of what it must have been like in the days of the tsars.

Forty-five minutes later, I was leaving, having signed more than twenty autographs and greeted numerous people. I walked out the door I'd entered and got my bearings again before walking the planned route past the Hermitage and back to the Hotel for my meeting with Gina. I am quite pleased with myself and even more confident that I'll be able to perform well as both an actor and a spy. Thirty minutes later, I am sitting down with Gina to discuss the afternoon's activity in detail, as well as my role as a spy.

"Well, George, you finally have your first opportunity to help," Gina opens, her voice kind.

"Great," I answer. "I am willing to perform any task given to me."

"That is wonderful, but as we've told you a number of times, your only task is as courier," she reminds me, sighing. It is frustrating that they seem bent on limiting me, but once I show them what I'm capable of, she'll realize they aren't using me to my fullest potential. It was the same way when I started on stage. They put me in small roles, but, one day, I took a chance, got noticed, and got the lead. Spying and acting are the same game on different stages.

Gina's instructions are short and to-the-point. I guess the less complicated, the more likely a successful outcome. "Take this Hermitage brochure and the Russian currency I have for you, and go sit on the stairs of the museum to read the brochure." She hands me the items. I look at them as she speaks. "Vladimir will be coming there. He will approach you with an offer to sell you a small drawing of the Hermitage. He will come up and ask if you are an American and if you would like to buy a drawing to take back to your home in the United States. You will ask how much, and then give him the currency. It is that simple."

"It sounds simple," I say, looking up from the brochure.

"Under no circumstance are you to show any reaction to his presence, nor have any conversation implying you know him," she says.

"Okay," I say.

"George, it is most important that you immediately return to your hotel room after the exchange. Do not spend any time with Vladimir other than the time needed for the transaction. When you get to your hotel room, take the painting, and in the back upper right-hand corner, make a small slit, and remove the microfilm. Take the film, and place it in the special lining of the suitcase Franco gave you. Put the suitcase away in your room with the rest of your luggage."

"Understood," I say, excitement now threatening to explode within me. I'm not nervous at all. This is far simpler than I'd expected. "Don't worry," I assure her, when I notice she is still looking at me.

"Okay. This is just your first mission, and there is a lot riding on this," she warns. "I will contact you upon your return."

"Alright," I say, and she seems to finally relax and trust me. Then, she leaves my room to allow me time to prepare for my errand.

I have about fifteen minutes before I leave. I've only been back a short time, but, now, the weather has changed from bright to cloudy with a light rain. It hardly seems a time for a man to sit outside reading, but they know what they're doing. I don a raincoat, pull my collar up, place a hat on my head, and put on a pair of sunglasses. I check myself in the mirror. Why in the world did I put sunglasses on when there is no sun? Now, I look like a spy, so I take the glasses off and put them in my pocket. I leave the hotel, walking slowly towards the Hermitage, where I sit on the steps and begin reading the brochure. From the corner of my eye, I see Vladimir approaching. It took every bit of fifteen minutes for him to wind his way through the mass of tourists in the square waiting to enter the Hermitage. When he approaches, he asks the prearranged questions. Proceeding on, he offers to sell me a painting of the Hermitage. After the exchange of currency and drawing, I ask Vladimir to sit down.

"Is there anything I can do to help the cause?" I ask.

"One of my men is working as a merchant sailor on the merchant ship, the *Alexander Gorsky*," he begins. "I've been unable to contact this man and receive some important documents on the purpose of a future sailing of the *Alexander Gorsky*."

"How can I help?"

"If you could ask for and receive a VIP tour of the port, maybe he could pass microfilm on to you," Vladimir answers.

"Sure. I will try to get a pass," I answer. I'm doubling my impact with this one simple task. Franco will be quite proud when he realizes all I've done. I take my sunglasses out of my pocket and place them on my face. We spend a few minutes talking, and I am feeling very good.

"RUN!" Vladimir suddenly yells. Startled, I look over my shoulder and see six men running towards us. They are having a hard time fighting their way through the throngs of tourists in the square.

"I will get to the port," I yell, as I take off running. Three of the men have broken away and are now chasing me. I dodge back and forth through the crowd, pushing past people and being careful not to lose the picture with the microfilm. How in the world do these men know what we were doing?

The sunglasses make things a bit darker and harder to see, but I don't dare take them off, for fear of being recognized. I break out of the crowd and turn one corner, and another. I loop back around to look from where I came. I see the three men have given up on their pursuit of me; I run up some stairs and am able to see the entire square behind me. The three men have joined the other three and have Vladimir surrounded, leading him away and depositing him in a waiting car.

I now start a fast walking routine. I need to get to the hotel, but I don't want to alert anyone to me or my plight. There is a metallic taste in my mouth, and it hurts under my ribs on the right side. I am really out of shape, even with all the rehearsing. When I arrive at the hotel, I am still breathing hard. I check over my shoulder as I enter the lobby and then hurry to my room, heart pounding in my ears.

I get in my room and lock the door behind me. The phone rings and startles my heart into a gallop once again.

"Did you enjoy your walk?" Gina asks, her voice friendly.

"Yes, but could you come to my room please? It is rather urgent."

I have already been warned not to have any important conversations on the phone, because someone may be listening. She doesn't answer. I hear only a click. I dread telling her the whole story, but realize that I must. Too soon, there is a knock on my door. I'm not surprised at her reaction when I tell her everything. She is furious.

"Franco needs to hear the entire story and will make any adjustments or decisions necessary. I will go find Franco. You meet us in the lobby at seven for the party," she hisses at me before slamming the door behind her.

The evening's events will be hosted by the cultural affairs chairman, Alexander Kapersky, and his wife, Marina. There will be a lot of government officials, dancers, actors, and musicians introduced to the members of the American tour. What if I am recognized there? Fear snakes through me a moment, but I remain calm. I cut the microfilm out and put it in the suitcase. No need to get caught with it in my room in the picture.

With several hours to go until the beginning of the party, I decide the only thing to do is to try and put the afternoon's debacle out of my mind. My plan is to take a professional nap. My professional ritual, whenever something is weighing on my mind is simple: close the blinds, unplug the phone, put on my pajamas, and get under the covers. This time, it will be hard to nap. I have messed things up and need to make them right. Nonetheless, I will try. So I put on pajamas and get under the covers. No sooner do I close my eyes, but there is a banging on my door. I open the door and Franco barges in. The litany of obscenities is enough to curl a sailor's toes. "I warned you—don't get involved!" he screams. "How could you have gone above my head? You compromised Vladimir and, most likely, the entire mission."

"But I—" I begin, but he silences me with a raised hand.

"Did they recognize you?" he asks.

"No. I really don't think they did." I talk about my disguise. I believe I convinced Franco they did not know who I was, but, to be safe, he has me throw away the coat, hat, and sunglasses I was wearing at the meeting. I hate to do it, because they're beautiful, but my protests are met with a cold silence.

"DO NOT DO ANYTHING ELSE," he booms—his voice deep and a bit menacing. "We are part of a team on this, and there is no time for a star or a solo. We work as a team, or we all will crash and burn."

I am angry that he would imply that I'm not a team player. I know how to work as a part of a production, but I am not accustomed to sitting in the chorus. I am a star. I am the Actor. The mission is named after me, and I intend to do my part.

"I will evaluate the information you obtained from Vladimir regarding the port and will now try and seek out any information leading to the possible compromise of our tour." Franco opens the door. "See you at the welcome party."

The Party

The main ball room of the hotel is filled with more than three hundred guests. Vodka is flowing, and the best caviar in the U.S.S.R. is offered to everyone. Introductions are made, and, most of the time, I am introduced as the actor from the United States. I am not sure how many of the guests have any idea of what Broadway is all about or realize how big a star I actually am in the United States, but they all nod politely and seem impressed.

After an hour, Alexander Kapersky goes to a microphone to greet all of the guests. He speaks first in Russian, then in English. He makes special mention of certain politicians, Russian stars in attendance, and introduces his wife, Marina. The speech goes on for twenty minutes and is the typical hot air of men in his position. He tells everyone how happy he is to welcome the Americans and their tour. He loves America and hopes this is the beginning of a wonderful and long relationship between the two countries. I take a liking to Alexander's style, and immediately hope everyone I meet is as nice and cordial as the cultural affairs chairman—even if he does seem a bit full of himself.

I notice Gina and pull her aside. "I really liked Alexander's words and hope to see more of Mr. Kapersky," I say.

"George, don't believe everything you see and hear."

My expression must have told her I needed further explanation, because she continues, "Manager of cultural affairs—that's a laugh. This man is really the second in command at the KGB. He is the second most powerful man in the U.S.S.R. He is ruthless and will kill anyone who gets in his way or just looks at him the wrong way."

I look up at him, trying to reconcile her description with the man I see.

Gina continues, "If he ever finds out you were the man on the steps at the Hermitage, I would suggest you cover your private parts. So now—and I can't warn you enough—feel free to talk to Kapersky, but be very careful in any conversation you have with him."

The eighteen-piece orchestra strikes up "Give My Regards to Broadway", and Gina starts to walk away. Everyone is asked to dance and to continue enjoying the food and drinks.

Kapersky's beautiful wife, Marina, comes over to me. "Might I dance with the star of this production?" she asks.

"Certainly, ma'am." The two of us take the dance floor, and, at the end of the number, we approach the bar and toast the success of the tour.

"I was once an actress in Russia," Marina begins

"That is wonderful. Where did you act?" I ask.

She begins to talk, and we have a natural bond in theatre. She shares with me all about her previous acting and how, as a very young actress, she studied with the great and aging Stanislavski. I enjoyed hearing from an actual Russian actress and ask her opinion on the Stanislavski method of acting. I talked about how method acting is all the rage in the United States—practiced by the likes of Marlon Brando, Stella Adler, interpreted by the acting teacher Lee Strasberg, and taught at an acting school called The Actors Studio.

The hour passes, and I have no idea how much vodka has been served. I'm feeling a bit free with my tongue, but I'm trying to remember Gina's warning. I look around to see many of the guests have already left. Then, the orchestra begins playing its last song. Marina moves close to me and whispers in my ear, "I would very much love to see you again."

In the past, I knew exactly what the whisper meant, but knowing that her husband is the second most powerful man in Russia—ruthless to boot, and not forgetting the Hermitage incident—I give her an appropriate answer.

"Marina, I would love to see you again. When you and your husband come to see the show, please come backstage to say hello, and the three of us can go out afterwards for dinner and drinks."

Saying goodnight and leaving the ballroom, I meet up with Gina and walk her back to her room.

"I couldn't help noticing how much time you spent with Marina and how much attention you both gave each other," Gina says, clearly still very angry.

"Marina was an actress. We discussed so much about the theatre and acting. She even studied under Stanislavski," I say, wistfully. "I invited her and her husband to come backstage after a performance, and suggested that the three of us could go out for drinks.

Gina seems relieved for the first time. "About this afternoon," she begins, "if anyone can smooth over any problems from earlier in the day, Franco is the one."

That is a tremendous comfort. I understand my mistake this time, and, next time, I will be much more careful. We both say goodnight and return to our respective rooms. I only hope that Gina, knowing my proclivity in romancing the other sex, will believe my explanation of talking about theatre with Marina is true.

CHAPTER 9

THE PHONE CALL

Just over a week after the welcoming party, my phone rang.

"George, this is Marina Kapersky. Please don't hang up?" The opening came out so fast it was as though she thought that was a standard greeting for Americans.

"I'm not going to hang up," I assure her. "What can I help you with, Mrs. Kapersky?"

"I know you implied you didn't want to see me alone, but please listen to me. I need to meet you. It is urgent. I have to tell you something. I know it will be of the utmost importance to your government." Marina's voice was urgent.

My heart shifts from a trot to a full gallop. This will not go over well if I am being spied on.

"In fact," she continues, "it could be the biggest news story of the year, possibly the decade." She takes a very long breath and blurts out, "I would also like to see you again, too."

I am intrigued to hear about Marina's important information, but I also—for some inexplicable reason—have the need to see Marina. "Marina, what about your husband? And where could we meet privately?"

"My husband is in Moscow for the next two weeks, and it is safe to meet with me. I know where we can meet and not be seen. I have a friend with a houseboat on a quiet spot on the Neva River. They are away, I have a key, and they have let me use it before."

I consider again what Franco and Gina said. I think about what happened with Vladimir. I know all of this, but I need to make it up to them, and this time *she* is approaching *me*. She is asking me to be a courier of something, and that is exactly what I'll be. Maybe the information to be given to me may put me in good standing with Franco.

"Okay," I say. "I will meet with you."

"Wonderful." Her voice is lovely, but her relief reminds me of how much pressure she must be under. So much sadness has washed clean from her tone, and it makes me sad for her. We agree to a time to meet later today.

"George, outside of your hotel is a bus stop. Take the bus marked Neva River. The word will look like Peka Heba to you," Marina explains.

"Thank you for that. I wondered how I would understand the writing," I laugh. She laughs, too. I can't help thinking what a pleasant sound her laugh is.

"I understand. Your alphabet looked quite odd to me when I was learning to speak English, too."

"Okay, so I get on the Peka Heba bus," I repeat, realizing I may be flirting a little bit, but more to make her laugh than to have sex with her.

"When you get to the first Neva River bus stop, exit the bus and walk approximately a quarter of a mile away from the direction you have just come. On the right, you will see a houseboat painted blue. There are no other houseboats on this part of the River, so you won't be confused. I will be looking for you, and, George, thank you for seeing me."

The Houseboat

It is somewhat a short bus ride, and when I arrive—as promised—Marina is waiting for me. I keep walking down the gangway connecting the land to the boat's dock. We give each other the traditional European welcome kiss on both cheeks.

"Please," she urges, "come inside."

I go below deck, where there is a small table covered in an assortment of pastries, a bit of jam, coffee, and tea.

"Please, sit down," Marina says.

She is beginning to look nervous again, but I sit down and wait to learn why I was invited here.

"I want to explain some things to you, so you understand why I am doing what I'm doing," Marina begins.

"You don't have to justify yourself..." I begin, but the look on her face silences me. She needs to say these things, I believe, far more than I need to hear them.

"I am abused by my husband, mentally and physically," she says. "I realize many still think that women are merely an extension of their husbands and laws do little to protect us, but I have never believed that, and I'm ashamed to now be in this position."

"It isn't your fault," I assure her. "Men will say almost anything to win a woman." The admission stabs me in the chest and, while no abuser, I feel the talons of guilt sinking deep into my flesh.

"My marriage was never very good, and the last two years we haven't had a good relationship at all. In the early years, we had a somewhat active sex life, but we haven't slept together for several years." She said it all as though she were discussing the plot of a novel, not her own life.

"I'm sorry?" I say. I have spoken only a few hours between the party and today, but the things she is revealing seem a bit forward. I must have had it on my face, because she looks at me and giggles.

"Do I seem forward, George? Maybe I do." She spreads some jam on a small square of bread, "I have read so much about you in my husband's file that I feel I know you." She takes a bite of her bread. "And I certainly know that you have no modesty when it comes to the topic of sex."

"What file?" I ask, suddenly concerned about the mission and my life.

"We'll get to that in a moment," she says. "Don't worry. They aren't interested in you."

That allows me to relax a little.

"Alexander worked his way up the ranks at the KGB to second in command, and, on his journey, didn't have much time for me. Two or more weeks every month, he is at the KGB's Moscow headquarters, leaving me all alone in Leningrad."

"Many men have a busy professional life," I offer, hoping to defend myself, as well as Alexander. If my wife were to sit down and paint the tableau of our marriage, what would she say?

"That might be so," Marina continues, "but for a woman who was active and had a mostly successful acting career, not having any purpose or direction in life is difficult. Alexander knew me as an actress. Who knows, maybe that was why he wanted to marry me." Her eyes look a bit glassy as she recalls her earlier life. I don't think her tears that threaten to break loose are because she misses his love— I think she misses the love she *thought* she had.

"Once married, he forbade me from acting or a career of any kind. I tried being the dutiful wife of a high-ranking official in the KGB, but I was becoming bored by the lifestyle thrust upon me."

"You didn't have to marry him." I say, hoping I don't sound insensitive.

"I realize that," Marina acquiesces, "but he was a very different man when we were courting."

I love the use of the old-fashioned word "courting". It made it seem so sweet, until I considered what she was telling me about life after the vows.

"But I really don't want to talk about that part right now," she changes gears. "I want to tell you why I called you here. See, as careful as he is in the business affairs of the KGB, he has the habit of leaving important papers around the apartment and on his desk."

"That is quite surprising," I say. Franco and Gina seem to be very cautious. I cannot imagine the idea of them leaving classified documents lying about.

"I think it is because he drinks so much vodka at home," she says, ruefully. "It makes him stupid, careless, and mean."

"If that's the case, it is a wonder he's gone so high in the organization," I say.

"Maybe you're right. I don't know," she says, waving away my comment. "But I want to tell you about what I found out."

"Okay. I am eager to hear it." And I truly am.

"No one is ever allowed in the apartment, other than me. That is why he feels so free to leave things out, I think."

"Possibly." Or maybe he just doesn't like people over. I wonder which it is.

"Over the past few years, when he is gone, more and more I've been reading his memos and documents. Normally, there isn't much there of any real interest," she says with a dismissive wave of her hand. "It is little more than trying to create scandals or find out information on opponents. Much of it bores me."

I nod.

"Then, a few days ago I saw a file out that said, 'The American Actor.'" She smiles sardonically. "It was a dossier of George L. Toomey. I read all about your career on Broadway. All of it confirmed what you'd told me at the party. That was why I thought that I might be able to trust you. In Russia, it is really hard to know who to trust with kids turning in parents and wives informing on husbands."

I look around the boat, as if indicating my understanding of her last point. She laughs heartily, "This file also documented the countless escapades of bedding down actresses you starred with on Broadway."

"I would like to find out who told the KGB about my sex life," I say, not denying what she already knew.

"On the last page of your file was written, 'CONCLUSION: GT is of low importance. Rich American loves women, NO NEED TO FOLLOW.'" She shifts in her seat. "I think that is another reason I can trust you. They aren't watching."

"I guess this is one review in which I don't care if the writer says I am not important to watch," I say. "Is this fairly recent?"

"They update him every few days. Since he is out of town, there hasn't been anything new at the house. Why? Should you be on their radar?"

"No," I say quickly, hoping this is true and that the Vladimir thing really did go away. "I just wanted to make sure."

"Well, this is now the important part," she leans forward, as if someone nearby might hear. "I clean the apartment, water the plants, and do the laundry. We have plenty of money to pay for help, but I don't want to wait for him to be home so it can get done. It is also an outlet to keep busy and prevents me from becoming more bored than I have already become."

"Understandable," I say, considering all of the things my family had done to fill the George-less moments of their lives. Despite my goals, sitting with Marina was making me rethink the way I'd interacted with my family and how much time I'd not given to them. Once again, guilt started to take me, but, as before, I shoved it back and focused on what I could do now: help Marina and help America.

"A few days ago, while I was finishing my chores, I found a file that had inadvertently fallen behind my husband's desk. It was wedged tightly between the desk and the wall and labeled KGB—TOP SECRET. I thought it might be a very important document, and I was bored, so I read it while I drank my morning coffee. There were many documents inside, as well as personal notes written by several high-ranking KGB officials. One page was most sensitive, and that was when I realized maybe I shouldn't have opened and read it—but by then, it was too late." She stops talking and focuses, instead, on her teacup, running her finger around the rim over and over.

"What did it say?" I ask her, not because I'm prying, but because if this was why she called me out here, I need to know what's happening.

"It was a summary of a major mission. In the document, it said, and I'm quoting the best I can from memory, 'The main goal of *Operation Castro* is to supply and transport the latest, highly sophisticated missiles and rockets to Cuba. All armaments will have the range and the ability to reach key cities in the United States.'"

Immediately, my ears perk up, and I wish that I'd asked Franco to join me, or at least Gina. Why hadn't I? I guess because I'm attracted to Marina, and I don't really need their help. I just need them to believe me, and they might not on something this big without proof.

"'The KGB will offer full military and financial support to Castro to build up his military and his government,'" Marina continues. "'The Castro government, being less than a year old, must not be allowed to fail. All missiles and armaments will travel by freighter and will be listed and labeled as medical and humanitarian supplies. URGENT!!! NK has approved this operation and wants it to move forward at once, without delay.'"

"Are you certain of this?" I ask, stunned by what it would mean and even more stunned that the Russian Three had been right.

"I am quite certain," she says. "I pretended I was memorizing a script for a play. There may be a word or two off, but the meaning is completely unchanged."

"That could be catastrophic to the U.S.," I say, thinking about how close Cuba is to our country and how many cities a missile could hit.

"Which is why when I knew I had stumbled on something important, I had to reach you. This might be my chance." She hesitates a moment before continuing, "I might as well be honest with you, upfront."

I listen, as if I am not aware of Marina's comments about her husband.

"My husband and I are married in name only. He is rarely in Leningrad, and we see each other less and less every year. I agonized over the decision to have called you at all; however, the night we met at the party at the hotel, a feeling came over me. I could trust you. More importantly, you might be able to help me. It was this feeling that prompted me to phone you."

"This is an awful lot to process," I respond, somewhat overwhelmed. "Let me think for a moment."

We leave the little table and move to a large, circular couch in the living room of the houseboat.

"The missiles will be transported on the freighter *Alexander Gorsky*," she adds. "I believe your government might be interested in seeing the papers? I can show you the document."

That's it, that's it, I am screaming silently inside of my head. "You have the document?" I turn and look at her. "I thought you only memorized it."

"Of course I have it," she smiles. "But you don't speak or read Russian."

"No. I do not," I smile. She really is a wonderfully smart woman. Now, I have a decision to make. This is exactly the subject the Russian Three were talking about in Florence—and it is what Vladimir wanted to find out about—it is armament movements on freighters at the ports. I remember Franco's loud and clear statement at out meeting in Florence. *It is top priority to find out what the Russians are planning.* Of course, the next statement was pointed at me, *Don't get involved.*

I think Marina's information trumps anything Franco has said in the past. She was reaching out to me. I agreed to meet with her, but I'm not really doing anything beyond carrying the information to him. So what if it isn't on microfilm? This is a spoken tip, *with* documentation. I realize I can't tell Gina or Franco anything until I obtain the documents. Then, I will be able to make a decision. I have to feel confident Franco would want to know about the conversation I just had. Maybe this information will get me back in Franco's good graces.

Marina continues, breaking in to my mental ramblings. "I am telling you all of this with the hope that you may be able to tell the proper person in your government about this conversation and see if they can help me."

If I only connect her to Franco or Gina, is that really breaking their rule to stay out of it? I think again about what she just said: help her. How does she want me to help her, and can I actually give that help?

"What kind of help do you need?" I ask.

Marina relaxes, and I see her body sink back into the couch, as if a long ordeal is now past. "There are two things I need in return," she says. "First, for turning over this top secret report, your government will transport me out of Russia, grant me political asylum, and relocate me in New York. Secondly, I think I am a somewhat attractive woman and a good actress—I would like to resume acting and want you to be my mentor in helping me with my career in the United States."

The second is no problem at all, but I'm in no position to offer the first. I am fairly certain, however, that Franco can. Even while I'm still thinking, Marina leans forward and kisses me, not in the European way, but romantically. Warmth engulfs my body, and, for the first time in my life, I am taken aback by the chemistry in the kiss and the embrace. I know I shouldn't let sex get between the bigger need starting to form, but my feelings for Marina are too strong. I feel a need to not only possess her physically, but also to help her. Maybe once we are free from the problems here, we can have a life in America together. We could give each other what we've both longed for. I can have a companion who loves the theatre as much as I do, and she can have a partner who will care for and appreciate her in a way she deserves.

We walk hand-in-hand into the bedroom, where we make love. Not just any kind of lovemaking, but a genuinely caring form of lovemaking, in which both of us are more interested in satisfying the other first. I know it has been a long time since I felt so warm and satisfied. We tangle ourselves in each other's embrace until we are both exhausted.

"I cannot remember the last time I felt this way," she breathes. "I certainly never felt this with Alexander."

I bring her lips to mine again, and we kiss deeply. It is Marina who breaks our embrace. "I must see you again. Let's have lunch tomorrow at my apartment. Alexander is away, and we can be all alone."

The domestic meal appeals to something I'd thought was either dead inside of me or that had never existed. "That will be great."

"Good. I'm a great cook, and I will prepare a deluxe culinary spread for you."

We both force ourselves to get dressed after another kiss and embrace. "I'll see you tomorrow at lunch," I say.

"I'm looking forward to it."

"And I'll see what I can find out about you getting into the U.S."

"I'm looking forward to that, too," she responds, kissing me one more time and then taking a step back, so I can turn to leave. I leave the houseboat reluctantly to begin my journey back to the hotel.

CHAPTER 10

THE TOUR ENDS

I step up to the door and push the bell. Almost immediately, Marina opens the door and looks down at the flowers I'm holding for her.

"Welcome," she pulls me inside and kisses me. "It has been a very long time since I was excited about preparing a romantic lunch for anyone. I have bought meats, cheeses, Russian bread, and Russian wine for our luncheon. I made sure the table was set with my finest china and silver. I wanted this day to be special in every way for the two of us."

"It will be," I promise. I haven't talked to Franco or Gina yet. They are busy with their own work and probably think that I'll stay out of trouble from now on.

"Why don't I show you the documents first, and, then, we can enjoy lunch."

"That sounds like a wonderful day." I smile. "Business before pleasure."

She returns my smile, and hers is full of promise. She gets the documents out and makes a copy of an important page on a small photocopier in the apartment, then hands it over to me. We discuss the content with her pointing to things and translating the words for me. More than once, she looks a word up in the dictionary and proves to me what she is saying is true. It is unnecessary, because I would have trusted her without the dictionary.

"I don't work for the KGB, but I'm sure the content is real," Marina says as she begins to put a few things away.

"If you believe they are credible, I believe you are credible," I reply.

"Excellent. Let's eat."

True to her word, Marina is an amazing cook. Sardis has some competition on its hands. If Marina comes to America and cooks food like this for me, I may never eat out again. The thought brings me to another. After seeing the document in person, I now feel I can trust her and tell the whole story about the tour. The words come out slowly. "I am a courier and know the right people who will be able to get you out of Russia. When I get back to the hotel, I will start the process and will let you know the outcome."

She is so happy that she jumps up from the table and hugs and kisses me. After finishing our lunch, we move to the living room to enjoy a pastry and cafe. I have been honest and vulnerable with her, and she has been honest with me. I feel I can give her something she needs: protection and a better life. I can provide for her. I provided for Carol and the girls, but she rejected me. She hated our apartment. She hated our life. She even hated the sand, for crying out loud! Marina wants those things. Already, this tour has been so much more than I could have hoped for when I agreed to it.

Overcome with emotion, I put down my plate and lean in to kiss her. For the next hour or so, we hug and kiss on the couch. We are necking like teenagers, and I don't care. Gradually, the necking becomes more, and we make beautiful love on the floor. Afterward, I hold her, and she talks about her love of the theater and what life will be like when she escapes Russia.

Too soon, I have to get back to the hotel to prepare for the evening's performance.

"I want to see you so badly tomorrow," I say. "But tomorrow is matinee day, and it will be difficult to get away."

"I understand." And I know she actually does.

"We will be together in two days. I promise to have an answer, regarding your political asylum, when I see you in forty eight hours."

"That is good enough for me." She smiles broadly, and I see a radiance in that smile that I've never noticed before. It is far lovelier than the expensive clothing she wore the day we met. It is better even than this lavish apartment. It is the look of hope.

I quickly return to the hotel. I must talk to Gina as soon as possible. I have no idea how fast these shipments are moving, but I'm certain that they are eminent. I manage to find my way back to the hotel again and bust through the doors, heading up the steps.

"Mr. Toomey," the bellman greets me, "I have a message for you, sir."

I step over to his desk. He hands me a note in a sealed white envelope with my name written neatly on the outside. I open it, trying not to be so eager as to arouse suspicion, and read it quickly. Gina had to go out of town for two days on business and will see me when she gets back. I am disappointed. This means I've broken my promise to Marina, and I'm even more concerned about the sensitivity of my information. How is it that they can leave me unprotected for two solid days?

The Kapersky Apartment

Alexander walks in the door without a word. Marina was certainly somewhere in his house, but it hardly mattered to him anymore. She had become nothing more than a tuxedo for him: pull her out and display her at government events and functions, then return her to the closet.

"You are home?"

Alexander turns and sees Marina standing in the doorway, a startled expression on her face and a feather duster in her hand.

"Da," he replies. "I am home." Things had become too intense in Moscow at his meeting, and he is glad to be able to come back to his desk at home and read through things, without any of the quarreling and jockeying endured at the office.

A number of files are out on the desk, but not the most urgent one, the one Khrushchev sent him home to deal with. A bit of fear, just a bit, starts to make his head hurt, but he pushes it back. He won't allow such feminine emotions as fear or love stop him.

Never mind. He will get answers from her. He stands up and sees the gap between the desk and the wall. There, wedged in a crack, is the file. If this were ever discovered, there would certainly be hell to pay. He immediately puts all of the files in the safe and locks it. For the next hour, he reviews his notes on the Moscow meeting and the mission with Cuba. With this, they will cripple the U.S. and be able to push into Europe and maybe even get some allies to launch into parts of America.

The sun is getting low in the horizon, and he checks his watch. It is about time to leave. "Marina," he yells as he slips on his coat and picks up his hat.

"Yes?" She comes down the hall, now dressed more appropriately.

"I have a dinner meeting and will be back tomorrow," he informs her, putting his hat on his head.

"Fine."

How is it possible she still gets upset that he doesn't spend more time with her, when she really doesn't like his company?

He takes a few steps to the door and turns. "I forgot to ask. How was your week?"

"Fine," she repeats, turning and walking back down the hall.

The next morning, he cannot get to the apartment fast enough. He hopes beyond hope that Marina is there. It is just after eight in the morning, and Marina has always been an early riser. Hopefully, that habit hasn't changed.

He reaches their door, pushes his key in the lock, and turns it.

"Marina," he yells, still trying to pull the key out of the door. He finally gets it out and closes the door. "Marina, where are you?"

"Alexander, I'm—" He slaps her across the face before she is fully in the room.

"How dare you!" he screams. He backhands her with his fist closed, sending her sprawling across the floor.

"Alexander, please," she begs, but her voice is little more than a stick scratching on glass to him. A nuisance that keeps a person up at night and something you vow to cut down in the morning.

"How dare you!" he growls, kicking her in her side again and again.

She draws up her knees, trying to protect herself from the blow, but he only kicks harder. Every injustice he has suffered. Every disdainful glance from her. All of her mockery of him as a man. He will extract payment as he kicks her again and again.

Finally, his foot hurts a little, and he jerks her up by her hair, flinging her to the couch. She sits up, her face already turning black and swollen. A dribble of blood runs down from her mouth, a bit more from her left eye and even more from her nose. She lifts her hand up to touch her face, and he sees two jagged red nails that have snapped off.

"Marina, I know everything," he screams. She looks at him, uncomprehending. "I know you met the actor at the houseboat. You were followed. You had an affair." He pulls out his eight-millimeter projector. "I know you have seen files."

He pulled out the film he'd had developed the previous night before his dinner meeting. "There you are with him on our floor." He throws the box that had held the film at her. It hits her in the face. He likes that.

"Alexthander." Her mouth is swelling, making a subtle lisp. It makes him hate her more.

"Shut up!" he screams. "And you are in my office here, giving him something. What did you give him?"

She doesn't move. Doesn't talk. She only draws her knees up to her chest. "Alexthander," she implores once more.

"No, you listen, Marina," he says, putting the gun in his holster, so he doesn't shoot her too fast. "I need to know what these papers are you're looking at."

She says nothing. He grits his teeth, absolute fury taking over every inch of his body. The quality of the film is not very clear; he could only see basic activity taking place in the apartment, not anything specific. He needs to know exactly how much that actor knows.

He hits her again and again, until his hand hurts, but she won't speak. She just keeps lisping his name. He goes in the kitchen to wash his hand and hears her crying in the next room.

"Are you ready to talk yet?" he screams. "You know, I've handled men, I can handle you."

"I never want to see you again," she screams back.

He's had enough insults from this woman. He is no cuckold. "I can certainly oblige." He raises the pistol and puts three bullets in her forehead and face. Blood splatters back on him, staining his new shirt around the cuff. Even in death, this woman is a bother.

He holsters his pistol and walks to his office phone. He dials his office at the KGB. "I need someone to come to my apartment and get rid of my wife's body. No one should ever be able to find it."

"Yes, sir," his assistant replies on the other end.

"And connect me to extension 34." Although Alexander wants to go immediately to the hotel and kill George Toomey, he needs to talk to his superior first. When the man answers, he decides that Alexander should return to Moscow. It is further decided not to alert anyone in Leningrad of the situation, until they know what the American actor knows and who he may have told. They would discuss next steps over the next two days: how to handle George Toomey, the compromised document, and the cultural tour.

***

Two days pass. I haven't been able to reach Marina, and I'm going crazy. Every few hours, I check the front desk for messages, just in case my phone isn't working. She hasn't called. Gina will be back today, and I need to talk to her about what I have and what I know. If she's in danger, we need to get her out. I pace around my room, but I cannot stand it any longer. If I don't hear from her in two hours, I will go to her apartment, just to make sure everything is fine. The phone rings. I snatch it up before it finishes its first ring. Hoping it is Marina, I nearly call out her name, but, thankfully, my senses reengage, and, instead, I answer with a desperate, "Hello?"

"George, what have you done?" Gina's voice is urgent. "Don't leave the hotel. Wait for me. I will be there in five minutes."

What have I done? I try to think about what she could mean. Was everything with Vladimir coming to a head? I hadn't done a thing on that since they told me to back off. Now, I have two mysteries: Marina and Gina.

In about three minutes, Gina rushes into the room. "What the hell have you done, George?"

"What do you mean?" I ask, genuinely trying to figure out what I did wrong now.

"Our operatives in the KGB have told us that you have had an affair with the wife of Alexander Kapersky. Are you crazy?"

"I...I..." I start to stutter an answer, but it falls flat. I have too much to tell her for my brain to catch up.

"And," Gina starts to yell, then looks at my hotel room door and lowers her voice. "And, they also said you received a top secret document, but no one seems to know anything about any document."

I try to explain it all to Gina. It wasn't just an affair—I really care for Marina, and she for me. I tell her about the request for political asylum in the United States. In addition, I had agreed to help with Marina's acting career in New York. I show Gina the document in question.

"I was coming back to tell you that day, but you left me a message saying you'd be gone for two days. I couldn't find you, and you said no phone conversations, so I did nothing but wait," I say, feeling the need to defend myself. "And Marina called me over. I didn't seek her out."

Gina looked at the document. "Holy Christ, this is important."

"So you understand it?" I ask.

She glares at me. "Do you think I'd be on this assignment if I wasn't fluent in Russian?" She looks back at the document. "I have to tell Franco about everything immediately."

"I know. That is why I've been waiting for you," I say, trying to help her see that I'd done the right thing and hoping she'll help me get Marina to safety.

"George, Marina will not be going to the United States. She is dead."

How could this happen? I struggle for an answer. I cannot understand why this happened to her. Why hadn't Gina been here to get the message? Who killed her?

"You better get up and compose yourself. They are coming to kill you and to get the document," Gina says flatly, with no more emotion than if she were telling me that she preferred black pants to navy blue.

"What have I done?" I ask, and I mean it both ways. What did I do that was so wrong? What horrible fate overcame Marina because of me?

"I have to break our cover and go to the U.S. embassy to make a secure call to Franco," Gina says, showing me absolutely no sympathy. She doesn't care that the woman I cared for is dead. Is this the way all spies operate? I'm angry at all of this, but I need Gina to get out. So I won't tell her now what I feel.

"George, stay put while I go out, or I will kill you myself," she threatens—and she shows me her gun for emphasis. Then, she is gone.

I am left pacing back and forth, muttering to myself, "I just wanted to help everyone; I just wanted to help everyone."

The hour passes. It is the longest hour of my entire life. Gina again rushes into the room and yells out, "They are on the way to kill you. We must leave. Grab the suitcase with the microfilm in the lining, the Castro document, your passport, and nothing else. Follow me." I pick up the items, and she takes the document from me.

"There is a car downstairs to drive us to a secluded airport. Franco will be flying there in a private aircraft," Gina says, looking up and down the halls as we run. "The airport he is using is out-of-the-way and only used infrequently by rich Russian businessmen who have bought private planes and are learning how to fly. There is no tower or flight plans needed, and Franco's plane can fly low over the trees undetected."

I follow her, wondering why she is telling me all of this. If they are on their way to kill me, they might be listening.

Once again, I realize how out-of-shape I am as we run down the staircase. Gina begins to pull ahead, and the pain under my ribs makes every footfall ache.

"Where are we going from there?" I manage to choke out as we run.

"We will all fly to Finland to hide out, until Franco figures out the next step."

I never ran as fast as I did down the stairwell in the hotel and into the waiting car. When I dive in the backseat, I feel, for the first time, that I actually might make it. As the driver speeds away from the hotel, I turn around. Everything I had, except for this suitcase, was still in that hotel. I watch the hotel fade away. I also see a black sedan.

"There is a car following us," I yell to the driver.

"I figured," Gina says, muttering a stream of expletives. "I'm guessing four on board," she says to the driver.

We break out of the city and onto the country roads, from pavement, to gravel, to dirt.

"George, you get down in the seat," Gina yells. "Down on the floor would be even better. If they start shooting, I want you out of the way."

The last thing I see before I'm on the floor is a farmer's tractor. We swerve around it, but clip a car only moments later.

Gina cusses, and the car goes faster.

"They are keeping up with us, no matter what," the driver reports.

"Just keep pushing it," she urges.

I hear a ping, followed by another. It sounds a bit like hail hitting the windows when I was a child living with my parents outside the city limits. Only this isn't the calming sound of youth. They want me dead.

Another bullet hits the car, then another, shattering the back windshield. I cover my head with my hands and stay low.

"George, we're almost there," Gina says. "Franco will cover us when we get to the airport."

I'm scared, really scared. I'm also sad. And I'm sorry that I didn't try to find Franco or Gina, so that I could have told them about Marina.

I hear two more gunshots, and, then, I feel something wet. I reach up and feel my head. Blood. I carefully feel around for the injury and look up. Gina's dead eyes stare back at me. There is far more, but I turn away. As my mind reconstructs the horror I just witnessed, I realize that part of her skull is gone.

"We're almost there," the driver yells back.

"Gina's dead," I scream. Somehow, I'd forgotten there was another person in the car.

"Are you sure?" he yells.

"Pretty sure," I yell back up, not willing to look again.

"It's going to get windy for a bit. These roads out here are like tight esses," the driver says.

I feel the car move from side to side, and hear Gina's body flop to the seat.

"I see Franco's plane," the driver yells over the sound of the wind coming through the back.

I hear a smashing sound, followed by an explosion. In that instant, I know we've hit some bomb left from the war or something else and that I'll be dead before my next thought.

The car slows only slightly. "Well, four less people chasing you," the driver says. "They just smashed into a tree back there, and the car exploded."

Since I'm not being shot at, I sit up. Franco opens the door of the plane as the car slows.

"Let's go," Franco yells as soon as I open the door.

"But the things…" I say.

"What things?" Franco asks, watching past me as I quickly climb out.

"The suitcase and documents," I answer. I reach in around Gina's body and find the suitcase and the sleeve that held the document.

"Do you have everything now?" Franco asks, pushing me to the airplane.

"Franco, Gina…" I say, trying to form words.

"I'll get her. Get on the plane." I hesitate. "Grab him," Franco orders the driver. The man has to be at least five inches taller and forty pounds stronger than I am. He grabs me and pulls me along by the arm.

I'm still buckling when Franco gets on the plane and puts Gina's body in a seat. Then, he closes the door and yells, "Take off."

"I am truly sorry for Gina's death," I say quietly to Franco. "I know you have lost your best agent."

Franco never takes his eyes off of Gina. He runs his finger gently across her lips, then her chin and takes her hand. "I have lost more than my best agent tonight. Gina was my wife."

CHAPTER 11

FLIGHT TO FINLAND

The flight to Finland had to be the most bizarre of my life. Gina's covered body was in a seat on the plane, and, for Franco, it was business as usual. He started developing and discussing various plans for ways to eliminate the problems I created for everyone without showing much emotion—all while having his dead wife on board the plane.

"We will land at a small airport, just north of Helsinki," Franco says. "You will hide out in Finland for several months. Once things have blown over, or at least settled down, you will fly back to England and onto New York."

"Where will I stay?" I ask. "I don't know the language."

"Don't worry, most people speak English here. I have arranged for a small apartment, used in the past by the CIA, just north of the private airport," Franco assures me. "Since you will be there for a while, we have created an identity for you. People will learn the occupant of the apartment is a sports writer from New York. He will be writing a story about Helsinki, ten years after the Olympics."

"A writer?" I ask, incredulous. Couldn't they come up with a better story than that? I am an actor. I know nothing of writing.

"Yes," Franco continues. "A writer. You'll also study if tourism has grown, what became of all the athletes, stadiums, ski jumps used for the venues, and whether all the money spent to bring the Olympics to Helsinki was worth the investment…stuff like that."

I sit quietly. There isn't much more to say. When we land in Finland, several CIA agents meet the plane. One takes charge of removing and handling the remains of Gina. Franco bends down to kiss his dead wife, showing some emotion for the first time since her death. When I consider my reaction to the death of a woman I only knew briefly, I wonder how Franco is holding up so well.

Two more agents drive Franco and me to the apartment in town. It is a small, quiet town, and the apartment is not very large. He says that here I should be able to walk around and not attract too much attention.

"Okay," Franco says, "some basic housekeeping." He picks up an envelope, about nine inches by eleven inches, dumping the contents on the table. There is local currency to purchase clothes and personal items for my stay. "I need to go into town to make a phone call," he informs me.

"Should I shop now?" I ask, wanting to find some way to occupy myself.

"Not until I get back," Franco says, without looking at me. He walks out the door and closes it tightly behind him.

I watch outside for Franco to return. I'm not allowed to leave. There isn't much to do here.

"Well, you are really great at what you do," Franco yells as he comes in the house. From his tone, I am quite sure he wasn't trying to be complimentary.

"Thanks to what you did in Leningrad, an order was handed down from top echelons at the KGB. All cast members and crew on the tour will have to leave Russia immediately. Everyone was given one hour to be on buses heading to the airport. All will be subject to thorough searches of all their luggage and personal belongings. Your room at the hotel has been sealed off, ransacked, and all of your remaining suitcases and personal belongings taken by the KGB to their headquarters." Franco looks up at me. "You will never see any of that stuff again."

I decide it is best not to respond.

"Also," Franco continues, "the American Ambassador has been summoned to the Russian foreign office, called on the carpet, and expelled from the country. And, of course, your life is in jeopardy."

I'm not sure what to say. We've not been here very long, and I didn't think I should show him the document on the plane, finding out who Gina was and all.

"I need the document that has caused this mess," Franco says. I give it to him, and he starts reading. I guess I should have known that he would understand Russian, but I nearly explained it to him. His eyes grew wide.

"This document is one of the most important pieces of information ever received by the United States intelligence community," Franco says.

"So, you didn't know what I had?" I ask, feeling that I have, at least, done something useful.

"No. The KGB does not know which document, in actuality, was turned over. Our sources tell us that the KGB thinks Kapersky shouldn't have killed his wife so soon."

I try to ignore how callous the KGB was. They didn't care she was killed, just that her husband killed her too soon. It makes me angry, and I feel a tear about to surface. I think that would be insensitive, considering Franco lost Gina, and I force myself not to cry. I try to think about the good my actions caused. What I have done will go down in history as a great espionage act. I have made my mark on history, and, with any luck, what I have done will lead to the end of the Cold War.

Rules

"You will have to understand, governments have rules when it comes to warfare," Franco explains.

I nod, wishing this was just me researching a part for a play and not my life at this moment.

"The Geneva Convention specifies how you kill combatants, how prisoners of war are treated, the way you protect cultural property, the means by which you protect the civilian population, and, most importantly for us, defining the role of a spy," Franco relates.

I am about to ask if that means I'm a real spy, but, when I open my mouth, Franco shakes his head. "Don't get me started," Franco exclaims. "I guess one should say please, thank you, and excuse me for dropping bombs on your city, and pardon me for stealing your secret documents."

Clearly, Franco and I were not thinking the same thing. He continues on about how the intelligence service has separate rules of conduct. If a courier gets caught, one would be expelled from the country. Once the line is crossed to spy, and the spy is not in military uniform, he or she would be killed. A spy is the most dangerous form of government service devised by man."

I guess being classified as a spy isn't all benefits.

"You crossed the line, George," Franco lectures. "The Castro document you acquired is very important. In all my years working with the CIA, this is the most ironic situation I have ever seen. Your government is indebted to you; however, the United States government will disavow knowing you, any relationship with you, and any knowledge of your activities. You did a good job by doing a bad job. If that isn't an oxymoron."

"Why? I didn't do anything wrong," I say. Suddenly, I see myself fading from immortality to one of the faceless masses of the forgotten, like the codebreakers who broke enigma but were rewarded with obscurity.

"One cannot take it upon one's self to acquire, in any manner, sensitive and classified documents of any kind, unless the CIA has given full approval of the methods of obtaining those documents in advance," Franco explains, as if speaking from rote memorization and not conviction.

"But I—" I begin.

"But nothing, George. We made it very clear to you. We told you you'd only be moving items from point A to point B, nothing else."

"She called me. I didn't ask for the documents," I try to defend myself further.

"This is difficult for me to tell you, George, but your government wants you to disappear. They want no publicity, no mention of George Toomey anywhere in the world. There has to be no chance Russian agents can get to you, interrogate you, and murder you." Franco just keeps talking as though he is recording something for later use and not talking *to* me. It is almost as if I'm not even in the room. Does nothing I say have any impact on this? "The CIA has threatened every producer that if they hire you, they will never get government clearance and documents for them to produce a show in Europe again."

"In fact," Franco says, trudging on, "the CIA has already started putting pressure on the theatre community never to hire you again. You are an actor without a stage. Your agent at William Morris will not accept nor return your calls. You will not be welcomed in New York." For the first time, Franco looks at me, and I can see this does impact him. "I am truly sorry, George. I will try to help you any way I can."

I cannot breathe. I have lost my wife, daughters, career, Marina, and caused the death of Gina. For the first time in my life, I will be without my agents, lawyers, and business managers to discuss my career moves. I must put myself at the mercy of Franco to plead my case with the hope he can take it to his superiors for review. Deep down, I know there isn't going to be any change in the CIA's decision. You cannot be both invisible and a star on Broadway.

"I will be leaving for several weeks," Franco says. "First, to bury Gina in the family cemetery in Florence, and then on to the United States for a top planning meeting with my superiors in the CIA."

"I understand," I acquiesce. Of course, I will be most anxious to hear the outcome of this meeting—to find out what fate has in store for me. I will be really alone for the next couple of weeks, except for CIA agents visiting me every so often to check up, and some interviews for my so-called sports article I am writing. It will be like solitary confinement. There is no television, practically no one to talk to, and my daily walks will not give me any real socialization. I expect the time to go slowly. *How am I ever going to accept going from the toast of Broadway to a flop in Finland?*

THE CIA MEETING

It was a rough couple of weeks for me. The realization that my wife, Gina, will never be coming back hit me the morning of her funeral. She always helped me during sad times in our family. We had a way of communicating that transcended language. I managed to put on something presentable, deciding if I looked awful, everyone would understand. Seeing them lowering her casket into the deep hole dug by cemetery workers was my breaking point. I don't cry easily, but I completely sobbed. After spending a couple of days with Gina's family, it was time for my trip to the United States. It is not a trip I am looking forward to, either. I thought I had George under my wings, but I never expected for him to do so much damage to the cultural tour. I was instrumental in developing and implementing the tour. Maybe the agency will find George's information to be of value and be more lenient, but that has never been my experience in cases like this.

I step in the Director's office and share greetings and thank them for their condolences. Then, it starts.

The Director repeats all the rules I had so carefully, and on many occasions, previously given to George about the role of courier and spy. "And you made this clear to him?" the Director asks.

"Yes."

"Well," the Director goes on, "no one is ever able to plan in any way, collecting, copying, or taking and disseminating any information from any foreign government without the express, advance approval of the CIA. The consequence is completely disavowing knowledge of any person involved in the unauthorized activity."

I know the rules, but, still, I listen, as he continues on with a long list of actions against George. I am somehow hoping that I will find an out for George. A way to keep my promise to him, so he doesn't rot in obscurity after finding a document that may have literally saved the United States.

The Director promptly turns his anger towards me. "Why didn't you tell him, in no uncertain terms, that he was a courier, NOT A SPY?"

At this point, it is useless for me to defend my actions by listing a long laundry list of rules I had already given George so many times in the past. I just need to get through the meeting, leave Washington, and hope my record would not be tarnished in any way by his actions. If I lose my job at the CIA, I really will have nothing.

It is not a long meeting. Those present *did* recognize the importance of the information obtained by George.

"Why can't that count for something" I ask, after pointing out again that Marina had called him to her house, and that he had not asked for sensitive material.

Nothing I say is going to make a difference. The decision has been made. Someone has to pay in the name of diplomatic expediency; therefore, no one at the meeting has any interest in giving him any credit for his actions.

"It is for his own good," the Director continues. "We have to make sure George will get no work in the theatre. We can't chance the KGB finding him working on Broadway or even off Broadway."

"We could give him a new identity," I reason.

"Okay, you can hide him, change his identity, and get him an apartment," the Director says. His smirk irritates me, because he acts as though he is talking to a petulant child. "I don't want to destroy this man's life, but if the KGB finds out what documents he actually received from Kapersky's wife, it would destroy their usefulness. And you can imagine what they'd do to get it out of him."

"But he is an actor, just like we are agents," I say, trying one last time to speak up for George. I understand that they need to protect him, but maybe he'd be safer in plain sight? "It isn't just what he does, it is who he *is*."

"Well Franco, it is quite obvious your actor caused a lot of shit for the agency. We really got caught with our pants down. Not at the knees, but *all the way down* to YOUR ankles. The KGB has sent three agents from their Moscow headquarters to New York to find George and learn which documents George received from Marina Kapersky. If that wasn't enough, we have a crazy, demoted, destroyed, and devastated KGB agent, Kapersky, wanting to kill George on sight."

"He didn't mean to cause all of this. He didn't realize the depth of what he was getting in to." I try again, already knowing that the Director had just as much at stake in keeping George alive as I did. Losing him takes away our one advantage.

"For his own good, and for ours, too, get The Actor out of town. Franco, you still are the point man for this operation, but don't let any Russian get George. I hope you understand that if they get him," he pauses a moment, as if getting ready to say something, and then seems to change his mind, "you and I will have our pants down lower than our ankles."

"I understand."

"I will get back with you soon," the Director dismisses me. In the interim, I am still in charge of handling the repercussions from cancelling the tour, paying salaries, reassigning people—explaining without explaining. On top of that, I'm still in charge of the continual management of George, until such time as any changes may take place. I guess it is a sign that the CIA still believes that my ability to run an operation was still intact. At least that is what I thought.

***

Franco has finally arrived back, and I couldn't be happier. Although I was deeply concerned about the results of his meeting with the CIA, I was still looking forward to seeing him.

"Well, it is a mixed bag," Franco says to me as soon as he walks in the apartment. "First, the good news." When he said it, I hoped he meant *really* good news and not just moderately okay news. "Tomorrow, you begin your journey to England, and, then, back to the United States."

While that was good, that was a travel itinerary—not what I'd classify as good news.

"Is there anything else?" I ask, really hoping that isn't all there is.

"George, besides Kapersky trying to find you, the KGB headquarters in Moscow also wants to find you and learn which documents Marina gave you. It is best for you to leave town and hide at your Cape house."

"I would rather be in the City. It is bigger than the town on the Cape, and I can hide better." I tell him, still trying to process all that has changed in such a small amount of time.

"We really feel it would be better for you to go to--."

"Please!" I cut him off with the exasperated word. "I cannot handle the quiet right now. I need to hear the cars and go for walks where I won't be noticed."

"Your wife has sold the Park Avenue apartment, which means you no longer have a place to live in New York." I try to catch my breath. I left my money in Russia. I have no idea how much I have in America, since I counted on the income from this tour. Now, I am without a residence.

"Don't worry" he says, "I have arranged for the CIA to rent an apartment for you in New York. It will be a small place at 122nd Street and Riverside Drive."

"Well, it is a start," I say. Franco looks annoyed at my comment, but I'm pretty annoyed with him right now, too, so I guess we are even.

"It will not be fancy, nor like anything you've been accustomed to in the past. However, this spot will enable you to live unnoticed, with anonymity, and to truly get lost in the big city, until everything you have caused has calmed down."

Calmed down? Does that mean that they're going to do something with what I learned? Were they keeping me in obscurity to protect me from the U.S.S.R. and from the press in America? Franco is holding off on the real answers I wanted.

"What did the CIA say about my actions?" I ask, unable to hold on any longer.

"George, they were not pleased—for exactly all the reasons I told you prior to my trip."

I am stunned. How could they not understand what I'd done for them? I'd done even more than they asked.

Franco continues, "The good news is that I am still in charge of the remains of the tour and the mop-up of any damage as the results of your actions. I also will be able to look out for you for a while."

That was the good news? I guess Franco's response to my question must be considered positive. That's me, Mr. Positive. The only thing I have left in all of this is trying to keep a positive attitude. In the past, I have always been able to lift myself out of the doldrums by thinking about others worse off than me. In this situation, as hard as I try, it does no good. They want to block me from my theatre, erase me from the memory of history, and hope everyone forgets that a man named George Toomey ever existed. Gina is remembered. At least Franco still has a job. I am the one who really wanted to make a difference. Fate opened that door, and, now, I'm punished for doing what any other person would have done in my situation. It doesn't seem even a little bit fair.

The next morning, I pack up the small number of articles I have purchased in Finland and wait for the car to arrive to transport me to the airport. At least this trip won't have bullets flying all around, and I have to assume nobody will be killed. On the car ride to the airport, I think about going home. Who am I kidding? I do not have a home or a family waiting for me. Hell, I don't even have an apartment. I have nothing. And this is how I get to restart my life.

CHAPTER 12

RETURN TO NEW YORK

RETURN TO NEW YORK: PART I

Returning home from the tour was a far different experience than leaving on the Queen Mary to Southampton. Coming home, I had no bon voyage party. I was not in first class. To keep a low profile, we used the same small Helsinki airport we'd arrived at when escaping Russia to fly to London. My arrival in the countryside of London was also very low-profile. I landed at a small airport in the countryside used by the RAF during the Second World War for raids and bombing runs on Germany.

When I arrived, Franco met me, and we sat and talked for a short while, waiting for the new plane to fuel and prepare to take us to New York. My time in the horrible little town has done nothing to squash the awkwardness I feel inside. I had relentlessly made a play for his wife, and Franco had never said a word.

"It looks like they are ready for us." Franco observes, and I step out of the small waiting area and out to the tarmac. The air is saturated with the smell of fuel and soil. A damp mist—thicker and wetter than fog, but not quite rain—makes my hair and skin immediately damp. It is an appropriate setting for an abysmal exit.

"Thank you for everything, Franco," I say, reaching out my hand.

"I'm going with you," he replies, a tired smile on his face. "I said that they're ready for *us*."

I nod and step on the plane. We are the only passengers onboard a four-engine turbo prop plane. The flight promises to be long and exhausting. If Franco had told me Gina was his wife at any point, I certainly would have left her alone. I figured she was just playing hard-to-get. I had a co-star like that once. She was the one who made me chase the longest—even longer than my wife—and, after eight months, I finally bedded her. I'd not pursued her exclusively, just like I hadn't pursued Gina exclusively, but she was still a focus.

Now, I will be riding for hours on a plane with the husband of a woman I'd not only tried to bed, but also managed to get killed. Add to that the fact that he is responsible for my protection, and I'm not sure how he does it. I know I couldn't.

"There will be quite a few changes when we get to New York," Franco advises me, not looking at me. The plane feels empty as we fly along over the water that, not long ago, I'd danced, sung, and relaxed on.

"Like what?" I ask. I'm a bit worried about what kind of rules they might now impose on me with everything that happened. What if they make me live like a prisoner in this apartment? What if I'm not permitted to see my friends? My New York life was a good one, and I'd told everyone I'd return an international celebrity. Now, I'll have to tell them all that I'm not, but I won't be able to explain to them why. Dinner parties could be pretty awkward for a while.

I think about all that has happened and try to mentally prepare to live a bit less flamboyantly when I return. I will contact my agent to see about a small role and spend time with my friends. It won't be what I'm used to, but I can make it work.

After more than an hour of silence has passed, I drift off to sleep with these thoughts. We sleep most of the way across the Atlantic. I didn't have much to say to Franco, and he, I am sure, didn't want to say anything more to me. I wake when the plane starts making a different sound. It startles me at first, but, then, I look at Franco.

"We are getting close," he assures me. "They are slowing their speed."

Franco must have known my thoughts, or felt them, himself, before. I still don't care much for flying, and these sounds don't endear me to it at all.

"How much longer?" I want to get on to this low-key version of life.

"For safety and security, and to arrive back in the States unnoticed, it was decided to land at New York's Marine Air Terminal in Queens, New York," he explains, his voice flat, as though reciting a manual, rather than talking to me.

"Oh," I respond, wondering if he is unhappy with the decision or if his frustration is with me. To be safe, I decide I won't say anything else until we land. Thankfully, that is only about thirty minutes later. The landing is a bit bumpy, but I am thankful to be back in America and New York.

Franco leads me off of the plane and into a building where we receive courtesy of the port, allowing both of us to quickly move through immigration and customs. A car and driver, supplied by the CIA, is there to take me to north of Riverside Drive and 122nd Street, my new home. It's wonderful to see the New York skyline again through the car's window on the drive past the City.

We pull up in front of a rent-controlled building in an older part of the City. When I left New York, I lived on Park Avenue in a twelve-room duplex with a balcony, a doorman, and a breathtaking view of the City. The windows of this apartment overlook a small park, and, as the name implies, the river isn't far away. Broadway isn't far away either. At least it is something.

Franco takes my few remaining possessions out of the trunk and sets them on the ground at my feet. I guess I will have to learn to carry my own luggage again.

I look up at the side of the building. It is about six stories high. Not as high as my previous place.

"Are you ready?" Franco asks. He isn't quite as put off by the atmosphere as I am.

"Yes." I manage a smile. "Let's go."

We walk in, and Franco takes me to the elevator. That is at least good. I won't have to be on the ground floor. When we step off, we go down a hallway that is only two people wide and smells old. Not the quaint old of a mansion outside of town, but the old smell of something that has gone past its usefulness and is now entering a stage of neglect.

It isn't smelly and decaying—it is just not new and vibrant. We stop in front of the door, and Franco pulls out the key. He slides it in the lock, and something about the sound wakes me up, and I am overcome with guilt. I remember the once-old, now-new buildings in London. Buildings that once had the wonderful scent of age and history, but now carried the smell of fresh paint and rebuilding that comes after a building is bombed, walls bloodied by bodies, and dreams shattered.

If my goal had been to make my mark, hadn't I done it? I was just like all those nameless and faceless soldiers who came home from the war in London to find their previous way of life destroyed and a new, harder one taking shape.

I must remember to keep my frustration in perspective. With that resolve, I steady myself and prepare to follow Franco in the apartment. This place was a one-bedroom with high ceilings, a sunken living room, and a pretty large kitchen. It isn't horrible, just a bit cramped. It is only slightly smaller than my hotel room in London, and I had found that to be lavish. I will find a way to enjoy it here.

"The apartment will be paid for as long as you would like to stay," Franco says, handing me the keys.

"Thank you," I answer, taking it all in and finding it hard not to show my emotions, which fluctuate from moment to moment between gratefulness and depression.

"I told you on the plane that things would be changing," Franco continues, stepping over to a small table in the corner and taking a seat.

"Yes. This is a change," I sullenly answer.

Franco looks around, a smile of sudden comprehension. "I suppose this *is* a change, George," he says. "But that wasn't the change I was referring to."

"It's not?" I ask. What other change could he possibly mean?

"We've rented this apartment under a new name," he says. "You are now George Thompson, until further notice."

"George Thompson?" I demand, my frustration no longer staying down. It screams to the surface with all the power of a rubber band that has been stretched as far as it will go and then suddenly released.

"It's a small matter," Franco says. He is clearly surprised that this has evoked such a strong response. "You can still use the name Toomey for calls to old friends in the theatre, but it is imperative that you use the Thompson name for everyone else."

He offers no further explanation, and I haven't the energy to try to get one out of him.

The apartment has modest furnishings, and that, combined with my few clothes, will have to be the beginning of my new life. I have some savings, unless that is gone with my wife and daughters. For the first few days, I rested at the apartment and enjoyed reading the paper. I also bought a few more outfits and some things to make this place feel a bit more like my own.

It is cooler outside, but I still go out for walks regularly to clear my head. I've had more time off since meeting with Franco that first day in my dressing room than I have had since I was a very young man. I don't really get updates on what happened to the cast and crew, nor do I want one. I feel bad that the production was shut down by the Russians. Even with me gone and the other things tied to it, it was a really great show, and people would have loved it. I am tired of my break, so, after five days in the apartment, I decide it is time to get back to work. I call my agent, David, first, to see if he'd like to meet at Sardis.

"David, please," I say to the pleasant woman who answers. "This is George Toomey."

"One moment, Mr. Toomey," she says. Her voice is kind and quite young. David seems to be constantly surrounded by beautiful women. I guess it is the nature of things in our industry. You have to always be beautiful in every way.

"Mr. Toomey?" a voice comes back on the line, jarring me from my mental ramblings.

"Yes," I answer.

"I'm sorry. He is not available."

"That is alright," I say. "Just have him meet me a Sardis at 1:30 PM."

"I'm sorry, Mr. Toomey," she continues, her voice not quite as pleasant. "He is not available to you."

"What do you mean?" I ask, horrified. "He is my agent."

"I'm sorry, sir. He simply asked me to relay the message to you that he is not available."

I'm too stunned to say anything more. Maybe if it weren't so unexpected, I'd have had some kind of wonderful comeback or some kind of fight in me, but I'm too shocked. It cannot be possible that he won't take my calls.

Just a short while ago, the commissions and fees I paid him provided for most of his overhead. Now, he says he won't even talk to me.

"Thank you, then," I concede, trying not to reveal the full extent of my disappointment.

"Have a nice day," she says, some of the sweetness momentarily returning.

Does she really care if I have a nice day? I go to my fridge and fix a sandwich. Suddenly, I don't want to go to Sardis for lunch anymore. I feel completely naked and exposed…even a bit vulnerable. Through all of the problems these last few weeks, I always had the assurance that when I came home, I could make things work, because I had people here who would help me. For the first time, that belief has been shaken.

I eat my sandwich slowly, considering my next step. It's hard to know what to do when so much has changed. I have been on an upward trajectory for years, each part building upon the success of the previous one. Other than my attempts to crossover to film—which had been thwarted—I have been bigger with each role.

I decide to call Kermit Bloomgarden next, to let him know that I'm available early to join the national tour of *The Music Man*. I had planned on having David do that for me after we talked, but, if he's decided he no longer needs my commissions, I won't force him to take them. I consider a moment whether my contract stipulates that I'd have to pay him, since we discussed the project. I will just refuse to pay it. If he won't take my calls, I don't have to take his.

I clean up from lunch and look for Bloomgarden's number. It is either in all my things at my old place or somewhere in the U.S.S.R. Instead, I call the main number, where I am transferred from office to office, until I reach his assistant.

"I'm sorry," she says when I introduce myself. "He isn't available at the moment. Could I take a message?"

She is very friendly, not at all like David's assistant had been. I gladly give her my number. "Tell him that I'm done early with my other project, and I'm now available to take the part of Harold Hill in *The Music Man* national tour."

"I will certainly tell him, Mr. Toomey," she says. "Thank you so much for calling."

With that now done, I feel better, and I decide to go up the street to buy a few things. I get a suitcase—since mine are all gone—and I also get a new raincoat and a couple of pairs of slacks. It is a productive afternoon. I pick up a sandwich from a shop and take it back home to eat.

THE ACTOR?

It is nearly four in the afternoon when I come back to my apartment. A bit early for supper, so I put the sandwich in the refrigerator and turn on the radio. The phone startles me, and I look up to see that it is now five. I must have dozed off. I turn the radio off and grab the phone.

"This is George T—" I stop myself. Should I say Toomey? My cover is blown. However, if I say Thompson, it will confuse the people calling me. For a long moment, I debate how to answer, and, finally resolve the matter by repeating, "This is George."

"Hi, George, this is Stefanie Williams." I don't know a Stefanie Williams, so I'm not sure if she's looking for the real me or another version.

"Hello, Stefanie, how can I help you?" I ask.

"I am a production assistant for Kermit Bloomgarden," she says. I feel heat on my cheeks, as though someone has turned on an oven and blown it at full broil on my face. The shame of the moment is almost overwhelming. "He wanted me to let you know that the role of Harold Hill has been cast."

I thank her quickly and get off of the phone—the full understanding of my predicament clear. I can forget about being hired in New York, no one will even talk to me. The CIA certainly knew how to implement a campaign to discredit me. While I had worked to try to help our country, my country was working to erase me from memory.

I had to get away from this apartment and everything it had reminded me of. I stomped out the door, nearly forgetting my keys, and went down to the street level. Finally outside, I'm able to get control of myself and put things in perspective. My reintegration wasn't going to be quite as easy as I had expected. In fact, I was starting all over again, but I'd done more with less. I had become famous as George Toomey. I could do it again as George Thompson.

I hail a cab and get in. "Sardis, please." The sandwich can just sit in the fridge. I need real food. I ride, trying to cool off a bit before I get there. There will certainly be some talk, but what is most important is for me to have a story as to why I'm back. I finally decide on just telling the truth: The Russians kicked us out. Everyone knows how the Communists can be.

That decided, I wait the few remaining minutes to get to Sardis. I'm so hungry! Not just for food, but also for people to talk to. I need connection. I need a woman. I just need to put all of this mess behind me!

I hadn't bothered to call ahead for my table, but that is fine. It is still early enough that Sardis will have it ready. They always hold it and seat it last, in case I'm coming. I step in the door, where the familiar smells help me relax again. I'm greeted with startled glances and quizzical stares.

"Hello, Sir." I turn. I've never seen this maître d' before. His face is polite, but he doesn't seem to recognize me at all.

I look past him to the blank spot on the wall. My picture is gone! It was removed. This whole city and everyone in it is determined to drive me from town or completely mad—or both!

I spin around, stumbling into a man stepping through the door. "Hey, aren't you..." he begins to say. I shake my head and push quickly out of the building.

Out on the sidewalk, I hail another cab and give the driver my address. It is like I can't breathe. There is an incredible weight on my chest, and my stomach rhythmically clenches.

"Hey, buddy. Not in the back," The cab driver calls back, and I hold up my hand in answer.

I no longer exist. Actually, it is worse than that. I exist, but I am no longer welcome. I am a *persona non grata.* I am like one of those untouchables in India. I won't even bother trying to call other friends. Certainly, none of them will take my call. To be associated with me is to end a career.

I get to my apartment and fall through the door. To sob would be far too feminine, but my throat feels like I swallowed my own fist. I lock the door and go straight to my bedroom. I no longer have an appetite. I only want to sleep.

This is not how this was supposed to be! I have had my wife leave me, lost my kids, lost my possessions in Russia, a woman was killed for talking to me, and Gina died protecting me. These were all bad, but, without my career, who am I? I kick off my shoes and fall across the bed fully clothed, begging for sleep to come and take me from this nightmare of living.

Return to New York: Part II

Without much to do, I think about ways to hide who I am. I've always kept myself fit, clean-shaven, well-coiffed, and well-dressed. Therefore, I decide to embark on a new challenge. I haven't shaven in nearly two weeks, and, now, I have a reasonable beard and mustache. I've gained at least a few pounds already, but, by next month, I'm certain it will be more. I'm also letting my hair grow longer, but only until I find a new barber. Since my clothes have gotten a touch snug, I've also found some new pants that aren't at all the style I previously wore.

This morning when I looked at myself in the mirror, I was, at first, disgusted at what I saw, but not many now would recognize this one-time star—so mission accomplished.

I kept on trying to find something to keep me connected to the industry I loved, but to no avail. Suicide did cross my mind several times, but, even at my lowest point, I couldn't bring myself to go through with anything of the kind. I still fight to keep on going. I will never give up.

On several Wednesday matinee days, I headed for the theatre district to walk around and watch the crowds rush to various theatres. Walking through Shubert Alley, I would often stop and spend time listening to the crowds talking about the shows and stars they would be seeing. Occasionally, when a show had closed, I spent hours watching the show being loaded out of a theatre. The scenery, lighting, and sound equipment were left outside the theatre on the sidewalk, waiting to be loaded onto trucks for removal. I would get as close as I could, without drawing attention to myself. There was a wonderful, distinctive smell of a show emanating from the painted scenery and equipment. It transported me backstage to one of my past shows.

The exit doors to the street were usually left open for the load-out, so I would walk to the last row of the orchestra and sit quietly, watching all the activity. It is really hard to put in to words what that felt like. It was bittersweet. It was sweet to be in the theater again, but I felt even more bitterness over what I had lost.

It has now become my routine to go over to watch a load-out. It is something to look forward to and to make some kind of break in my boring routine of waking up, gaining weight, listening to the radio, watching a television program, preparing meals, eating meals, cleaning up from meals, and going to bed.

I go through the open door at the back of the theatre, and it still amuses me how no one recognizes me, nor seems to be bothered by me. I even think for a moment how funny it might be to get a job moving sets.

I watch things move around for quite some time, completely lost in the familiarity of it all.

"Sir." A voice from behind me booms, making me jump.

I turn around and look up at him. He is large—certainly more than six feet tall, and I'd guess at least 250 pounds of muscle. I think I've seen this stagehand on other shows. It is easy to remember someone so large, even if you don't generally pay attention to the people around you.

"Sir, you aren't allowed to sit in the theatre," he says, his voice less intimidating, but no less gruff.

"Certainly," I say. "I'm going."

His eyes widen, and he looks me over, pausing at my midsection, squinting at my beard, and, then, honing in tight on my eyes. "Don't I know you?"

"I don't think so," I dismiss him quickly, and I get up and move out of the theater. Once outside the door, I look over my shoulder a few times to make sure he didn't follow me, and, then, I slow down and continue with my normal Wednesday routine.

The Wednesday matinee trips into the City ended around 5 PM. As I did each time before I left the theatre district, I took one last walk around before heading to the subway. I will have to eliminate 'sitting in the theatre' from my routine. I cannot risk being discovered. While I hadn't really thought it a big deal before, it might be wise to keep my profile low. I self-consciously rub my belly. I really hate being overweight, but I simply have no motivation to try to shed the weight. What role am I trying to secure?

A Ford Dealership in Queens New York

"The biggest Ford dealer in New York is on Queens Boulevard in Queens," Boris says. "It is so big that most customers have already shopped around and come in with prices from other car dealerships written down or memorized."

"As long as we can get through fast," Gregori responds.

"People come in knowing they are going to buy, but wanting the best price," Boris assures, pulling open the door and holding it for Gregori.

"Can I help you gentlemen?" The man's nametag said James. He smiled broadly, no doubt because of the black tailored suits they both wore.

"I want a new Ford Econoline truck," the man on the right said firmly. "It must have a rear and side door. I will give you cash and will need it delivered in 24 hours."

"We have one here," James said, leading the man to a van halfway down the lot and gesturing, as though he is a child proudly displaying a school project to his father. "Is that agreeable to you?"

Gregori and Boris walked around the van. It would be fine.

"I like it," Boris says in Russian.

"You can speak English, Boris," Gregori answers, looking around the inside of the van.

"I know, but it is more fun when they think I don't know how," Boris laughs, looking at Gregori through the back of the van and smiling. "It is what I do for entertainment."

"You mean when you're not working a hit?"

"Exactly." Boris chuckled slightly and closed the door.

They didn't worry about speaking Russian in front of him. Certainly, James was accustomed to working with immigrants, since the dealership is in Queens.

"Yes, this will be fine," Gregori concedes in his heavily accented English.

"We have just a few papers to complete the sale. If you will come to my office," James says, nodding and leading the way back to the building.

It took longer to fill out the needed papers to register the van than it had to make the entire sale. They used a New York City address, and the owner of the vehicle was listed as the Maintenance Department of the Embassy of the Soviet Union.

In twenty-four hours, the van was delivered and the two men took the Ford to a custom van shop in Queens, where specific modifications were to be made.

"The back of the van must be designed like the inside of an ambulance," Boris says. "I need a gurney attached to the floor. All of the windows in the back should be blacked out, and I want a long shelving unit to be installed for medical supplies."

"You'll have it in forty-eight hours," the man promises. Gregori didn't bother to ask his name.

In a back office at the Russian embassy in New York, they meet with a senior official they are to call "Mr. Luka".

"It is a top priority is to find George Toomey," Mr. Luka says. "From our investigation, Toomey is non-gratis in the theatre community, but everyone in the embassy is certain he will spend time in the theatre district."

"Pathetic," Gregori mumbled.

Mr. Luka paused briefly but didn't comment. "You will continually cruise the area from 42nd and Broadway to 52nd Street and Broadway, between Eighth Avenue and Sixth Avenue.

"Da," Boris says, nodding.

"When you find him," Mr. Luka continued, "Put Mr. Toomey to the back of the van. Sedate him immediately to get him in the van, then administer an injection of scopolamine. This will loosen his tongue, so he can no longer hide the truth. Find out what was in the documents he received from Kapersky's wife."

The plan was simple enough. Gregori nodded and looked at Boris.

"I love this kind of assignment," Boris enthuses, the lust of violence in his gaze.

"We will assign a third agent to do much of the driving, so the two of you can work in the back." Mr. Luka says.

"Good," Gregori replies.

"He will probably have gained weight, grown his hair long, and, it is likely that he will have facial hair," Mr. Luka continues. "You must study his features and recognize his basic look, so you can recognize him, no matter how much weight or hair he has added to himself."

The assignment was clear. Gregori and Boris had done many such assignments, so, after a brief rundown of timeline, they start their hunt.

A Wednesday matinee was the first time they found a male in Shubert Alley. Even from a distance, Gregori recognized a man with the same features of George Toomey. They had a third man, Petrov, driving today. He pulled the van up and stopped on the 44th street entrance to Shubert Alley to watch the movement of a certain male who was standing for a while, leaning against show posters adorning the walls of the alley.

A tall New York City policeman approaches the van. "No parking or standing here. Now move on."

"Drive around," Boris instructs. "Gregori and I are going to follow the heavyset bearded man."

Petrov nodded and drove on.

"He's over there," Gregori said, noticing the man walking aimlessly down the street.

The two men fought their way through throngs of theatregoers who were leaving their afternoon performances.

"Do you see him?" Gregori asks, the sea of people seemingly swallowing him up.

"No," Boris said. "And we can't grab him anyway without the van."

With so many well-dressed bodies in the way, the two men temporarily lost sight of the heavyset man with beard. Boris cursed, and Gregori tried, again, to see through the current of people moving up and down the alley.

"I'm sure it was him," Gregori says. "We will come back tomorrow. If he was here one day, he'll be back."

Boris nods, and they start down the street to wait for the van.

Return to New York: Part III

I realize there are two men dressed in black suits, black ties, and carrying briefcases following me. I'm not sure how long they've been behind me, but they look like the same men who were behind me last Wednesday. I start to move quicker. The men continue to talk to each other, but their pace begins to quicken as well. I pass through Shubert Alley and stop to wait for a moment, discretely turning back to see where they now are. They've stopped and are now joined in conversation with a third man. How was it that they recognized me? Certainly, this weight has done nothing but make me unattractive and make running much harder to do.

I start to move a bit faster. The men pick up their pace as well, although their faces don't show the exertion I feel. A bead of sweat rolls down from my neck to my back, tickling me as it rolls. I always found sweat so unattractive, even under stage lights, and knowing that I'm certainly soaking my shirt disgusts me.

Trying to lose the two, I attempt to move quickly towards the 42nd Street subway station. People are in my path, and I work my way through them while trying not to draw attention to myself. The two men continue to follow and board the same subway train, sitting close to me. My heart is thudding in my chest, and I'm terrified. America, and especially New York, should be a place where a person can come and disappear, but these men have found me after only one month of trying and are now less than ten feet from me, planning to do only God only knows what kind of horrors to me.

I try to figure out what to do next. Should I get off at my regular 116th Street stop, or leave at another stop? The 116th Street station, also known as the Columbia University stop, approaches. *If I get off here, they could follow me home, but if I get off somewhere else and get lost, I might be an easier target.* I vacillate between the two options for quite some time before finally deciding that it is smarter to get home. I move to the doors, preparing a quick exit off the train. The two men follow me. When the doors open, I go out as quickly as I can without drawing attention to myself. *If they realize that I know that they are there, what if they start firing at me, or something worse?*

I dart up the stairs and out onto the street. A car swerves away from me, and the driver blows his horn. I keep running, expecting at any moment that I'll feel the sting of a bullet behind my right shoulder or the center of my chest. Another car is coming fast, but I run across oncoming traffic on Broadway. The sidewalks are full of the masses returning home from work. I guess this is a lucky break. I glance back quickly and see no one. I run down the hill, towards Riverside Drive, and pause to really look behind me. I have lost the two ominous men following me. I take a quick right onto Riverside and gather up all the strength I can to continue running towards my apartment.

I don't want to wait for the elevator, so I sprint up my steps, taking them two or three at a time, until I am up to my apartment. No sooner do I get through the door, than I immediately call Franco to tell him about the two Russian agents following me. We talked for quite some time, with me recounting everything that happened and Franco periodically stopping me for clarification.

"I think we need to have all of your movements watched by our agents, and be with you on your next trip into the theatre district," Franco says firmly. I'm glad he saw this as a real threat and didn't try to tell me it was my imagination.

For the next week, I spend time watching out my window, in case the men have returned. There are plenty of men who wear the same style, so it is hard to say, but I don't notice anyone in particular watching my house.

At 5 PM the following Wednesday, the two men are following me again as I leave 44th Street to return home. This time, I feel safer, however, because there are two CIA men watching everything and following me home on the subway. If they were going to shoot me, they would have done it already, so, certainly, having the CIA agents following me will be enough to get them. Once Franco finds out why they are after me, maybe I'll have to move again. I can't think about those things right now. Instead, I wait in my apartment for Franco to return.

I hear a tap at the door and the key sliding in to the lock—Franco's greeting.

"George?" He yells, and, while I am walking to the living room, I hear laughter. I come around the corner and something about me makes him burst out in another shout of laughter. "Sit down."

There is a long pause while I wait and try to keep from getting anxious.

"They are not Russian," Franco finally says, although, clearly, he wants to laugh again. "They are two students from Columbia University Business School, working in an intern program in the City. They leave the City daily around 5 PM and return to their apartment on Riverside Drive." I plop onto the couch and let out a loud laugh and a larger sigh.

"I imagine you scared them pretty good, showing up," I joke, finally allowing myself to laugh with him. We both laugh and release so much with this common enemy. I look at Franco again, and, finally, the tension feels gone. I don't think there ever was any with him. It was all me.

With the laughter subsiding, Franco gets serious again. "The students are not a threat; however, Alexander Kapersky is another matter."

Just his name causes my breath to catch. A shiver briefly passes through me. "I imagine so," I reply, somberly.

"Because you have slept with his wife, stole his top secret files, and caused his demotion at the KGB, he wants you dead." Franco's voice was flat, but I'm certain that is not because he is uncaring, rather, that he is always focused on work and how to keep me safe.

"When you say it like that, Franco, I sound like a real S.O.B."

Franco says nothing, except to continue to plow into his thought. "He is a most vindictive person, and, no matter how long it takes to get to you, he will wait. We will do all we can to protect you."

"Thank you."

***

That conversation was years ago, and Franco has kept his promise. I continue to find ways to keep myself busy, although the theatre is still closed to me.

It is now 1962, and not much has changed in my boring life, except that I am getting older. Today, something a little different happened. It seemed a minor thing, but it has absolutely changed my life and also solidified my need to remain hidden indefinitely.

I awoke this morning and started the daily ritual of leaving to buy coffee and purchase the morning papers. The headline on the top paper got me first:

SINCE PRESIDENT KENNEDY ORDERED A FULL NAVAL BLOCKADE AROUND CUBA A FEW DAYS

AGO.... FREIGHTERS WERE STOPPED IN THE BLOCKADE TRANSPORTING MISSILES, DISGUISED AS MEDICAL SUPPLIES, TO THE ISLAND.

IT HAS NOW TURNED IN TO A STAREDOWN. THE CUBAN MISSILE CRISIS WAS A STAREDOWN BETWEEN JOHN F. KENNEDY AND NIKITA KHRUSHCHEV... KHRUSHCHEV BLINKED

It was the story of the year, although I knew it way before it broke. The story in the paper went on to say that a top CIA undercover operation, which included many agents, uncovered and intercepted top-secret communications. The interception of communications allowed President Kennedy to know in advance of missile movements to Cuba and to be able to take an offensive position, before the freighters even left various ports in Russia.

For a moment, I thought of Marina, Gina, the tour, and my life before. The human brain is an amazing thing. All of those images and memories from the Queen Mary, first class over to London, through the streets of the war-torn city, to Leningrad, and the escape back to America. All of those images passed before me in a single moment.

I looked back at the news story. No agent's names were used in the story; the head of the CIA accepted thanks for everyone from a grateful nation. Promotions were given, raises to the whole team involved, and the President went on television announcing that the operation was one of the greatest undercover operations in United States history. I don't suppose I'll get to meet the President. Things like that don't happen. Instead, I read statements from the President in the paper. The President said, "A U.S. U2 spy plane flew over Cuba and uncovered missile sites in the country, which led to the United States taking action."

If anyone was watching me this morning, they would have noticed the slow walk of a broken man going back to his apartment. They would have seen the posture and facial expressions of a defeated individual. It wasn't any better when I returned home. I turned on the television and watched the continuous stories. They depressed me even more. I was responsible for the success of the whole operation, yet no one would ever know my name, nor my role in the Cuban missile confrontation. I will never be able to say anything. Although the story is now out, the Russians will be still interested in eliminating the one person responsible for the whole situation. I am all alone: no friends, no family, no one to love or be loved by. I wasn't sure how I could go on and survive.

The brain is a funny thing. In the midst of all of this, I suddenly started to worry about a variety of things, one after another. I worried about my health and about my future. I ran down the list of the many other worries that seemed to dance in and out of my mind daily or weekly. Then, a new worry in my life raised its ugly head. I still had the summer property on Cape Cod, but hadn't visited it since before I left for London. The property was using up my last financial resources for taxes, upkeep, and a caretaker to visit and make sure there was no damage from storms and hurricanes. I know it is inevitable that I will have to sell the property, as I will need the income in the future.

The publicity on the Cuban Missile crisis heightens the possibility that Kapersky will be looking for me to settle the score. Being in New York might just not be the right spot for me right now. While a big city can help you become anonymous, I'm still recognized from time to time.

I decide to change up my routine. With the CIA paying all of the expenses of the apartment in New York, it is time to get away and visit Cape Cod. It will be a perfect hideaway from any harm. It is also a time to explore the idea of finding a smaller and less expensive place on the Cape and deciding upon plans for my future.

The trip to the Cape will not be like the others I've taken. In the past, I went by private plane, and a limo would transport the whole family in style. For this trip, I will take the bus to Hyannis and, then, a short cab ride to my home in Dennis. I am looking forward to getting back to the Cape, and although my ex-wife didn't like it, walking through the sand in my bare feet is something I can't wait to experience once again in my life.

CHAPTER 13

OLD CAPE COD

Just like in Patti Page's song, I am very fond of sand dunes and salty air.

Patti Page was a dear friend of mine. She came to almost all of my opening nights. On the wall of the Cape house is her autograph on a piece of sheet music, "Old Cape Cod."

To George, I love being with you on Cape Cod. Love, Patti.

I think about that wall hanging as the bus travels over the Sagamore Bridge and onto the Mid-Cape Highway. Even though I'm not traveling here the way I used to during the trip, all tension, depression, and worries almost magically disappear. In the past, I had the same feeling returning to the Cape, after a long week of performances in New York. I can't remember seeing the bridge during my trip in by private plane. Maybe that is why this trip is more magical for me. When I flew by private plane, I had missed seeing the wonderful approach to the Cape. Today, I will savor every moment, because it is something in my life full of wonderful memories that hasn't completely faded.

Arriving at the house was a beautiful sight. I hadn't been here in years, although, seeing it, I'm not sure why. The house looked as lovely as it had the last time I walked out the door. I couldn't tell it had been abandoned for so long.

I walk closer to the house. Although the storm windows are dirty, the caretaker has done a marvelous job with the outside. I turn the key in the door and am immediately overcome. It is now obvious the house hadn't been lived in for a long time. The furniture is all covered with sheets, the air is heavy with dust, and a stale smell hangs like a dense fog. Spider webs hang from many of the fixtures and lamps. The dust clings to them, creating a dirty, yet delicate, lace. Had it been darker, this might have conjured images of haunted houses or things that frighten children, but, since it is still light, it reminds me more of comfort, familiarity, and memories.

I realize that I'm rambling in my own dreams and decide that it would be best to start cleaning. I call a cab to go into town to buy cleaning supplies, buckets, and gloves. I have never cleaned anything before, and I'm not quite sure what to buy. The older woman at the market was very kind and helped me buy all that was necessary to have the house completely cleaned, from top to bottom.

I return home with my assortment of mops, brooms, buckets, and chemicals, ready and eager to overcome this new challenge. I assume the project should take the rest of the day. The view is still magnificent, and I spend as much time as I can looking out over the ocean while I clean windows and counters. Throughout the morning ,I stop for just a bit to reflect on some of the good times I've had here.

By late afternoon, I need to get away from the house to pick up a few more supplies and a few groceries. I call the cab, and we take Route 6A to the local market. The trip reinforced my feeling of how quaint and beautiful the north side of the Cape is, and has always been. Now that I've completed some basic house cleaning, my next priority is getting a lobster roll, fried clams, and onion rings from my favorite lobster shack. They are as delicious as I remembered. Being here lets me pretend that my life is normal again. I can imagine that I'm still the star of Broadway and my life hasn't been taken away from me by a few mistakes and a couple of bad circumstances.

On the drive back home, my stomach and heart are both full. Here I am, still George Toomey, the actor, to all the natives.

The next few weeks, I am completely at rest, spending hours sitting on my private beach and sleeping. One day, I dreamed of my two girls running around in the sand, swimming in the ocean and building professional sand castles. When I looked up, I saw the empty sand and realized just how much I'd missed. Oh, how I wished I could turn back the clock and have the whole family back together again.

Weeks went by, and I started to come to grips with the fact that I could no longer afford this place. It was a part of who I'd been and no longer could be. I was going to have to make the phone call I'd been avoiding since even before I got here. While I hadn't fully appreciated my girls then, now, I truly missed them and I saw them in each room. Happy memories that we'd made together, when I was still their hero and my future had seemed like it would stretch into endless perfection.

In the kitchen drawer under the phone, I searched for my book of business cards. The real estate broker who had originally sold the house to me was still in business, and I placed a call to her.

"Hi, Linda, George Toomey here," I say. Although I have to be George Thompson, I can't in this circumstance. The house is still in my name—I kept it in the divorce—and Linda had been a guest a few different times when we entertained business or professional connections at our home.

"George, are you at the Cape?" she asks. I am not entirely sure why that is important, but I let her know that I am and why I'm calling.

"Well, I'd be happy to help you with your house, George," she says, and I am certain she was already mentally spending her commission on the place.

"Does tomorrow fit in your schedule?" I ask.

"Certainly," she answers, quite eager. "What time would work best for you?"

I don't want to say it really doesn't matter, since I have absolutely nothing going on in my life.

"I don't have much going on tomorrow, so I can be fairly open," I offer. I am an expert liar now.

"I will be there at 9:30 AM. Is that alright?"

"That will be fine," I tell her.

We exchange a few pleasantries, and she seems genuinely surprised to learn of my divorce. Once we hang up, I sit in my chair, completely exhausted.

The house has so many wonderful memories. It has entertained the likes of Irving Berlin, Richard Rodgers, Cole Porter, and countless Broadway producers. Weekends of lobster and clam bakes. Many a dark night, guests would skinny dip in the warm water and enjoy a nightcap on the deck, overlooking the ocean.

I fell asleep in my chair and only woke up about twenty minutes before Linda arrived. I quickly showered and changed and was drinking coffee when she rang the doorbell.

"I am here to see George Toomey," she announces, her tone polite, but distant.

"It is good to see you again, Linda," I answer.

"Oh, George," she sputters, looking me over. "It has been a long time."

I try to ignore her embarrassment, as if I hadn't even noticed. Maybe it is good that I'm no longer recognizable to even those who knew me for years. It does sting a bit, because I know the change isn't a positive one.

We exchange the usual greetings and small talk before she jumps in to a conversation about the real estate market on the Cape. We talk about an offering price for the property and a possible contract date.

"I am selling this place, but I'm also interested in buying a smaller house, depending on how much this one sells for."

"Wonderful," she says, smiling broadly. "We will have to wait for the next stage, but I'd be happy to show you a few places while you're up here."

"That would be nice," I agree, using all of the acting skills I had to hide the pain I was feeling at losing this house.

"I'd like to stay here as long as possible. I won't move until it is sold," I resolve, my voice very firm. I want her to know that this is about business and not desperation. I understand businesspeople. If she thinks that I'm desperate, she will try to sell cheap or raise her commission.

"That will be just fine," she assures me.

Before she leaves, we exchange more chitchat, and I go back out to the beach. The beach is my daily routine. At low tide, I could walk for miles, simply enjoying the peace and tranquility.

And that was how it began. I went on long walks to enjoy the last moments here. Then, when Linda started showing the house, I went on more long walks. After several weeks, I had developed a perfect tan, and I even lost some weight. It was nice, because even the new clothes I'd bought after I started gaining weight had grown quite snug on me when I was in the City.

Being at the Cape is exciting. There are lots of people coming and going, and I enjoy talking with the people at the small shops. The most exciting part of being at the Cape is being able to forget most of my worries, hardly ever thinking about the Russians and their threats Franco had shared with me.

This morning, while I was eating breakfast, Linda called. I would have normally missed her call, but it was raining today, so I couldn't go out for my daily walk. She had good news. There is a couple from Danbury, Connecticut offering to buy the house and pay exactly the price I had asked. I tried to be happy with the news, but in reality, my wish would have been to keep the house. She will call back later with the date for passing papers.

Now, I am looking around and trying to motivate myself to pack up the personal items I have here and get ready to move them to my new, smaller house. The one that doesn't know George Toomey. The home George Thompson will own.

Leningrad

"We found him." Kapersky could barely contain his excitement. A KGB agent in Boston had seen a real estate offering announcement appearing in a Massachusetts paper. "There is a house in Dennis, Massachusetts, and it is the home of, and is being sold by, our George Toomey, to a couple from Danbury, Connecticut."

"No wonder we can't find him in New York; he is at Cape Cod, Massachusetts," Kapersky says. The excitement of having this man finally eliminated almost makes up for the years of irritation and wrong leads. It almost does, but not quite.

"Leave immediately for Boston," Kapersky orders the two agents. "Find a third person you trust. When you get to Boston, drive to Hyannis. Check into a motel and plan everything out. I want no foul-ups." He turns and looks at first one man, then the other. "I want no excuses."

"Understood," they both assure him.

"Good. Stay an extra day if you must, in order to make sure you can do this and do it right."

They left, and Alexander drank his vodka. He should have word in a couple of days, three at the most. The thought warms him almost as much as the drink.

The three men slept the first day in their hotel room. And the leader sits in his chair. None of them use their actual names, and, on this particular one, he is using the name Igor. He has worked for Mr. Kapersky for many years. He'd nearly lost his job—and his life—when the team he'd sent after Toomey in Russia failed. Failure was usually punished with a bullet or noose. Somehow, he'd become useful enough that Kapersky hadn't done that, and, now, Igor was on an important mission again. He must be back in the inner circle.

The time change was eight hours backward, and after that and the long flight, it was better to sleep than to make mistakes. Igor sent Dimitri out to get breakfast at a local place and bring it back to their room. With Dennis only fifteen minutes from the hotel, they had plenty of time for breakfast.

"I have the Toomey address from the real estate listing," Avan reports between bites.

"Alright," Igor says. "Let's go through it one more time, so there are no mistakes."

They review the plan and drive to the house. Through the windows, they see George Toomey walking through the house. He has put on a bit of weight, but he is still recognizable. Same hair as the photograph. Same confident strut through his domain.

Igor is disgusted that this pretty boy has made them all look like fools.

Dimitri motions to the window, and Igor nods his approval. The men take out their guns, approach the door, and ring the front doorbell.

A man opens the door, and there is a woman standing at his side in the doorway.

Avan is the first one to push into the house and the other two follow. "George Toomey?" Igor yells, suddenly not so sure they have the right man. His face, while similar at a distance, doesn't have the same nose nor chin as Toomey.

"I don't know," the man stutters dumbly. The couple is scared, which is helpful, but it could also make them forget things.

Avan and Dimtri rush past the couple and start a complete search of the house.

"What do you want?" the woman yells.

Igor looks at her. She clearly doesn't understand who they are, or she wouldn't stand in the room with her arms crossed like she is.

"You have some nerve busting into our house," the man barks at them. Igor wants to smack him, but this isn't that kind of assignment.

"WHERE IS GEORGE TOOMEY?" Igor's voice is hard, but they remain angry more than scared.

"We don't know where he is," the man says.

"We bought the house from Toomey, and passed papers about an hour ago." Igor looks between them. Unfortunately, they appear to be telling the truth.

"Do you know where he went?" Dimitri demands, clearly sensing the same thing as Igor.

"To the best of our knowledge, Toomey has gone back to New York," the woman answers.

"When did you last see him?" Avan is growing impatient, and Igor looks at him, trying to silently calm him. It might have been a mistake to bring him along. When Kapersky told them to bring a third, Avan seemed like the best choice, but he is getting too excited here, pacing around and raising his gun to their faces more than once.

"We have never seen him. There was a lawyer representing him at the passing of papers."

"We don't know him. You need to leave," the man yells at the group.

"You shouldn't yell at us," Igor intones, his voice calm. "My friend over here," he indicates the direction of Avan, "is new at this and might shoot you, accidentally."

"You have no right to threaten us here," the man yells and turns to the phone. "I am calling the police." He picks up the receiver, and, immediately, Igor hears the popping sound of a gun. He doesn't have to look.

"I was saying it to scare them," Igor says, turning to Avan, "Not to tell you in code to shoot."

"He was going to call the police," Avan says.

"Did you touch anything?" Igor asks, looking at the other two.

"No," they both answer.

"Then run," Igor orders, leaving the front door open, as it was, and the bodies of the new homeowners lying in the front hall.

"Just drive quickly, but don't speed," Igor urges Dimitri. Kapersky will have them for sure for this.

"Hopefully, it will take a while to find the bodies," Avan says.

"And Kapersky?" Igor asks.

"Let's just get to Leningrad and worry about that later," Dimitri says. Igor sits back. Dimitri is right. He cannot lose his head.

Chapter 14

West Hyannis Port, Massachusetts

Many of the streets in West Hyannis Port are filled with small one and two-bedroom houses that are usually rented in the summer by the week, month, or season to renters who want to be close to the ocean. I found a small two-bedroom house and decided to purchase it with some of the proceeds from the sale of my oceanfront house in Dennis. I also purchased a small two-seater, red Triumph Spitfire for transportation. I can live off of the rest of the money from the sale for the next several years.

I try not to think about what I lost and, instead, focus on what I have. I don't have my own private beach, but the house is a four-minute walk to the beach, and I am able to take long walks passing Squaw Island, where some of the Kennedys' have homes. If I continue on walking and head towards the Kennedy compound, I will be able to exercise until the Secret Service, state police, and local police stop me. I only try it once. I don't want them to lock me up, because they think I'm after the Kennedys, or anything.

I fantasize about seeing the President. If only I could bump into JFK, I'd yell out to him, "It was me who told you about the missiles."

Just like in Dennis, the walks on the beach give me the time to think about my future, the amount of time I will need to spend at the Cape, and my plans for returning to New York.

I decided to take an extra long walk this morning after reading the newspaper. It seems like I always find out about big news events in my life from the newspapers. Headlines in the local newspaper report a double murder in my old house in Dennis. The body of a husband and wife were found in the front hall of the home, covered in sand. The newspaper story goes on to mention the front door was left open; wind forced sand and salty air into the house, forming a sand dune, covering the bodies in the front hall.

The article finishes with: If you're fond of sand dunes and salty air, you won't like this house.

Although I didn't meet the couple, I feel sad for the innocent pair. Their killers were looking for me, and they were just in the wrong place at the wrong time.

I immediately called Franco, who confirmed what I already assumed; the double homicides were meant for me. Kapersky sent a hit team to kill me, and, now, after another botched attempt on my life, the KGB believes I have gone back to New York.

"Do not come back to New York. You will be safer at the Cape."

"Are you sure?" I ask. It seems like out here, I am more likely to be spotted than in a city of millions.

"Yes. Stay there," he orders. His voice is calm, but firm, and his calmness gives me confidence. "The CIA will keep your apartment in New York, and, at any sign of danger, I will send agents to the Cape to watch over you."

"You haven't steered me wrong before," I concede, and, suddenly, I understand a deeper meaning to that sentence. I hadn't listened to him before, when he was trying to steer me right. If I had, I might still be performing on stage and—.

I stop that line of thought. It won't change anything and will only upset me. The murder in Dennis has changed my thinking. I am resigned to staying in West Hyannis Port longer.

The line is still silent, and I begin to wonder if Franco is waiting for me to say something else. "I guess my safety concerns are somewhat lessened, with so much police presence to protect President Kennedy in and around Hyannis Port and West Hyannis Port," I say.

"That is very true," Franco agrees.

"And I look completely different," I say.

"Don't describe yourself over the phone. I have heard enough to have the mental picture, and I don't want to risk anyone hearing you somehow," Franco warns.

"I thought you said I am safe here." Then, I hear Franco's muffled laughter. I have gained more weight, grown a long ponytail, dyed my hair blonde, and added glasses to my appearance—allowing me to feel comfortable in the fact that nobody will recognize me, but he must have been told about it.

"Be safe, George. And we'll be in touch," he promises before hanging up.

I walk extra-long, because I have a lot to think about. If I am going to stay on the Cape, I need to figure out how I will spend my time—like a job. I wonder if anything in my acting background could help me find a job to add to my income. There is not much potential on Cape Cod to keep a professional actor busy for twelve months of the year, especially since I cannot use my real name.

I think about contacting one or two of the few summer theatres in the immediate area. I called The Cape Playhouse in Dennis first. They are the most famous of all the summer theatres, and I could earn something with them. Hopefully, I could get a role for one of shows for the next summer's season.

"I would like to audition," I say, after working my way through various gatekeepers.

"You will need to call New York," the woman advises me. She is quite polite, which is nice. "All auditions and casting are now done in New York, where shows are produced and packaged for summer tours."

"Thank you," I say, completely defeated. Since I can't go back to New York, I can't audition. I had been right. There isn't much work on the Cape for professional, full-time working actors.

Since there is no acting potential, I start reading the papers to pass the time and hope that something will open up. Of course, in a small town like this, there is not much material written about theatre arts.

Still, I keep reading and find a small advertisement. "Barnstable High School, in Hyannis, is looking for an individual: part-time, to help with the staging of the yearly musical." It could be fun to work with young actors. Certainly, no one would recognize me, and the small salary will help stretch my savings a bit longer—hopefully until I'm able to go back to the City.

I apply for an interview, using the name George Thompson. Without any experience I can point to, and, since I can't reveal my background, I will really have to sell myself and fudge on my experience. That's what actors do—no matter what is asked of them at an interview or an audition—we always say, "We have done it and can do it."

***

"Mr. Thompson, the position is yours, if you'd like it," the man on the other end of the line says. I remember him from the interview. He was a very kind—albeit very distracted—man about fifteen years older than me.

Maybe they bought my story, or, maybe, there just weren't many applications for the position. Who cares about the reason; I got the job. I was excited as I was when I was told I was hired for my first professional acting gig.

I begin to really enjoy working with student actors, and find there are many talented actors in the high school. Some have shown an interest in pursuing an acting career, and, for those students, I enjoy directing them even more.

"Great work again, Tom," I say as we're cleaning up after rehearsal. When you're part-time working with the students, you do whatever needs done.

Tom Willingham, a freshman student, has acted for many years and is always willing to stay late and talk about the craft. When he was very young, he auditioned for any child role needed in the high school musical. Soon, people learned that if any amateur theatre company needed a child actor, Tom Willingham was the person to call. His parents had made the time needed to take Tom to all the auditions, rehearsals, and performances. It was a big commitment in time for the whole family, because Tom was usually cast in the roles he had auditioned.

"Have you decided what shows you're going to do next year?" Tom asks as we put away the last costume and double-check that the closet is locked.

"What role would you like to play?" I ask him.

"I don't know," he says, but his smile tells me he has a role in mind. "Since tonight is the last performance of the year, I'll wait a week or so before I try to figure out our next show for the fall."

Each year, I cast Tom as the lead in the shows I'm directing. Tom has a real natural talent for the stage. He reminds me of myself, when I was first bitten by the acting bug. I only wish I could mentor the boy's acting career more, but I can't disclose my real identity. More importantly, I can't make the calls to agents, directors, and producers I once could have to help the boy get his foot in the door.

Seeing all the young students reminds me of my two daughters, who I haven't seen in a long time. Tom is just a few years older than my oldest daughter, Jody. I spent many a moment trying to picture how they would look today. I cannot give them my address, because it could jeopardize their safety, and there was no record of any attempt on their part to contact me while I was overseas. Of course, why would they? I'd only been gone a while. To them, it was no different than when I'd been on Broadway.

"Mr. Thompson?"

I look up and realize Tom is staring at me.

"I'm sorry," I say.

"It's okay. I just wanted your thoughts on these notes."

He hands me a script he's been reading, and I look at the notes he's taken down. It is so rewarding to be able to spend many hours talking to Tom about his craft. Teaching him how to audition, method acting, stage movement, makeup, playwriting, and the fine points of musical comedy will be my way of being able to mentor Tom.

"Have you looked in to any of the acting schools, drama coaches, or theatre programs I told you about?" I ask him while I scan his notes. Since I cannot use my name, I tell him various ways to break into the theatre. All this information will help Tom in making decisions on which path to take after graduating from high school. Even though he doesn't know my true identity, he trusts me, and I think that is another reason I love to help him.

I work that part-time job for several years, directing some of the very shows I starred in on Broadway. The time has passed, and I find myself thinking often of my dream of going back to New York permanently and possibly to be cast in a Broadway show again. But, despite the years in hiding, the dream is eluding me, and I try to push it from my mind. I have been able to visit New York several times over the years, but I usually go back quietly, so as not to bring any attention to myself.

That is until this last month. I think it is time to go back. It should be safe by now, and if it isn't, will it ever be the right time?

"I understand," Franco says when I tell him of my plans. "Honestly, I wish you would find a job outside of New York for a little while longer."

"Since I have been able to keep my real identity a secret for so long, I believed I can continue the George Thompson life back in New York," I reason.

Franco doesn't answer immediately, but to my shock, he doesn't tell me he will call me back either. "Give me a minute," he says. Then he puts me on hold.

While I wait, I think about what a move would mean and what I'll do if they say no to me. I could just go anyway.

"Be careful," Franco advises.

I'm startled by his voice suddenly in my ear.

"I always am," I answer.

"You can go. We will be listening to communications and watching out for you, but, if we're going to try it, now is a good time," Franco concedes.

So I will head back to New York. Telling the high school administration about my plans was a bit tougher than I'd expected; the students were tougher still. They all cried, and I realized how much a part of my life this small group had become. What was once just a part-time directing position has turned into a full-time job, and one of the most respected roles at the high school.

Everyone loved the new character I'd created: Mr. Thompson. He is the man I wish now that I'd always been.

No one wants to see me leave, and I know it will be very hard for Tom Willingham. He has come to lean on me for almost every decision he makes regarding his current and future acting plans.

Tom will be a senior next year and still needs my continued help in mentoring and advice. The time has come for me to leave for New York; to once again, as I had done so many years earlier, to search out a career in the theatre. As for Tom, he will have his first experience of being alone in making his career and theatre decisions.

"There is no way I can convince you, Mr. Thompson?" Tom asks. He has just received his first taste of rejection. He couldn't sell me on the idea of staying.

"No, you can't," I say. It was like leaving my girls all over again. I had spent so much time with him that I would miss him terribly. Just like I missed my girls. And I would wonder about what he made of himself, just like I do my girls.

"Well, then," he pauses. "Thank you for everything." He reaches out and shakes my hand.

"Never give up. Many will try to destroy your enthusiasm, but you now have to have the drive and the fire in your belly to go forward. Stand on your own two feet, and do what is best for you and your career," I offer. It was the best I could give him.

Since I have sold my Triumph Spitfire, Tom drives me to the bus station to catch the bus to New York. As I leave his car, I can see a tear rolling down his cheek. I don't look back; not to embarrass him. In the years to come, he will have to learn tears dry up with disappointments.

Now, I am on the bus, and the City of New York is only four hours away. The same old city, but my brand-new life.

Chapter 15

Broadway at Sea

Upon my return, the apartment was exceptionally dirty. Except for a few visits in the past years, I spent practically no time there. Unlike when I went back to the Cape, I was now able to afford a cleaning person to do the heavy cleaning. Coming back to New York, with the hope it would be my final move, was a wonderful feeling. I will miss the Cape, all my acting students, and especially Tom, but I am still glad to be back, and near to Broadway. In truth, I could have had the best of both worlds; New York during the winters and the Cape in the summers. I could have done that if life had turned out differently, but, now, I must continue to be extremely careful. There is always Alexander Kapersky.

When I came back to the City, Franco and I decided that I would continue using the name George Thompson. I am going to clean up my appearance, but will keep the long hair, beard, and slightly dyed blonde hair, for at least a little bit longer. This spare tire around my midsection, however, will have to go.

Shortly after returning to the apartment and meeting with the woman I'd hired to clean the place, I left to walk down the street. It is liberating to again buy and read the trade papers, and to catch up on theatre news from when I was away. I will resume my daily routine of purchasing the daily *Variety* and *Backstage*. I walked around for a couple of hours to give the cleaning woman time to fix the place up. I sat on a bench and tore open the pages and read. When I got home, the place looked great again. I thanked her and went immediately to my table, where I spread out the papers and culled through almost every story and casting announcement for anything I could follow up on. There really isn't much today, but getting familiar with what is happening has helped me feel more a part of things and will, hopefully, help me when I start to audition.

Since I didn't have much luck yesterday, this morning I rushed out and bought the trades again. I also picked up a pastry and coffee on the way back to my apartment. I spent more time reading about the current status of the industry. Many of the names of the major players in the theatre were new to me. New shows, listed as opening on Broadway, were foreign. I have started to worry that my Broadway may really be in my past. I'm going to start aging out of some of these characters, and I'm starting all over again.

I don't allow myself the luxury of pity, but I do allow a bit of frustration. Everything seems to be the same as the day before, until my eyes fall on the story of a new producer named Maryanne Michaels, who has set up a production office to produce and direct shorter versions of Broadway musicals to be performed on cruise ships.

Under a section for auditions in the daily *Variety* was a notice from Maryanne Michaels's productions. Open call for actor's singers and dancers, for the Broadway musical *George M.*, the musical bio of George M. Cohan.

I keep reading, hope building in me for the first time in a *very* long time. There is a part that piques my interest, the role of the lead's father, Jerry Cohan. The audition is in a week. While I was working at the school, I did exercises with the kids, but I haven't worked myself hard in nearly a decade now. I put down the paper, move the furniture to make space, and begin training to work on my singing, dancing, and acting. Thank goodness I decided to exercise more. Most of the extra weight is gone now.

I keep rehearsing, all the while expecting to have the police show up because of a neighbor complaint. I'm sure it wouldn't be the first time they had to go out on a noise complaint late in the night. Of course, they may notice it now, since the apartment has been completely empty for so many years. It is a risk I'm willing to take, if it means returning to stage.

When audition day finally arrives, I hail a cab and try to relax. It is nearly impossible, because the same nervous feeling in my stomach takes over my whole body. I feel now like I did more than twenty-five years ago at my first audition.

"Here you are," the man says when we arrive in front of a building with lines stretching out the door and around the corner. The open call is for anyone without an agent who wants to audition. I never had to worry about open calls in the past, because I was always sent to an audition by my agent and at a particular time. Many times, I wasn't required to audition at all, because the role was written especially for me.

I pay the cab driver and get in line. A few people start small conversations, but most of us are absolutely focused on the audition. This was my chance, and I am concerned by the number of people I see who are my age in line.

Three hours passed until I was called in by the stage manager. I am shaking, and if I hadn't worn an undershirt under my dress shirt, I'm certain I would have sweated through. I still had long, blonde hair, glasses, and was a few pounds—but only a few—overweight. Certainly no one would recognize me. At least that is what I am hoping.

Several people sat at a table, none of whom I knew, nor even recognized from the old days. This made me a bit less nervous, because I only had to focus on acting. I read my part of the script with the stage manager. I think I read it pretty well. Then, I sing several songs.

At the end of my audition, Maryanne Michaels approaches me, "What is your previous experience in the theatre?"

"None," I lie. "I came from Cape Cod, where I directed high school students in musicals." That much was completely true. I add, "And performing in amateur regional theatres on Cape Cod." That was a lie.

"I'm really impressed by your audition and surprised you never performed professionally."

"Thank you," I say, already getting excited. This cannot be the way she treats every person who reads.

"You have a lot of talent, and I would like to offer you the part of Jerry Cohan," she says. "You can keep your long hair. We will tuck it up under the wig."

"Thank you," is all I manage to get out. The acceptance means more than acting. It means I'm really good. Even as George Thompson, and not Toomey, I have talent.

"Rehearsals will start in a week in New York, and, then, the cast will be flown to Miami to board the *Ocean Queen*, for seven-day cruises to the Caribbean," she says. "Welcome to the cast."

"Thank you," I say again, realizing I sound dumb. At least it is easy to believe this is my first role.

Maryanne smiles at me, as if she has seen it all before. "The general manager of the production company will be calling in two days to discuss the contract, salary terms, and rehearsal schedule."

Terms, I laugh on the inside. I would have accepted any salary, just to act in any kind of a musical again.

The show is based on the Hollywood film *Yankee Doodle Dandy*, with a score of George M. Cohan songs. Although my part is small, I will be is able to sing and dance to some of the most iconic Cohan songs. The time passes quickly, and, already, we begin to rehearse.

The rehearsal period is pure joy for me. I sit for hours, watching and listening to the actors singing and performing their roles in the show. Rehearsal period is four weeks long, but it goes by very fast. I wish it could be longer, but I will be able to listen to the music and enjoy the stage again, because my contract is for an entire year. For the next year, I will perform. It is like a cool drink after a very long, hot day in the sun.

After the four weeks, the entire cast leaves for Miami to board the *Ocean Queen*. I have been given my own cabin. Although very small, there will be privacy. I think about my last trip on a ship, and it makes me smile, the pain of what I lost soothed a bit with this new role. As I had hoped, the first day on board is to familiarize the cast with the ship. There are no guests, but, instead, we get a tour of the stage and the wings, and, then, we have to participate in a mandatory lifeboat drill.

The person overseeing our training comes to the microphone during lunch on the second day, "You are all part of the social staff," he begins. "You will be required to meet and greet the passengers as they embark each week on their cruise." I was not aware of this responsibility, but I really didn't care. I would do practically anything to be back on any stage again.

There will be several days of rehearsals on the ship, and the show will be performed three nights a week, allowing all the passengers to see the show.

The first day out, I was struck suddenly with the flu. When it wasn't gone the second day, I was sent to the ship's hospital.

"You are seasick," the doctor pronounced.

"That isn't possible." And I get ready to explain my experience on a ship, but, then, I pause. "No one in my family gets seasick," I continue.

He just nods his head knowingly and gives me some pills. Over the next few days, I learn the proper way to handle the malaise and quickly settled into the routine of performing and the weekly activities on board. The year passes by quickly. At the end of the year, Maryanne Michaels has come aboard to rehearse the cast, clean up the show, and make it fresh again.

I sit in the theater seats, watching everything on the stage, and Maryanne approaches. "You have had rave reviews from the passengers, and the social director gave great positive responses, too."

I knew there was applause, but I had no idea how well-received my work was. "Thank you for telling me that," I say. I am truly humbled.

"I would like to make you an offer," Maryanne says.

"Certainly. What is it?"

"I'd like you to star in my next production, *Damn Yankees*."

I am shocked, and I simply look at her. She must have misinterpreted that as me holding out because she continues.

"You would play the comedy lead—the role of the Devil (Mr. Applegate)," Maryanne says. "This would, of course, call for a raise in salary, a paid vacation, and rehearsals of the show in New York, until we return to the *Ocean Queen*."

"I would love to do that," I say. I will have a month's vacation in New York. A call to Franco is in order, because it has been quite some time since I have spoken to him. It isn't easy on the ship, and I've been busy.

"That is great, George," Franco says when I tell him the news. "It is a good idea to stay on ships."

"He is still looking?" I ask. Somehow, I'd hoped that he'd forgotten me by now.

"Alexander Kapersky has increased his efforts to find you, and he wants you dead," Franco warns.

"How long will I have to run?" I ask. The excitement of my news is now draining.

"He has lost all of his power with the KGB, and, as I told you previously, was destroyed by the fact that you had an affair with his wife," Franco says. "My sources at the KGB tell me Kapersky has a pledge to kill you, no matter how long and how much effort it will take." I self-consciously look over my shoulder. "The one good thing is that Kapersky has no idea where you are or how to find you."

So I've stayed on the ship.

Damn Yankees is widely accepted by the cruise passengers. In fact, George Thompson becomes quite the celebrity on the open sea. I love the adoration everyone gives me. I won't lie. In fact, I've liked it so much that, for the last five years, I have appeared in five different musicals from the golden age of the 1950s musicals. It looks like I have proven I am a consummate star—even if it is just on the ocean.

After five years, it is time for me to tell Maryanne that I will not be renewing my contract. I must finally go back to New York. I have been on ships long enough.

"Just one more year," Maryanne implores.

"I don't know," I say, but she is a very persuasive producer.

"Just one more year," she repeats. "I will double your salary, give you more time off, and I will move you to another ship—*The Regal Fantasy*, with an entirely new show."

With all she has done for me, I reluctantly agree. "But this will be my last contract. Under no circumstances, will I perform at sea any more after this contract has expired."

So, I begin the process again. Back to New York for vacation, four weeks of rehearsals, and then onto *The Regal Fantasy* for a year of weekly performances.

Again, I received excellent responses from the audiences on the *Regal Fantasy*. Although I enjoy all the acting, singing, and dancing I do, it is starting to take a toll on my physical well-being. In fact, I haven't been feeling well lately. I think it is just the motion of the sea.

I was extremely proud that I had never missed a performance on board. I fought through many illnesses, including colds, the flu, and all kinds of minor ailments. It came as a big surprise one night during a show—whether from the heat, glare of the spotlights, or because I hadn't eaten much during the day—that I became lightheaded. Although I had experienced something like this before, this time it was entirely different. I can't completely explain the feeling, but without any warning, I fainted on stage.

Chapter 16

Last Days on the *Regal Fantasy*

I open my eyes slowly, trying to remember where I am and what I was doing before falling asleep. The room is completely unfamiliar, and my mind is sticky, as though I am waking from a hangover. I begin to make out images—first, I notice a bright light, then, the large silver thing holding it. I look around and see surgical equipment hanging over the hospital examination table.

I feel something in my hand. It is someone else's hand.

"Welcome back, George." It is Ingrid, and she is as beautiful as ever. I'm not sure how I got lucky enough to find such a wonderful woman on board, but, since we met about ten months ago, she has been my constant companion.

"Thank you," I say, shifting slightly, but still holding tight to her.

"You passed out on stage and have been out for a few hours," Ingrid explains, holding my left hand in her right and stroking the side of my face with her left. It feels wonderful to have such a caring touch.

"A few hours," I answer. "That doesn't sound good."

"It isn't." She's very matter-of-fact, and I'm momentarily scared. Will this mean I have to quit acting? Will they remove me from the ship immediately?

"What will this mean?" I ask, trying to read some kind of answer in her eyes.

"I don't think you'll have to leave today," she says. "The doctor didn't say anything about that. So, you will still have these last few days with me."

"I guess it is a good thing to be sleeping with a nurse," I joke, and she smiles. I love her smile. It is friendly and flirtatious and wonderful.

"We have been monitoring your vital signs since you passed out," she continues, a small smirk still painted on her lips, "And the doctor seems to think it was nothing more than dehydration or overworking yourself."

"So you were worried," I say, and smile. She recognizes that smile, and, in response, she bends down to kiss me. Although brief, the kiss is full of promise of what is to come. I believe I will be quite well.

"I wasn't *that* worried," she teases, "but I will go let the doctor know you're back with us."

She squeezes my hand before walking away from the gurney. I still feel her kiss on my lips. The mind is a funny thing, and memories are even funnier, because after she walks away, I remember a bit of when I was young. I remembered how my mother would kiss me on my forehead when I wasn't feeling well as a young boy. It has been a very long time since anyone showed me any sympathy for a physical ailment. When I started grammar school, my father reminded me that I was a young man and that I shouldn't need kisses and hugs to feel better.

I put my fingers to my mouth, trying to make it look like an itch when, in fact, I want to touch where Ingrid's lips had touched. My father was a good enough guy, but I think he was completely wrong about the power of a kiss.

"George." I turn and see David, the doctor, standing beside the gurney and Ingrid a few steps behind. Another nurse, who appears to be on duty, based on what she is wearing, is not far from his right arm.

"Yes, sir," I respond. Then, I glance over at Ingrid, who playfully blows me a kiss. She reminds me of a child standing behind her father who is getting into mischief because she knows she won't be caught. I smile back at her.

"Hi, George." I look back at David and realize he is looking at some papers on a metal clipboard and not at me, so I decide not to answer. "I am not sure what may have happened that caused you to lose consciousness." He drops the clipboard to his side and looks directly at me. "The good news is that all of the tests performed are normal, and, other than rest, nothing more is needed for now."

I am not certain that I was completely satisfied with his account of what may have caused the episode, but I don't say anything. He is, after all, the doctor. He simply appears to be in too much of a hurry to spend time helping me figure out what is wrong.

"So, I am fine?" I ask, trying to draw out some kind of information. Just because I'm not sick doesn't mean that I'm completely well. I've never passed out before, and I'd like to make this my last time.

"I'm sure you'll be okay for the next few days," he assures me. "But it might be wise to visit a doctor in New York for follow up when we dock."

"I will do that," I agree, glancing at Ingrid for comfort. She knows how to relax me.

"In the meantime," he says, "you should spend the rest of the night sleeping in the hospital, and, in the morning, you may go back to your cabin."

"I can watch him," Ingrid says. David turns to her and then back to me. Some sentiment crosses his face very briefly, but I'm not able to discern exactly what it is, possibly a smirk.

"That should be fine" he says, looking between the two of us, then, to the nurse assisting him. "Report anything you see that is unusual, but I'm sure you'll be just fine."

I watch David walk out. I'm not exactly thrilled about staying here for the night, but it is already fairly late, so maybe it is best.

"So, are you okay with me taking care of you?" Ingrid asks, leaning over, so she is only inches from my face.

"Yes," I say. "That is the kind of treatment I am delighted to accept."

"Well, I cannot wait to take care of you," she says, pulling a chair over beside my bed. "And I'll start by sleeping here tonight."

"You don't need to do that," I insist. "It is far too uncomfortable."

"I'll be fine," she replies, her voice ever calm. Certainly, she has learned that after years of dealing with patients.

I changed the subject. There was no use arguing with her, and I really am happy to have her with me for now. Instead, we talked about the things we normally spoke of: life, funny stories on the ship, our families, or whatever else came to mind.

"You should try to rest, George," Ingrid urges.

"I just rested for hours," I complain. "I don't want to rest again."

"That was hardly resting." She smiles. "Your body was recharging and healing from the torture you put it through. Now, you need to actually rest." She pulls my blankets up, and I smile at how nurturing she is.

"I need a kiss before I sleep," I say. Ingrid leans down to kiss me. She smells wonderful, like lavender mixed with bandages. It is a comforting smell, but still sexy. Our lips connect, and, immediately, I know that I'm completely healthy. I want to be alone with her. She tries to back away, but I hold on to her hand, compelling her to stay in the embrace a bit longer.

"Rest," she whispers against my lips. And I finally release her and close my eyes.

I hadn't thought I was tired, but the next thing I remember, I'm waking to noise and activity in the hospital area. It is morning, and the room is no longer dim and quiet.

Ingrid is still there, and, after a quick exam, David approves my discharge back to my cabin.

Ingrid can't wait to nurse me back to health upon my arrival in my cabin. She smiles and holds my hand while we walk out of the ship's hospital and back to my cabin.

Thank God for my understudy, who will perform the remaining performances of the week. The doctor will allow Ingrid to spend the remaining time needed caring for me, so our nights are now completely free. For the first time in ten months, we can have a leisurely dinner and a real evening date, something other lovers take for granted. Just walking around the outside decks in the moonlight, hand-in-hand, is as romantic as any ship's voyage can offer.

"I've taken off the day, and will be able to devote the entire day and night tending to your well-being, "she says, squeezing my hand as we walk.

"That sounds wonderful," I answer.

My cabin is only a short distance from the hospital, which is good. From the looks I receive from crewmembers walking through the crew quarters, I must look awful. We arrive at my door, and Ingrid holds out her hand. I dutifully give her my keys and wait while she unlocks the door.

"Okay, here we are," she says, swinging the door in and stepping through.

I walk in behind her and close the door. "I love you." The words come out so naturally, but I can't believe I said them. I haven't uttered these words in years, and I have never said them to Ingrid.

"I love you, too," Ingrid tells me. She is blushing slightly, and it endears me to her even more.

I have changed into another person since waking from my sleep. Actually, that isn't true. When Ingrid and I were talking last night, I started to realize how much I've changed as a person over these past few years. For all the years of bedding down any woman I could get my hands on, I wasn't afraid, this time, to express emotion. I also realize that I care more about her needs than my own. Last night, I wanted so badly not to be alone, yet I'd considered her comfort and wanted her to go back to her own cabin.

I'm not entirely sure when the final break from George Toomey to George Thompson happened, but, somewhere along the way, I became the character I had created. I had decided to become a new person—one I wish I'd always been—and, now, I realize I am actually becoming that person.

I realize something else, too. I now feel the time is right to tell Ingrid about my past and my life before we met.

I realize too well that everything must be put on the table, and nothing can be held back: the Broadway star of the fifties, the Russian tour, my relationship with Franco, the death threats, the deaths I caused, my affairs, the breakup of my marriage, the loss of my daughters, the Cape property, the years at the Cape, and, finally, expressing to Ingrid, for the first real time, that I now know the feeling of really being in love.

"Would you like to have something to eat?" I ask Ingrid. While I'm excited to tell her about who I really am, I'm also nervous. I'm nervous she may reject me. I am also nervous that she won't trust me anymore. *Worse still, what if she completely believes me, but she blows my cover? I will have to, again, start over.*

"I had something to eat…" she pauses and looks at me, "George? What's wrong?"

"I have some things I'd like to tell you," I say, but, then, realizing that is normally how bad news begins, I decide to say it another way. "I love you, and I want you to know all about me."

"I do know all about you." She smiles. "But if there is more to hear, I'm ready to listen."

I began the long, tedious explanation of my past—trying not to miss any of the various complicated details. Ingrid listens intently. She doesn't show much emotion, and I'm not sure if she heard all the gory details. I start to feel nervous, so I continue talking while I change my clothes. It gives me something to occupy myself with, and I don't have to look in to her eyes. I'm not sure if she had any reaction to my long conversation, but at least now I could feel comfortable. I told her about the old me; not the person she fell in love with on the ship.

"That is what I wanted to tell you," I conclude.

"I guess you're right—there *was* a lot I didn't know." She smiles. "I guess I'm a bit boring. The story I told you about me is the only story there is."

It isn't the reaction I expected, but I'll take it. She is still here. We begin to discuss plans for the rest of 1979. I guess my long banter about my past didn't turn her off, because she was more than willing to spend a future with me.

"I don't want to lose you," I finally say.

"You won't." She is very matter-of-fact.

"In three days, when the ship arrives in New York, I will leave the ship," I say, explaining the obvious. I feel like a young, lovesick fool.

"Why would that mean that you're losing me?" she asks. "You know where I'll be."

"But... what if you find someone else?" I ask.

"I would think you'd be more likely to do that than I would," she says, without a bit of negativity. "And, since I'm not worrying about it, I see no reason for you to worry."

She is right. I tell her so and listen to her plan.

"I will finish my contract through the summer, ending in September. Every Saturday, when the ship arrives in New York, preparing to embark new passengers on their seven night Bermuda cruise, you will visit me," she says.

"I will miss you so much during the week." Even now, it feels like a fist in my gut thinking about the long week stretching alone in my apartment, waiting for her ship to come into port, so we can spend those few, precious hours together.

"It isn't perfect, but one day a week is far better than nothing. After the summer, we will finally be together," she says, with far more resolve than I. Why am I so weak now? Maybe I should have withheld my declaration of love?

"I have a small apartment on Riverside Drive in the 120s, rented for me by the CIA, and I will make plans to look for a bigger apartment for both of us to move to together this fall," I say, trying to focus more on the time we'll be together than the time we'll be apart.

"Good," she responds, "I have a great friend in New York, but I haven't spent nearly as much time there as you have. You will be a better judge of where to live."

"When I was a big star on Broadway, I had this big Park Avenue penthouse in the high seventies," I say. "That would have been wonderful for us.

"I don't care about big apartments, as long as I can be with you," she says, snuggling deeper against my chest.

"You know," I begin, "maybe you could find a nursing position at some New York hospital, where the location of our apartment could be close-by."

"That would be perfect."

Perfect. The next three days are perfect. Every waking moment, and even some non-waking moments, we spend together. We don't let go of one another. She sleeps beside me. We eat meals together. We even shower together. Holding onto the minutes is like trying to hold water in our hands. It just flows by too quickly.

"I love you," I repeat to her. I am getting more comfortable in expressing my love for Ingrid.

"I love you, too," she answers, and, this time, she doesn't blush. It is progress. The war had scarred her so badly that she'd been afraid to give love. Now, she expresses it to me.

"We both have changed," I observe.

"I think you're right."

It is a simple exchange, but I'm so grateful for it. I am now in my late fifties and experiencing the kind of love normally reserved for the first loves of youth. It is a feeling that takes over my entire body. I look at her, and I can't catch my breath. Even right now, sitting only a few feet from her, my thoughts are lost on her. Our emotions have become all-consuming. We start to understand the feeling we both are experiencing for the very first time and can't deny; we don't want to lose any of the passion.

Neither of us wants to think about how soon I'll leave, but the last night finally arrives, and we don't stop our time together for a minute. Neither of us sleeps very much. I want to memorize everything about her. The way her voice sounds with that barely perceptible accent. The way her skin smells. I want to remember the curve of her hip and the way her fingers feel when interlocked with mine.

"Why are you staring at me like that?" she asks.

"If I told you, you'd just tell me to stop," I answer. "So why not let me just have my fun?"

"You are such a card, George Thompson, or should I say George Toomey," she says, swatting me playfully. I hold her against me and kiss her forehead. We make love, and, after we are through, I look at the clock. It is nearly 3 AM. At 5 AM, we want to be on the top deck of the ship as it sails past the Statue of Liberty. I will be able to sleep away the day in my lonely apartment in New York, but Ingrid will have to greet guests and return to her duties.

"Get some sleep, my love," I say. She doesn't answer. Her breath goes in and out softly, and I listen to it for a while before finally drifting off to sleep.

Too soon, the alarm screams, and we get up. I don't mind waking early—I've done it each of these last few mornings to squeeze every moment out of the day. What I dread is walking away from the ship and entering the life I'd known before. The one in which I existed without Ingrid—alone, in an apartment in the City. The one in which I was no longer an actor. I dread entering the next few months of waiting to move on to the next step of our lives together.

For now, however, my focus is on getting dressed, so we can go above deck. The deck is just losing the darkness of night when we come up top. June in New York is cool and beautiful. Sometimes, there is a light fog that comes off the water, but, today, it is clear. There is neither fog nor haze—only the few wisps of stringy clouds high up reflecting the oranges and reds of morning. The top deck of the ship is full of lovers embracing and kissing as the ship sails past the Statue of Liberty and into New York Harbor. It is like something from a book or movie, and I'm getting to experience it with a woman I truly love—and more than that—a woman I'm devoted to.

People begin to disperse, but we remain up top and watch the ship move quietly and slowly to its assigned berth at the pier. The *Regal Fantasy* will tie up at this pier every Saturday throughout the summer.

"I'm glad the rain stayed away," Ingrid offers, breaking the stillness.

"I don't think there could have been a more beautiful morning," I respond. "The little bit of cool humidity made the sunrise that much more beautiful."

It will be two more hours before the ship finally docks, luggage is unloaded, cleared by customs, and passengers and crew are allowed to disembark.

"Let's go back to the cabin," I urge. Ingrid silently nods, looking back one more time at the sun in its ascent. It is no longer a low, beautiful fireball. Now, it is high and bright, threatening a hot day.

I lead her back to my cabin to finish up some last-minute packing before I leave the ship. Now that the time has arrived, I'm eager to get off the ship, so it can be Saturday again, and I can see her. I hate goodbyes, and this one is slow and painful.

"Can you put this shirt in that bag?" I turn and see Ingrid, tears welling up in her eyes.

I set the shirt in the bag, and I hug and kiss her all over again. I remind her that it will only be a week—seven busy days—until we see each other again.

"Consider how fast the last three days have gone by," I say. "For that matter, the last ten months."

"I know," she says. "I am being silly. The time will pass quickly."

Someone knocks at my door, "George, we've cleared customs."

"Thank you," I answer, looking at Ingrid. "It's time."

She nods. I hoist one bag on my shoulder, and she takes my hand. I lift the other bag with my free hand. I take my bags, grateful to have so few possessions. I spent most of my time in costume and in swimsuits, so I haven't acquired too much on this trip. We walk, oh-so-slowly, to the disembarkation area of the ship and share one last goodbye kiss.

"I love you," I whisper in her ear, holding back my own emotion. Those words spoken so many times over the last few days are charged with emotion and promise.

"I love you, too." She kisses my cheek and neck, before turning quickly and rushing to the elevators to take her to the top deck. I disembark and walk down to the pier. Once I have my things, I turn and look back up. There she is on the top deck, waving goodbye again and again and blowing goodbye kisses to me on the pier. I cannot see her face clearly, so I imagine she is happy and beautiful. *It will only be seven days*, I remind myself. Then, I turn and begin to search for a ride home.

The pier is crowded, and people bump into me as I make my way to the street. Hundreds are lined up at least four deep near the curb, waiting for a cab to pull up.

I turn back to the ship and see Ingrid jumping up and down on the top deck, blowing kisses and frantically waving at me. I can't remember the last time anyone has shown me so much emotion.

After twenty minutes, Ingrid is still waving, although I'm sure by now her arm is quite sore. I realize that the hundreds have become only dozens of people waiting for a cab, and one-by-one, that group of people is thinning out.

I raise my arm, and a cab comes my way and stops directly in front of me. As I wait for him to open the trunk, I look back. Ingrid is waving, and I return the wave and repeat my chorus: Only seven days, only seven days.

"Thank you," I say. I reach down and pull out plenty of money for the ride and an extra-generous tip from the cash in my briefcase. Living at sea, where all of my meals and living expenses were covered, has given me a considerable amount of spendable cash.

The taxi driver carefully loads all of my luggage, briefcase, and personal belongings into the trunk of the cab. I am able to roll down the window and wave upwards toward the top deck, where Ingrid is still standing. The taxi slowly leaves the pier with Ingrid still waving, and I keep waving until we can't see each other anymore. Staring out the window, gazing at the ship, my memories of the last year of my life living and working on the *Regal Fantasy* pass by me. The ship finally fades in the background.

Chapter 17

THE CAB RIDE

I continued to gaze out the window as the cab starts its trip. Almost in a trance, I contemplate my future and what it has in store for me. It is hard to think about the pain I've endured these years and the loss of what I'd once felt so precious. Despite losing my family, my career, my identity, and—twice—nearly losing my life, I have been lucky enough to meet someone and fall in love with her. I am truly a fortunate man.

The rain starts all at once, as if the watering can of God were suddenly dumped on the City. The bright skies are covered in a thick gray blanket, and the inside of the cab sounds like someone is playing percussion on the roof and windows. The wipers squeak and squawk back and forth. I try to look out on the City, but the water is creating an impenetrable sheet. My breath is beginning to fog up the window, so I wipe it away. I had to open and close the window several times to clear the rain drops. It is like the weather is mourning with me. I laugh at my own sap. *Love has turned me in to a softie, I guess.*

Going from the Port of New York to Riverside Drive and around 122nd Street in upper Manhattan is a quick entry onto the West Side Highway, and, then, an approximately fifteen-minute drive northbound, but I want to take a longer route.

"Please don't take the West Side Highway," I ask. "Instead, head over to the theatre district and drive around."

"Alright," the driver acquiesces, clearly reluctant, "But as soon as we get to your apartment, I need to rush back to the piers for another fare from passengers still disembarking the ships."

"I understand and will gladly pay double the meter charge for your trouble," I promise, certain *this* will take away any reluctance. He nods without another word. I think my offer is very generous, but he keeps looking at the meter, in the mirrors, and shifting, as though anxious to get back to the pier. I understand he wants to get back to the pier and pick up his next fare, but this small side trip shouldn't add too much time.

As the cab moves closer to the heart of the theatre district, I start seeing familiar sights; theatres I played in and restaurants I have eaten at. It has been years and years since I last saw what makes the Great White Way, well, great.

The cab arrives in the heart of the theatre district: 45th Street and Shubert Alley. The rain has subsided quite a bit, and I can start to make out more of the buildings and the signs. There is deep ache in my chest. Even though I've been acting, I've never stopped wondering how different my life might have been if I'd chosen another path. I never stopped loving it here.

"Will you please stop?" I ask. I thought it would be enough to drive by, but the memories are flooding me too fast.

"I have other fares I need to get to," the driver protests.

"Keep the meter running while I walk around and through the famous Shubert Alley," I say, pretending not to hear his objection. He certainly won't drive off and lose this fare and my tip.

He grunts something back at me and puts the car in park. It is amazing; it has been more than eighteen years since I last appeared on Broadway. Of course, I'm no longer the man who appeared on Broadway. I'm a new man now.

Likewise, Broadway is all new. It is no longer the place I remember eighteen years ago. The show posters lining the walls of Shubert alley promote shows I've never heard about. *A Chorus Line*,

Sweeney Todd, *Annie*, and *They're Playing Our Song* are all totally foreign to me. The famous Astor Hotel once bordering Shubert Alley has been torn down, and in its place is a monstrosity of a building. What memories I had spending many a night at the Astor Bar: entertaining many of my leading ladies and meeting with producers on future show projects. I had a beautiful room facing Times Square, always ready for the moment I needed to go upstairs to have a more serious conversation with a starlet. While the memories are all still fresh, I realize I'm now an outsider here. The shows and the people are gone.

I turn back to the cab and see the glaring frustration on the cabbie's face. I will have to come back another time, when I'm not rushed and the weather is nicer. I go back to the cab reluctantly. For the second time today, I'm forced to turn away from something I love and return to this cab.

"Please drive up a few more blocks north, then east and south," I request as soon as I get in the cab, "so I can see the full boundary of the Broadway District."

"Sure," he says, and he quickly puts the car in gear. The theatre district is very quiet at nine in the morning. The only noise this time of day is the trash collectors throwing trash cans back on the street and the various trucks making deliveries to local restaurants.

I watch the shuttle of activity. A truck pulls up and throws a package at the front door of first one theatre, then another. They are certainly the Playbills for the current performances. The sights, the sounds, and even the smells of the District are like a time machine taking me to my heyday of theatre. While I'm glad to be the man I am now, I still miss the George Toomey of the stage.

After all these years of being away, I have almost convinced myself that I could live without theatre. I'd accepted my fate and forced myself to believe that it is no longer important to me. But, as I watch theatres go by the cab window, I realize how much I do, indeed, miss the industry. As much as I try to convince myself otherwise, in truth, acting on the ship didn't fully satisfy me. There is still a burning sensation in my gut to get back to work as an actor on Broadway.

Unfortunately, it doesn't even matter that the CIA shut the industry down to me—I've aged out. No producer, even if they wanted to, would hire me. There just aren't any parts for fifty-nine-year-old leading men.

The rain starts up again as the cab finally heads for the West Side Highway. It is getting stuffy inside the cab, and I'm anxious to get home now, so that I can put the painful memories away and start preparing for Ingrid in my life.

The taxi turns northbound and immediately stops.

"Great!" The driver exclaims, muttering a few oaths. I'm certain more than one was meant for me and my delays. We sit in bumper-to-bumper traffic, rolling a few feet and then stopping, over and over, from West 56th Street all the way up to 72nd Street. At 72nd Street, traffic begins to thin out, and the cab surges forward. Cars zip past, and I consider whether it is better to allow him to drive at this speed or to distract him and make him angry by asking him to slow down.

A few times, a car moves out in front of us, and the driver slams on the brakes before making a hard left and right to go around the slower car. I hold on to the door, trying not to let him see how nervous his driving is making me—not that he'd care.

We zip up all the way to 96th Street, where the other cars are all driving as fast as or faster than we are. I hadn't remembered such reckless driving when I lived in New York, but maybe I didn't care then.

We change lanes, and the cab feels a bit like it is sliding, but he rights it quickly, and we continue on in this ridiculous race to nowhere. I look at other cars as they pass us or we pass them. We are so close together and yet driving so quickly. Suddenly, I remember escaping Leningrad. I feel a bit sad remembering what happened that day. Watching the other car smashed up. Watching Gina die. The speed takes me back to that day, and I feel my pulse thudding in my chest and in my ears. An invisible hand or force or something is now pushing me back against my seat and, then, against the partition separating the front seat and back. Outside the window, there are no longer cars and buildings, but only blurry shapes. I feel my head hit the back seat again and hear squealing just before my head smashes into the window, I'm not sure which. I feel myself slipping off to sleep. I have the sudden thought that the cab driver has lost control. Then, just as quickly as it starts, it stops. The car is no longer moving. I'm barely awake. I can see bent metal in front of me, but I also see sky. I struggle to comprehend.

The first bystanders rush to the scene of the crash. I look up at them, pain overwhelming my senses. I see a young couple and a dog. Is it their dog?

"I have never seen a crash like this," he says to the woman.

More voices. A young man's voice yelling. I fight to open my eyes and stay conscious. My eyelids simply won't respond. Things are getting dark around the edges. The voices barely make sense.

"Would someone please run back to their house and call the police, fire, and ambulance?" a young man is screaming. "The driver has no pulse. I will start CPR until the paramedics arrive".

Dead? The driver is dead? A woman's voice. Is it Ingrid? The voice is so far away. I hear her giving commands. Someone pushes against my neck, and another hand presses my wrist. I hurt, and their fingers make me hurt more. The fingers let go. "The occupant in the backseat, who was thrown from the car, is barely breathing, but does have a weak pulse. It appears he has landed on his head, but is still alive."

Is that me? Are they saying *I'm* still alive?

Everything is dark. I hurt, and I've given up trying to open my eyes. It is too hard. I hear more footsteps and voices. "There is not much we can do until the ambulance arrives," someone says. "It is taking forever for the fire department and the ambulance to arrive."

I feel heat. Is hell real? The thought terrifies me. Then I hear someone yell "fire" and "back up."

Muffled voices now, "The ambulance... fire department... the police are here."

More sounds. Hissing like water on a skillet. People yelling. Hands on me.

"We have one dead, and one nearly dead. Let's get oxygen on the living victim, secure him to the backboard, secure all of his limbs, and get him on the gurney." I want to speak, but my mouth doesn't work.

"We must transport fast to the hospital, or he won't make it." I want them to call Ingrid, so she can come to the hospital with me.

"Head for Mt. Sinai Hospital." Everything hurts, but pain and consciousness are starting to fade.

"It is the closest, and they will be able to handle this kind of trauma."

Darkness.

***

"Did anyone see any identification, or any personal belongings of either the deceased or the living patient?" A cop barks out. Peter Alan had been a Paramedic for just over a year, but it wasn't getting any easier to look at these accidents. The cop bent down next to the living patient. He had to be the fare in the cab.

"I have been a cop for twenty years and have never seen such a horrific crash."

Peter turned to look up at who was speaking. It was that same cop.

"Yes," Peter answered, securing the man to the backboard, "it is pretty bad."

At least Peter knew his stomach wasn't completely soft. If even this cop was bothered by it, maybe he really did have a reason to be concerned.

"I am puzzled about the lack of ID," the cop continues speaking while Peter finishes securing the man.

"I guess I will put in the report that all personal effects and identification of the two victims were burnt up in the car crash."

"That sounds like a good idea," Peter says. He didn't want to seem like he was ignoring the other man—he was just focusing on making sure the patient was secure before they went to the hospital.

A couple of firemen help lift the stretcher into the back of the ambulance. Peter climbs in the back and begins working on the radio.

"We have a male, approximately 55 to 60 years old, badly injured in a roll over on the West Side Highway," Peter says to the hospital.

He watches the patient as the driver winds them through the busy streets on the way to the hospital. Four people meet them at the doors.

"The trauma team is ready in room one," someone barks, as he climbs out of the back behind the stretcher.

Peter gives a report while the doctors and nurses move the man off of the stretcher and onto their trauma room's gurney and begin cutting all of his clothes off.

"One of the cops said this was the worst accident he'd seen in twenty years," Peter adds. "The driver died at the scene."

"He is pretty bad. If we can save him at all, he'll have a long recovery," Dr. Miller says. Peter had worked with him on quite a few patients, and Miller knew his stuff. If he was concerned, this guy was probably going to die, too.

Peter went back out and cleaned the ambulance. It was a busy day, and he ran four more calls after that first one. The rain seemed to have washed the good sense out of everyone's head. The fourth patient was transported to the same hospital as his John Doe, so he checked in on him.

"He had a lot of broken bones and injured organs," Susie says. She was one of the nicer nurses there, so, when Peter wanted to check on someone, he always asked her.

"Does anyone know if he is a local or out-of-towner?" he asks. "There should be some way of knowing."

"Not sure," Susie says, shuffling a few papers. "So he'll be listed as a John Doe, and we'll see what happens. Right now, he is going up for surgery."

"Are they going to do anything to try to find out who he is?" Peter asks.

"The administrator of the hospital will take some pictures of John Doe and place the pictures in the newspapers. There may be some hope that someone will recognize the patient and come forward."

"Well, hopefully, he will wake up soon, and we can solve it that way," Peter says, but there isn't much chance of that.

"I think it is more likely we'll be calling in a priest soon," Susie observes.

"That's too bad," Peter replies. He needs to help his partner clean up and get back in service. They were running pretty hard today. "I hope the rest of your day goes better."

"Yours, too," Susie says.

CHAPTER 18

THE FOLLOWING SATURDAY

I didn't get much sleep last night; I tossed and turned the whole night. I haven't slept much at all since George left the ship. I can't remember when I slept and when I was up. Knowing I'd see George soon made it almost impossible to sleep at all. The ship that last week seemed to speed along on its path to the Harbor now moves painfully slow. The thought of holding George in my arms once again has me busting out of my skin.

I woke up at five in the morning to begin to get ready to see him. At five in the morning last week, we were holding each other and watching the sun rise. Now, I'm only hours from feeling him hold me again. My stomach turns around as I think about it. What will he think? Will he be just as excited to see me? Has he planned our time, or will we just make love and talk? As the water runs over my face and down my body, I think about the mundane conversations we had on the ship before he left. Those times together now mean so much to me.

I begin to think about George and our deep-thinking conversations about showering. We constantly debated the pros and cons of when to shower. George showers before going to bed, so as to be clean when retiring. Me, I shower in the morning, to start the day off fresh. It was such a ridiculous thing to talk about, but, right now, it makes me miss him. I even showered last night, because that is what I knew he would be doing at the same time. Then, this morning, I forgot and showered again. Maybe when he gets to the ship, we will find some time to fit in a shower. They say the third time is the charm.

Now that I am extremely clean, I get dressed and finish getting ready for the day. I take a leisurely walk to the top deck and observe this week's returning passengers, up early to see the ship pass the Statue of Liberty. The deck, as usual, is full of many couples kissing and holding one another as they prepare to end their week-long voyage. The sunrise and weather are ideal to be up this morning to watch the sights of entering New York Harbor. That is the wonderful thing about the summer in New York City; the weather is generally pleasant on the water. The mornings are a bit humid deeper in the summer, but it makes the sunset even more brilliant. The water cools the breeze as it blows across the surface. Only late July and into August does it start to get too warm to come out in the morning. I don't think I'll mind it too much this year, since it means I'll be that much closer to being with George.

This past week wasn't as bad as I expected. While I watch people begin to file off of the deck, I realize that all of the work kept my mind off of missing George. That made things so much easier. But, now, on the deck, there are so many memories of last Saturday, with George and me welcoming the day as we pass Miss Liberty, that time is beginning to slow down.

I will not stay outside long. The crew dining room will fill up fast, and I want to be cleaned up and ready for George as soon as he arrives. I walk down from the top deck and through the hallways. A few of the others greet me as I pass by, but, for most of us, it is a bit too early for pleasantries. We simply nod on our way to food and coffee.

I'm pleased when I arrive that only eight people are in line ahead of me, and nearly all of the tables are open. I get toast, a very small serving of eggs, coffee, and one slice of bacon, then walk over to a two person table on the far wall. It is only 6:15 when I check my watch, and I still have at least two hours and forty-five minutes until the passengers will disembark, and George can come on to visit me.

George will be at the pier at 9 AM, so I still have almost three hours to kill.

I pick at my food for about twenty minutes, but I'm too excited to eat much. I finally give up and return my tray of mostly uneaten food and half a cup of cold coffee to the conveyor belt. I start to walk out, when I notice a few of my crew friends arriving at crew mess. I wave, and they wave me over. They sit down at a table near the wall.

"Hi, Ingrid," my friend Stefanie says. Stefanie is from France, and I love talking about life in Europe with her. She is sitting with Patti, who is from America.

"Is everything going okay?" Patti asks, a slight smirk curving her lips.

"Of course," I answer. They know what today means to me. For the next hour, we talk about so many things. It is nice to have someone to talk to for a while. At least I am having conversations with human beings. I focus my questions on them, because I don't want to begin talking excessively about George and our great relationship. Sometimes, too much talking about your life with friends isn't good.

They have to leave to attend to their duties, but I have the day off, so I just start to walk around. In the distance, I can see the buildings that make up part of New York's skyline. It is very exciting when I think about experiencing this place with George.

I've spent a great deal of time the last week thinking about what George told me about himself before he left the ship. While it isn't hard to imagine him spending lots of time in the company of the ladies, when I think about his life being in danger and him hiding from people who want to kill him, it is a little scary.

At around eight-thirty, the ship is clear, and I decide to leave the ship and stand on the pier. I will surprise George when he arrives. Hopefully, he will get here a little early, and we can steal a few extra minutes from the day.

The passengers are filling taxis, just like last week. I turn and look back up at the ship to where I was waving feverishly only seven days ago. Although I seem to only think about George today, the fact is that I've actually had a very pleasant week. I know we can make this work. With us having our space during the week and the weekends to get to know each other, I think we really have a set-up that will give us a great start to a long-term relationship.

The time stretches on as people continue to leave. Then, I realize I am alone. I look around nervously, rolling up my sleeve to check my watch. Nine-thirty comes and goes. Where is George?

Ten AM: He hasn't arrived, and I'm a bit irritated. There is no one to call at the pier, at least that I know of, so I continue to wait, certain he'll be here any moment.

Eleven AM: He still hasn't shown up, and I'm now worried that something has happened to him. *What if those awful people found him and killed him?* I push the thought away. That is very unlikely.

Noon: No sign of George. I reluctantly, and with tears streaming down my checks, head back to my cabin.

I walk back up the gangway and call the front desk, just in case George slipped past me and is onboard. I ask them to check the guest list, and they put me on hold. I cannot imagine how he could have gotten past me, but I also cannot imagine why he isn't here.

"Ingrid?" a nasally voice asks.

"Yes."

"Sorry dear. George is not on board."

For the first time, I allow myself to consider the nagging fear that whispered to me all week long—George was a player. While on the ship, we were a great pair because there was no one else. George had no other options. But, now, there are clearly plenty of opportunities to find someone. I return to my cabin and look in the mirror. I look quite a bit older than I thought. I hadn't noticed it before, but there are wrinkles around my eyes and lips. The skin of my cheeks sag a bit, and I'm not as firm as I was in my younger days.

I lay on my bed, crying uncontrollably. Could George really be the same person he described in his long *mea culpa* two weeks ago?

Did he lie to me all along? Was it always his intention—even as we were kissing and passing the Statue of Liberty—never to see me again? I couldn't stand the questions anymore. I had to get off the ship.

I look in the mirror again, ignoring the wrinkles and trying to make myself look happy. I want to scream at the top of my voice, "I'm leaving," but I am certain no one would care, and it would only make me look like a bigger fool.

Once on land again, I walk to the phone booths to call my old girlfriend, Barbara Kenneth. Barbara was a nurse on the ships with me for many years and now lives in New York City. As I get closer to the phones, I begin to question my decision. She probably was not going to be home midday on a Saturday. I look back at the ship, but I can't do it. I cannot spend an entire Saturday in my cabin, questioning everything. I needed to do something, and if Barbara isn't home, I'll just find something else to do.

I dial her number, and she picks up on the third ring.

"I'd love to have you over, Ingrid," she enthuses after a few minutes of catching up.

"I'm so glad," I say. "Thank you. I just need to get my mind off of all of this."

"Of course you do," she says. That was one thing I loved about her. She never judged me and was always a loyal friend.

She gives me her address, and I promise her I'll be there soon. There is an empty cab as soon as I walk to the street, and a short ride later, I am at her apartment on the Eastside. I have a few hours before I have to be back on the ship, and the idea of seeing Barbara after such a long time cheers me up a little.

Walking to the entrance of her building, I notice so many couples walking hand-in-hand on the way to their weekend errands. My insides ache, and my arms feel a chill—the same chill I'd felt each time George released me from an embrace. My mind tries to replay memories of so many times George and I walked hand-in-hand around the decks of our city.

"Ingrid." Barbara hugs me immediately after she opens her door. "Sit down, and tell me all about your rotten lover."

She wasn't on the ship when George came aboard, but I begin the story of how we met, our long relationship, and how he broke my heart.

"That jerk." Barbara's voice is sharp. I look up at her, about to defend him, but realize she is right. "You need a break," Barbara says, quick to take an intermission from my story to give me a rest. "Any minute, our lunch will be delivered, so let's go to my wine rack and open a great bottle of wine."

Someone delivers lunch.

"Go splash some water on your face, and, then, we'll eat," Barbara directs.

The lunch takes my mind off what was hurting me so badly, almost. Having Barbara to visit on Saturdays would give me something else to look forward to. I am glad I thought to visit her.

"Tell me what you've been doing since you left the ship," I say.

"I did quite a few things for a couple of years," Barbara replies, "But I really love what I do now. Just recently, I accepted a nursing position at the Mt. Sinai Hospital, in the maternity ward, but it is such a huge hospital that you never get to know anyone personally. I'm thinking about finding a job at a smaller hospital."

"I can imagine it is big, but I think it would be fun," I say.

"It is, and, at first, it was a lot of work," she says, looking down in her glass of wine. "But, now that I'm familiar with the place, it is a fun challenge, rather than being intimidating. I just think I'd rather work at a place where I can get to know most of the people I work with."

"I cannot imagine anything intimidating you," I say. "You could do about anything when we were on the ship together, but you also loved getting to know everyone."

"Yes, it was just that there was so much to learn," she says. "Every department has a slightly different way of doing things. I also had to learn how to work with the patients. I only get to work with maternity patients, and I'd rather be in a post-op unit or the ER for a change."

"Are you going to try to find other part-time work or change hospitals?"

"Change hospitals," she says. "It is too crazy trying to schedule two places around each other."

"I guess I can understand that." And I do. I changed ships twice during my time on the seas and, although the job is the same, the work is actually quite a bit different on different ships.

"I must leave soon," I say, noticing the time. "The ship sets sail in about an hour."

"I'm so sorry to see you go," Barbara replies. "Let's do this next Saturday. I will come to the ship, and we can go for lunch to a fun restaurant in the City. If we have enough time, maybe we will go to a museum, or visit some sights of interest in New York."

Even though it was the same idea I'd had earlier, hearing her say it seemed to give finality to the whole George thing.

"Listen," she says, "Ingrid, forget about this man. He is a shit. You are pretty, have a great personality, and can find many great men—and I *guarantee* you will."

"It might be fun," I concede. "But I don't want to impose." Although she did a good job taking my mind off my man problem, she now came back strong with advice—advice I didn't want to hear.

"What imposition?" she asks, raising her hands and looking around. "I'm glad to have you. I just sit here after work most days. I would love to have a friend around." Then, she leans forward, her eyes intense, "Why not focus your attention on something positive. In September, when your ship contract is finished, why not move in with me? I will help you find a nursing job. You can stay with me for a while until you find an apartment. I am here for you, and you can start your life all over again."

I hug and kiss her goodbye, without promising anything, except that I'd see her next week. I got back to the ship about fifteen minutes before it set sail. I didn't have any plans for the afternoon before I was on duty, but the one thing I definitely did not do is go to the top deck to watch the ship pass the Statue of Liberty.

CHAPTER 19

UNIVERSITY COLLEGE HOSPITAL

LONDON, ENGLAND

I spent a very busy day saying goodbye to my patients. I had been a nurse in the ICU for many years, and leaving London for New York was pretty exciting for me.

"Joanna, how many more hours?" Jenny yells.

"Shift ends in three hours, seventeen minutes," I yell back. When Jenny started two years ago, I was one of the proctors during her orientation. When you work with critically ill patients, many of whom are unable to speak or respond, you need careful coaching during those first six months. That is particularly true when you work at the top teaching hospital with some of the highest acuity patients in the country. These are people who are too sick to say goodbye to me, or even to hear my goodbyes. At least I was able to give kisses on foreheads, and squeeze many a hand of hopeless souls. I only worked with one patient per shift, but the patient changed each day. Many of these people were here for many days, so I either worked with them directly or assisted their primary nurse on a procedure.

In several hours, the staff of the hospital will be setting aside a portion of the cafeteria to host a going away party for me. I don't want to be too conceited, but I was a very popular and a well-respected nurse at the hospital. I guess that does sound a bit conceited. What I mean is that I made many friends here and trained many of the younger nurses. People know me here.

Although I am excited about my move to New York and starting another chapter in my career, I dread having to say goodbye to so many friends and colleagues who worked with me these many years. There will be many tears and hugs, and, as emotional as I am with my patients, I do not enjoy those feelings in my social and private life. Maybe it is a result of my upbringing. My parents left Russia after the War. They never discussed their feelings about the conflict with me, nor were they very warm towards me in my early childhood. You might say that even to this day, they are not the warmest or most loving parents. I guess I inherited a cold personality from them. On the other hand, I was able to connect with my patients. I fought for them, and, sometimes, *with* them, in order to help them get better. Sometimes, I may have been too controlling and overly pushy in my attempt to force them to work at improving their medical conditions. That was particularly true when they needed to complete some kind of rehabilitation before going to a step-down unit or a regular room. Maybe my coldness helped make me a better nurse. The patients' needs sometimes have to come before their wants, and I'm willing to be the bad guy.

The party began. I was right; most of my friends became emotional and were crying and begging me not to leave. Most of the ward staff, as well as the hospital administrative staff, of the facility were present. You would have thought I was the most important person in London. There were many glasses hitting each other as toasts were offered to me, and a table was loaded with going-away gifts everyone chipped in to give me. We celebrated, and a few cried. We shared funny stories, and, finally, everyone had to go back to their responsibilities at the hospital. This meant the party was coming to an end, and I would be leaving for the very last time.

I wanted to go back to my flat straight-away, but there was still some final packing to do in the evening to prepare for the following day's flight to New York. I realized there wouldn't be much sleeping this night, because of the roller coaster ride of emotions I was forced to endure the last twenty-four hours. It was approaching eleven PM when I had everything finished. I only needed to take a shower, wash my hair, and try the best I could to sleep. Heading towards the shower, the phone in my flat rang.

I wasn't in the mood to talk to anyone, and hoped that if I answered the phone, it wouldn't be a long conversation. In fact, it was very short.

I picked up the phone. "Yes," I said. There was pause, "Yes?" I repeated. Another pause, and finally "Yes, I understand." I hung up the receiver, took my shower, set out everything I'd need for the morning, and went to bed. It seemed that as soon as my head hit the pillow, my alarm went off.

My flight to New York was leaving London at four PM, and arriving in New York late in the afternoon of the same day. I tried to sleep during most of the flight, but I was excited about my new venture in New York. I watched out the window, watched the in-flight movie, and counted off the minutes until landing. Our arrival in New York was delayed, but it was still light in New York, a beautiful summer night. I had plenty of time to gather up my luggage and take a cab into the City. The flat I rented would not be ready for a couple of weeks, so my plan was to stay at a women-only hotel until everything in the rented flat was ready for me.

When I first saw the hotel from the window of the taxi, I realized my accommodations would be small. The porter helped me with my bags to the room, and I was right. It was quite small. Since I won't be staying there long, it is certainly comfortable enough for my current needs. I started to unpack, and, growing restless, I decided to take a short walk around the neighborhood before it got dark.

I wanted to find a casual restaurant in the neighborhood for some dinner and try to go to bed early to counteract any jet lag. The hotel was a convenient walking distance to the hospital. Eventually, my new flat would be even closer, and a much shorter commuting walk. The next day would begin my first trip to Mt. Sinai Hospital.

On my way to work, I stop at a local coffee shop to pick up some tea and a roll to gulp down on the way. When I arrive at the hospital, I go straight to the personnel office on the third floor.

"Joanna, it is good to meet you," the head of personnel welcomes me.

It was nice to be greeted this way, and made me feel right at home. "Pleased to make your acquaintance," I reply.

"I love your accent," she says, smiling, and, then, she turns to go down the hall.

I follow her into her office, where she next brings in the assistant personnel officer to meet me.

"All of the papers you said you'd need are right here," I say, presenting my British passport and all of the forms, credentials, and licenses I had previously obtained to allow me to legally accept employment in the United States. I went with the assistant to her office, where I continued to fill out more papers and answer more questions. It took all morning. While I was tempted to complain how terribly inefficient this was, I realize I'm paid for doing the things here, not when I'm at my flat, so I keep my mouth shut.

Around noon, I am given my hospital ID and pointed to the hospital cafeteria for a lunch break. When I walk in, I am reminded of my farewell party just a few days ago at University Hospital. The cafeteria looked eerily similar to the cafeteria at my London hospital. So this, too, made me feel at home. I humorously thought that all hospitals must work with the same design firm.

I ate quickly, and, after lunch, there were more meetings. I now met and spent time with the charge nurse of the ICU unit. The rest of the day, I would be introduced to all the heads of the various departments in the hospital. Of course, the majority of time in the afternoon was spent on the floor of the ICU unit. I had to complete a series of tasks in their orientation program to demonstrate competency in a variety of areas. My experience in London with critical care patients was the real reason I was offered the position at Mt. Sinai, and everyone felt comfortable talking with me, since I understood the basic medical jargon used in an ICU unit.

"Right now, we have a very unusual case," the charge nurse relates, taking me to a room close to the nurses' station. "He is a John Doe who was in a serious auto accident a few weeks ago."

"Yes," I say, quite excited by this case. "I heard a few other nurses talking about it."

The charge nurse looks through her chart. "I guess he's been here about a month, and he hasn't woken from the coma. No family, friends, or anyone else have come forward to identify the patient."

"How unlucky," I say. I am really looking forward to working with this patient and will ask specifically to be assigned to him.

"Actually, this patient is lucky to be still with us." The charge nurse says. "There were multiple fractures, internal contusions, and cerebral edema." She closes the chart. "There has not been a lot of forward progress in the past month."

I nod my understanding. All I've heard about him was quite true. Despite the tubes, he is a very attractive man. I really hope he will recover. That would be a true highlight to my career.

"Continuing on," the charge nurse says, walking out of the room and drawing my attention to some charts and binders, "we are experimenting with a new system to save costs and shorten recovery time. Our staff will stay with their patient through the recovery and rehab stages."

"That could be a good system." I answer. "But I'm not a physical therapist."

"Oh, we understand that. PT will still come in to monitor the patients and work with them; this is just as it pertains with oversight of day-to-day care."

"So," I summarize, "the idea is that we become familiar with the patient and are better able to spot issues."

"Precisely," the charge nurse agrees. "Because of your years of critical care experience at the University Hospital in London, you will be assigned to the John Doe case. When, and if, he comes out of his coma, and is taken off the critical list and moved to a non-critical unit, you will be responsible for his recovery and coordinating his rehabilitation.

"That will be lovely," I say. It is as if the fates are smiling down on me. I get one of the most difficult cases immediately after entering the hospital. Hopefully, I won't have too many angry looks from my new colleagues.

"I wanted to make sure it was alright with you to take on this most unusual case for your first assignment," the charge nurse says. "The woman who has been caring for him will be leaving on Friday for maternity. With the other people assigned—and your experience—I thought it a good fit."

I spend the rest of the day talking about some personal matters: my English background, my family, and my years of employment at the hospital in London. I even spent some time talking about my plans for living in New York. The charge nurse talks a little about the staff at the hospital, covering the various nurses and doctors who will be working with me on a daily basis.

I leave the hospital at five in the evening. It is nice to already have such a difficult patient and such a kind staff at my new assignment. I was a touch nervous about what would happen when I arrived here, but, now, it appears that everything is falling right into place.

CHAPTER 20

MT. SINAI HOSPITAL

I did get my good night of sleep, since I didn't have to be at the hospital until noon. I spent some time unpacking and purchasing some food to fill my tiny refrigerator. I plan to be at the hospital early, so I can begin reading up on the John Doe case, before his nurse gives report at shift change.

I arrived at the hospital at ten AM and begin reading. At noon, I take report and do my hourly assessment. Between the trips to his room, I read the month of charts and records in the case file, as well as talking to various nurses who have been involved. It has been a rough time for John Doe. He was close to death several times. The excellent staff of doctors stabilized his medical condition numerous times in the past month, and, for the last two weeks, he has remained pretty much the same.

No one knows his name, where he came from, nor where he was going when he got in the accident. It was good to learn the hospital administrator had placed his picture and his horrific story in several newspapers to uncover the real identity of John Doe. Unfortunately, no one has yet identified him.

I spend the day reviewing his vital signs, then taking and charting new ones. I hang prescribed medicine, clean up the patient, and change bed linens. As I gaze down into the face of John Doe, I can't help thinking that, under the swollen face and bruises, he is still very good-looking...

"My daily routine will take place each and every day, as long as you are in the hospital," I whisper to him. "Whatever the length of time it will take, Joanna Lee will be by your side."

"Joanna, would you like to join us for dinner?" One of the nurses is standing in the hallway and pointing to two other women. "We all have worked his case and wanted to tell you about some things that might not be in the chart."

"That would be splendid," I say. I toss the dirty linens in my hands into the bin and wash my hands. I am surprised to see it is already five in the evening. Time moves so quickly here with so much to do.

***

Close to the end of the day, a male visitor arrives at the hospital. The security staff at the front entrance directs him to the medical records department on the first floor and a sign greets the visitor: "Will be back shortly." He has a promise to keep, and only recently has he learned about who the man is in the hospital.

To kill time, he walks around the hospital and down to the cafeteria for a cup of coffee. When he gets back to the records office, there is a young lady sitting there, "How may I help you?" she asks.

The visitor replies, "I have come regarding your John Doe patient. I read his story in the newspaper."

"Yes, what about him?" she asks, her face the same.

"I know who he is." He looks around, a bit anxious now to get this finished.

She pulls a form out of the desk in the waiting room. "I need you to fill this out, please."

Patient's name: The name George Thompson is written down, instead of John Doe. Recently moved to New York and lives at 122nd Street and Riverside Drive. Has no family and no next-of-kin. The visitor continues to fill out the confidential form with the exact address, phone number, and other information requested and hands it back.

"Thank you so much," she says. "We have all been anxious to know who he is."

She looks at the paper. "So, his name is George."

He has kept his promise to take care of George. He turns to walk out.

"Sir," she calls out, "you have forgotten to sign the form with your name and address."

He walks back to the desk and completes the form.

Name: Franco Livingston: No local address: Permanent address: Florence, Italy. The visitor leaves once again.

***

"Really?"

I am taking care of my patient and turn around to see the reason for the exclamation from the ICU receptionist. The place is generally quiet, except for the whispered gossip and monitor sounds.

"Joanna, we have a name for John Doe," the receptionist says, holding her hands over the mouthpiece of the phone.

"What is it?" I ask. Everyone in the ICU seems to have stopped and their full attention is held by this one conversation.

"A gentleman came in to identify our John Doe patient in the ICU as George Thompson."

"So that is your name." I smile, feeling relief at hearing it out loud. "George Thompson. It is nice to meet you after all this time."

Word spreads fast throughout the hospital, and, soon, I have various people in the hospital walking in and out. People returning from dinner come up to see what other details there might be connected to this man. Other than an address, there isn't much.

I bend down and speak into his ear loud enough for only him to hear, "Hello, George, I know who you are; I am here for you and will make you better." I grab his hand and squeeze it lightly, so as not to hurt him.

I wanted to hold his hand for a while longer, but people were watching, and there is a lot of work ahead for me. I go to work immediately updating all the forms, charts, and records from John Doe to George Thompson. Finally. I am so relieved—everyone can put a name to the face.

Each day the following week will follow my daily routine. I still don't see much forward progress, but I am still happy his condition hasn't worsened. I think that if he has any sense of what is happening around him that just hearing his own name is a huge relief. This is going to be a long road to recovery for him. Every time I am with George, there is the feeling of a new—and, on more than one occasion—a stronger bond.

I work three shifts a week with George, splitting duties with three other nurses; however, I'd like to see if I can be the sole nurse involved in his care when he's ready to return home. That would be a forty-hour week, 8-to-5, Monday-Friday. I really doubt many of the other nurses will object. They like to work three days a week.

I come back from my days off to even more excitement than usual in the ICU. "George has come out of his coma," Cadie, a young, happy nurse, says as soon as I walk in to the unit.

I rush to George's bedside and see his open eyes staring at me.

"Hello," I say softly, but my only answer is his blank stare. I'm not upset. We have time to get to know each other. Taking a seat on the chair next to the bed, I begin holding and stroking his hand. Although he is out of the coma, I believe he is not really ready yet to communicate.

"George, "I begin, "You were in a very bad car accident about two months ago. You are now in the Mt. Sinai Hospital." I pause and let the information sink in.

Before long, I am joined by a team of doctors who want to examine George from head to toe.

"Don't push him too soon to communicate," one doctor advises. I want to argue, but I don't. In England, we are trained to get the critical patients on their feet quickly, not like American doctors who want medical teams to take their time. I want to get George on his feet and recovering faster.

Over the next two weeks, George shows wonderful progress on his road to recovery. He is able to speak short sentences with me, and the physical therapist starts some basic physical therapy to get his muscles working again.

"I was an actor on cruise ships for many years," he tells me one day.

"That must have been very exciting," I answer, charting his vital signs.

"It was where I met Ingrid." He looks away from me, as though her name is painful to speak.

"Tell me about her," I urge, wanting to know all I can about him, in order to do my job well.

"She is a woman I fell in love with on a cruise ship, but I don't know where she is now." It is a start, and I record the information on his chart, as well as in a notebook I'm keeping on him.

As days pass, he remembers more and more of the accident details. Not wanting to push George too hard, I ask him about his experiences on the Broadway stage. To my amazement, he remembers the 1950s in great detail. He talks about his shows, his parts, and his success as a Broadway star. Most of the names of shows are foreign to me.

"I once saw a show in the West End of London, while I worked at a London hospital," I offer.

"I was in London a very long time ago and really enjoyed my visit," he replies.

After another week, the head doctor on the team is very pleased with all the progress and feels George would do much better in the comfort of his own home. That means we will institute the new hospital's "One-on-One" program. A temporary date is set by the team, led by me, to bring George home.

"The doctors will make the final decision in a few more weeks," I say to George when I go in to tell him more about it. "Likely, the doctors didn't tell you much about it, but it will be wonderful and will help you get healthy much quicker."

"That sounds great," he answers. "I am anxious to get back to living."

"I'm sure you are."

I leave his room and am called over to the nurses' station. "You will be assigned to spend every day with him at his apartment," the charge nurse advises me. "Oversee and coordinate the entire medical rehab program. You will also have to look over the physical layout of the apartment, and make decisions on how the space will accommodate George's needs." But, first, she was going to send another team to look over the apartment.

It only takes a few days to get all of the approvals in place and for someone to check out the apartment and make the few necessary changes. By then, the doctors had given the okay to move George home. Two days later, everything is set, and the transport ambulance arrives to move him from the hospital to 122nd Street and Riverside Drive.

"I cannot wait to leave the hospital and finish my recovery in my apartment," George tells me while we wait for the transport ambulance. "And I'm really glad you'll be in charge of my care."

"I am, too," I say, and I truly am. I realized soon after George woke up that he needs me. George has no one and nowhere else to turn. I need him, too, for some reason I can't explain. It was worth the trip across the Atlantic to be a part of this. A man enters the room with a wheelchair.

"It looks like it is time to leave, George," I say.

I help him to his wheelchair, and the ambulance driver pushes him out. Many of the staff have come to George's room to say goodbye and wish him the best of luck. Everyone loved George and appreciate the hard work he put into his recovery. There are not a lot of success stories emanating out of the ICU, so, when there is a successful one, everyone is excited and happy to be part of the story.

We get in the transport ambulance for our short ride from 97th Street and Fifth Avenue to the West Side Highway and north of 122nd Street and Riverside Drive. George can see out of the rear window in the ambulance, but I don't tell him when we cross the area of the accident.

"It is a very beautiful day to move home," I say to him.

"It could be a blizzard or a downpour, and it would be a beautiful day to go home," he replies, his eyes never leaving the windows.

I decide it is best to leave him alone to focus on his thoughts.

We arrive at the apartment, and the physical therapist who has accompanied us goes to get the key from the super. We get everything moved inside, and I get George settled on his couch. Since he has no family, a few of us went in together to buy some staples that we put in his refrigerator. Remarkably, there is nothing moldy here.

"Did you have someone watching your house, George?" I ask.

"A cleaning lady came once a month, but I was at sea, so there was no food here to go bad."

"I guess that does make sense then," I say. "Well, I've put some food in there now."

"Thank you." He is looking out the window, his face quite sad. I would be sad, too, if I had lost so much time.

I prepare his lunch to serve him. "I will sit with you most of the day. No rehab work today; the program will start tomorrow," I tell him.

"Good, I don't think I'm up to it today," he answers.

The physical therapist explains the routine to him, and I listen. This will be a perfect program for him to get well again. I generally like ICU work, but it is also nice to have a patient working towards becoming completely well.

The physical therapist leaves an hour later, but I stay an hour after her to be sure there is nothing he will need. Around six PM, I help him into his pajamas and get his dinner ready.

"I will be leaving now, but I'll be back tomorrow at nine AM," I say.

"I will be ready" he answers.

"You should get a good night sleep, and always—and I stress the word always—use your walker when you get out of bed."

"I will," he promises. "See you tomorrow."

I leave, thinking how satisfying the day was and looking forward to George's full recovery.

On the cab ride back to my apartment, my thoughts turn to my role with George. My real work is about to begin.

Chapter 21

SEARCHING

My contract with the *Regal Fantasy* has finally come to an end. Barbara kept me busy every Saturday during the summer with visits to most of the exciting spots in the City. I moved into Barbara's apartment, but the day was bittersweet. Moving in with her felt like a I was resigning myself to the idea that George might never come back.

"I thought about trying to find George," I say, tossing another empty box on the pile.

"Or you could give up on the shit," Barbara returns.

"I wish you'd quit calling him that."

"It is the better of the two names," she says and looks at me with a bit of a smirk.

Even though she obviously doesn't like him, she knows I loved him, and her names were her subtle way of blowing off steam. Her steam was getting hotter the longer I was in the City, so it is probably best if I stop telling her about my search and simply do it when she is working.

I have learned one thing about this town: New York City is a lonely place if you have no one to share it with. It has been a lonely place for me, ever since George disembarked from the ship.

"It has been three months, "she says, breaking in to my melancholy thoughts. "You know this city has lots of other men, if that is your obsession."

"Not all of us love the single life." I smile at her. "There are real benefits to a man."

"And some real drawbacks, too," she quips, without the smallest bit of anger. She has found a much-fulfilled life single in the City. On the other hand, I have cried myself to sleep almost every night for three months without George.

"Things might be better visiting my family," I say, trying to change the subject and secretly hoping she won't call me on the diversion.

"I think that will be great for you." She cuts the tape on the very last box. "When I do have my momentary lapses into dating, family helps me pick up the pieces after the inevitable aftermath."

I laugh. "You are a hopeless romantic."

"And you, my dear, are simply hopeless," she says, lifting out a bit of my lingerie and twirling it around her finger before placing it in my drawer.

To most people, Barbara might seem like an angry person, but I've learned that it is really a dry wit. She isn't a man-hater. She only hates George for hurting me. If she'd met him under other circumstances, she would have loved him and would have been the first one to urge me down the aisle.

"I should fill out the paperwork to transfer my nursing license before I go see my family."

"That could be a very good idea. They're desperate for nurses, but the license can take a while to process. The endorsement applications aren't done every day, so yours would take longer than some."

I begin breaking down boxes in my room and stacking them up. The small tasks help me not think about George as much. I will go to Norway for a week's break, and, when I return, I will find an open nursing position in one of the many hospitals in the City. Once I get a deposit saved, I will move out of Barbara's place and locate a small, inexpensive apartment to live in near my job. When I'm not doing that, I will use every waking moment to furtively search for George.

"I need to get to the hospital," Barbara says. "The boxes will need to go down to the alley; they won't fit in the chute."

"Okay. And what is the number to the Board of Nursing?"

"It might be in the phonebook." Barbara is going into work mode, which means I have to follow her from room to room as she dictates. I think she does that because she has to chase the attending in her department while he gives patient orders to the nurses.

"I'll look there," I respond, trying to suppress a laugh, and the urge to say, *Yes, doctor.*

"I'll also check with the nurse manager about the job board." She closes the bedroom door halfway, so she can change, and I stand in the hallway, writing down the various names of hospitals she thinks might be hiring.

She opens the bedroom door, her transformation from best friend to RN complete. "You know where the food is, and there is a great deli just on the corner."

"I'll be fine," I say. "You are a huge help."

She pats me on the arm, and I walk back to my room, until I hear the front door close and the lock engage.

I hurry to the phonebook and call the headquarters of the CIA. No one has ever heard of George Toomey. Deep down, I know they won't really give me any information, even if they do know the man. That is how it is with spies. I remember George telling me he once lived in a duplex on Park Avenue in the seventies and also had an apartment, supplied by the CIA, at Riverside Drive and north of 122nd Street. I might not be a spy, but I could be an-above average detective. I will begin my search in these two areas of the City and see if they give me any further leads.

First, I take a cab ride to Park Avenue and 75th Street. I will walk slowly up and down each side of Park Avenue's apartment buildings and start asking doormen about George. The buildings look enormous to me, nothing like I had ever seen in Norway. The weather is pleasant, and it makes me feel a bit better about the adventure. The day sours as one doorman after another turns me away without any new information on George.

I walk a bit longer. The buildings seem to be a single unit, but, in reality, they are separate structures built up against their neighbors. There are as many four or five doormen on a single block, and there are blocks and blocks of buildings. It was a slow and tedious process. Some doormen were polite and sympathetic. Others were rude and dismissive. All of them gave me the same information: they had never heard of George.

The streets are always busy, without a single lull in pedestrians. It would seem someone is always moving somewhere on the sidewalk, and the only way to tell time is your watch. Even the sunlight is obscured by the buildings, making it almost impossible to use shadows to mark the passage of time. I really don't know how I had the stamina to carry out my search. I look down and realize I have been gone for almost four hours already. My stomach is grumbling in protest. It is nearly 3 PM. It is a good time to eat between the lunch and dinner rushes. There are two more doors on my block. I will go in there and then eat.

I approach the door, and a doorman rushes to open the door for me.

"Thank you," I say. I'm sure my voice is weary, but I gave up the chipper greeting about eight buildings ago.

"Of course, ma'am." He smiles and steps back. I wonder how he is pleasant all day. It has to be a boring and tedious job opening doors, accepting packages, and greeting people every single time they walk by. I've only had to do this for a few hours. This is what they do every day.

"I am looking for someone, and I hope I have the right building."

He looks at me, still friendly, but also guarded. He has transitioned from greeter to gatekeeper. "His name is George…" I start and then I spill out the story I've said more times than I ever planned. Each time the scab is ripped off the wound.

"Oh, I remember him," he says, with a smile. "Lovely family."

My heart sinks just a bit, but it is the best lead I've had. This could still be my break. I fight to hold on to the joy struggling to break out inside of me. "Do you know where I could find him?"

"I'm sorry, I don't," he says, still friendly. "George and his family moved out more than seventeen years ago, and I have no knowledge of where they have gone."

The pounding fist of disappointment thunders inside of me. This is finality. This was his building, the best lead I had, and, now, even he cannot help me. I start to tear up.

"Thank you." My voice cracks, and I walk out quickly, embarrassed by my emotion.

I know I must be strong and continue searching on Riverside Drive—but on a different day. Emotionally, I have nothing left, and I cannot face any more disappointment. I skip the last building on the block and hail a cab. It is a very depressing cab ride to the corner of 120th Street and Riverside Drive. All during the ride, my emotions run the gamut from *George really is a shit for doing this to me* to *Maybe something has happened to him*. No matter what the reason, I am all alone, and I am starting to think I can't handle it anymore.

I go home—well, to Barbara's home—and spend time looking through various books, not really looking at the words. I start to remember the stories George told me about his past philandering ways. Maybe I should have recognized the warning in front of me? I realize there is so much more bugging me than just not finding George. I realize that the doorman there was a connection to the old George. The one who had cheated on his wife and who, now, was mysteriously gone.

That night when Barbara came home, I didn't tell her about my search. I will wait until right before I leave. Instead, we talk about her day. She talks about her patient and her coworkers. She shares funny stories about people she saw in the City and other things that temporarily distract me from the ache deep inside my chest.

"I work a twelve-hour shift tomorrow, so I should turn in early," she says to me around eight that night.

"I'm just going to read a bit longer." I motion to the magazine I've been pretending to read since we finished cleaning up from supper. I'm certain she doesn't believe me. I walk to the window and look down at the City below. It is beautiful with its traffic flows and lights. People walk around laughing. I wonder if somewhere in this city of millions of people if George is walking around, laughing. *Does he even remember me? Does he ever think about me?* The thought reaches in my chest and squeezes my heart. I fight the pain and decide I should go to bed.

I sleep fitfully, images of George smiling and laughing with beautiful women clogging my mind, and I wake up once again more exhausted then when I went to bed. Riverside Drive detective work is going to be more difficult than my search on Park Avenue. There are no doormen in this area of the City, so the only way to try to find him will be to look at every directory of tenants in every building for a listing of a George Thompson, the name he used on Riverside Drive.

This time, I decide to take the subway to the area, hoping that I might, somehow, encounter him. I get off at his stop and walk up the steps above ground. The City has more people than either Barbara's neighborhood or George's other neighborhood. Like the other neighborhoods, I find myself staring at an impossible task. Dozens of buildings are crushed together to form a single city block. Inside each building are dozens of apartments. I walk up to the first and scan the names. Nothing.

Then, at the next building I do the same. Nothing there, either. I repeat the process down the block. A man—maybe thirty years old—has begun to stare at me.

"Excuse me," I greet him. "My name is Ingrid."

"Sam," the man responds. His voice doesn't invite a conversation, but I press on.

"I'm looking for a friend."

"'Splains your walking to each door, don't it?" His voice isn't any kinder, and I wonder if I should even continue talking. He looks around, as if trying to decide if anyone is watching us and, then, looks back down at me. "So why you telling me?"

"His name is George Thompson, and he lived in this area a few years ago," I say, hoping this man might say something that will help me in my search and get me out of this awful neighborhood.

"Don't know him," the man says flatly. Then, he starts walking past me and around the corner. I watch him go and wonder why he even stopped to say anything to me to begin with. New York is full of so many different kinds of people. There are wonderful, caring people, like Barbara. There are the playboys and the social elite you hear about on TV. There are also people like Sam. Those are the people who are just existing in a world that moves around them, but never will include them.

I continue to another block of apartments. It is a long and arduous process of reading each and every tenant's name on the apartment list. As if the Park Avenue experience was not enough of a failure, Riverside Drive turns out to be a complete failure. All that is left is to return to the apartment, and, after much soul-searching, informing Barbara of all my attempts to find George. When she arrives home later that night, her look is kind. She must see my fatigue. The tender lines around her eyes add a slight smile to her somber face.

"I couldn't find him," I say, by way of explanation.

"I'm sorry."

She walks to the door, and, after pushing it closed, wraps her arms around me and lets me cry. All the rejection and disappointment and anger from the day floods out in a few moments of crying. I'm so embarrassed that I'm crying like this, but crying feels so good.

"I needed to try," I say when the tears finally begin to slow down. "I love him."

"I know you do, hon," she says, giving me a squeeze and then stepping back to look me in the eye. "That is why he is such a shit. He doesn't deserve you." She smirks. "Come sit down."

I follow her to the table and sit down. "I guess it is time for me to find work."

"First, you should see your family," she says. Her voice is firm, and that reassures me. I feel so confused by so many things right now, but Barbara's certainty gives me strength.

"Yes," I say. "They will ask me about George."

"And you can tell them the truth or only part of it," she says, setting a glass of wine in front of me and, then, pouring herself a glass. Seeing her drink while still in her nurse's uniform makes me smile. It is like laughing at a joke at a funeral. When we are in pain, we laugh at ridiculous things.

"I should tell them most of it," I say. I'm not a good liar, and the trip will be so much worse trying to explain why I lied.

"You leave soon, and you'll be back sooner." She sips her wine. "I will keep asking about open positions in the City and hope to have a list of leads when you're back."

"Okay," I say. What more is there to say? What she says is perfectly reasonable.

"And stop searching for him until you get back."

I nod in agreement, partially because I'm too tired to search, but mainly because she was kind enough to call George *him* instead of *the shit*. I know I will be able. The looming fact is that when I return to New York, I may have to admit that George may never be coming back.

***

Even as hard as I tried, the seven days in Norway were the longest seven days of my life. Although I enjoyed seeing my small family and spending time with relatives I hadn't seen in years, I felt like a caged tiger—wanting so desperately to escape and get back to New York. I arrived back in New York late in the afternoon on a Thursday. With the time change, it felt like the middle of the night, so I took the long taxi ride from JFK to Barbara's apartment, ate a bowl of soup, and went to bed.

When I woke up Friday morning, there were fresh bagels, coffee, juice, and a note from Barbara.

I will be home about 3 o'clock, maybe 4. Let's go to a restaurant tonight and act like the young girls we actually are. I missed having my roommate around this week. Have a good day. — Barbara

I began by calling around to the list of hospitals Barbara had written down on a notepad.

"Hi, my name is Ingrid. I've been a nurse for thirty years and just moved to the area…"

"Just a moment, Ingrid," the woman at the first hospital says. Her voice is kind, but tired. I'm quite certain it gets tedious each day answering questions for job-seekers. I wait for about three minutes while the line is silent.

"Thank you for holding," a new voice says. "This is central nurse recruiting, how can I help you?" I repeat what I said before to the first woman.

"I'm sorry, we currently have no positions open, but, if you'd like to fill out an application, we hold them for one year and will contact you if anything in your skillset is open."

"Thank you," I respond. I take down the address and, then, I call the next hospital on the list. I do not have much success in contacting other hospitals in the City. I thought there was a nursing shortage, but not at the hospitals I contacted.

Barbara arrived at the apartment at 3:30 PM.

"How was the hunt today?" she asks.

I'm not sure if she is asking me about jobs or George. "Not much luck," I begin. "No one seems to be hiring, but I have a long list of places that want me to put in applications, just in case."

"I'm so sorry to hear that," she says. "There was no luck at my hospital, either. They just hired a bunch of people about three months ago."

Barbara and I go out to eat and have a wonderful time. I haven't felt so good since seeing George off the ship. I start to imagine a life without George. The thought stings, but I have to start to consider the idea that his ship sailed the day mine did.

As we pass a newsstand, I pause. "Wait," I ask Barbara, "I want to pick up the paper." There are a few different papers, and I buy a few and Barbara buys a few more.

"I like the comics—you can read the wanted ads," she says, handing the man the money and smiling at me.

"Way to salvage my pride," I smile.

We go back to the apartment and have a wonderful time looking through the papers together. For just a little bit that night, my sadness about George is gone.

"It feels good to be a bit proactive," I say, turning another newspaper page.

"And I like having someone around to talk to at night," she says. "This one looks like a possibility." She writes a few notes down and circles the classified ad and numbers it.

"How many have you found?" I ask.

"About eight leads for you to follow up on, plus the hospitals you already called."

"Well, if something doesn't come of it, maybe I should return to the sea." I smile weakly, because both of us know I don't want to go back on the cruise ship. That is a young person's game. Seventy-hour workweeks for six months at a time are grueling.

The rest of the week continues much the same way. I spent time looking for jobs, and I take on the responsibility of cleaning and straightening up the apartment. It is the least I can do for Barbara for allowing me to stay at her place and never asking me—nor allowing me—to pay anything towards the cost of the rent.

I enjoy the daily feeling of a routine and the satisfaction that the chores and job hunt gives me. The apartment is looking better than ever, and Barbara comments often. Behind a chair in the corner of the living room, I come across a stack of old newspapers. I pull out the help wanted section and put the rest in a pile for the trash. Two-thirds of the way down an image stops me. I cannot speak. The name on the paper says "John Doe," but I can see it is the battered face of George.

"Barbara!" I scream. Sobs burst from the bottom of my gut. I look at the date. It was only three days after I kissed him goodbye that this paper was published.

"What's wrong?" Barbara drops to the ground, where I'm clutching the paper to my chest.

"John Doe, John Doe," I say stupidly, hitting the paper with my finger. "It's George," I finally choke out.

Barbara takes the paper from my hands and scans the page. "My God, George is in my hospital. The shit is in Mt. Sinai Hospital."

I laugh, because her voice has changed. She no longer hates him. She is instantly softened.

"I want to see him," I blurt out.

"We can't," she says looking to the window, as if that explains it. I turn and look; the darkening sky says it all.

"Tomorrow?" I ask.

"Tomorrow morning, I will leave early. As soon as I get to the hospital, I will go to the critical care unit and find out if George is still there and any other pertinent information. I will return home for lunch—hopefully with some good news."

I take the newspaper back from her and sit on the floor. My task is now forgotten. The routine is done. I look at his closed eyes. The inset picture of the burned taxi. I see his precious, bruised face.

"I'm so sorry I abandoned you," I whisper. "I'm sorry I wasn't there for you when you needed me."

The picture doesn't move. I smooth the crinkles from the hug I gave it. "I will never leave again," I vow. "And nothing will stop me from getting to you any longer, my love."

I finish cleaning up the papers and take the paper with George's face in to my room and place it on my dressing table. It was time to prepare for another sleepless night, hopefully my last.

Barbara left very early for work the next morning, well before I awakened from my restless and very short sleep. At eleven that morning, I am up and dressed and waiting for Barbara to return from the hospital. All of my chores are done, so, until noon, I can only read and pace. There is no time to go out and fill job applications, or I might miss Barbara.

The door clicks as the lock opens. Barbara walks in and doesn't have the smile I'd hoped for. "Ingrid, please sit down. I have a lot to tell you." Her eyes are tired. In a daze, I fall onto the couch and await hearing all about the information Barbara has uncovered.

"George was in a car crash last June."

"I saw the date," I interrupt. "It had to be right after he left the ship."

"Probably. I don't remember the exact date right now. He was brought to Mt. Sinai in a coma and stayed in the condition for three months."

"Oh no," I gasp.

"Everyone knew the patient as John Doe," she says, not stopping. "He is out of the coma and has gone home".

Before Barbara could finish the story, I cry out, "Where does he live?"

"I went to patient records and found out the exact address where George lives," she says, as if rehearsing lines that cannot be interrupted.

"Where?" I ask. She hands me a slip of paper with the apartment address. I smile at it.

"I don't think it is a good idea to rush over just yet." I stop and look at her. *What is she saying?* I want to yell at her, but instead I stare.

"Let me meet with the nurse in charge of his rehabilitation to find out the condition George is in, and, please forgive me, if he will be able to recognize and remember you."

Suddenly, what she is saying sinks in. The coma. The photo. The charred taxi. The fact that I've heard nothing from him. My George might really be gone. Reluctantly, I agree.

***

"When can I go to see George?" I ask the moment Barbara walks through the door.

"I think I need to talk to you first. Sit down," Barbara says. For the second day in a row, I'm confused.

"Is it bad?" My heart thunders inside of me. If he doesn't remember me, maybe I'll still care for him. He has no one, and I'm a nurse.

"George is doing very well," Barbara says, immediately silencing the fear in my mind. "He suffered major trauma and will take a period of time to recover."

"Wonderful," I say. "Not that he's hurt, but that he's getting better."

She smiles. "I knew what you meant." Barbara is acting like a nurse and not my best friend. It worries me. "I met with his rehab nurse, Joanna, and she feels it is best if she reintroduces your existence to George before you actually see him in person. It won't be long—so just think waiting is for the good of George."

I look at her. That isn't the way it should be. I wonder for a moment what she might be hiding. Does she still not trust George?

"I know it will be difficult, but, when you finally see him, you will be able to resume your relationship, as if nothing has happened," Barbara continues, but I know she is hiding something.

"What is really wrong?" I ask.

"Nothing. I just don't agree with Joanna's care plan, but she is in charge of his care." Barbara looks angry.

"So you think I should go see him, too?"

"It doesn't matter what I think, really."

"At the meeting, I was taken aback by the response I received from Joanna," Barbara continues. "But she insisted that George needs a great amount of time to heal, both physically and mentally from his injuries."

"Does she know I'm a nurse?" I ask. I cannot believe George is being taken from me again.

"Yes," Barbara says. "I couldn't believe what I heard."

"What do you mean?"

"Joanna became quite agitated when I told her George has a lover who yearns to be with him."

"Agitated?" I think for a while about the different things I'd learned in nursing school, and nothing ever seemed to indicate that it was best to keep family away.

"I'm going to look into this Joanna person after lunch," Barbara concludes. She stood and went back to her room. I wait in the living room, hoping that everything will make sense again.

We ate lunch in almost complete silence. "Barbara, I have some serious concerns. In nursing school, they emphasized having loved ones around a trauma patient as the best medicine."

"I know," Barbara replies, poking at her potato salad. "So why is Joanna so adamant no one should visit until she says it's permissible?"

"My thoughts exactly," I say. "Do you think she's too involved?" Once again, the stories of the old George rumble around inside me. I'm terrified. *Have I found him, only to lose him again?*

"I might go to the nursing supervisor at the hospital to discuss my conversation," Barbara says flatly.

"You don't want to cause a political situation. You are a new nurse at the hospital, and this isn't worth making enemies."

Barbara nods. "But I don't like it."

CHAPTER 22

RECUPERATING AT THE RIVERSIDE DRIVE APARTMENT

Joanna couldn't have asked for a better patient than me, and I tell her that—frequently. Each day, I jump right into my routine of exercising for building up my muscle strength and my cardiovascular activity. I am way ahead of the schedule given to me by my physical therapists at Mt. Sinai.

At ten in the morning, the same as every morning, Joanna lets herself into my apartment with a key I have given her.

"Did you finish all your exercises again?" she asks as she puts down her bag of paperwork.

"Yep, showered, shaved, and dressed." I smile. "I think it is the theatrical training."

"That makes you a show-off," she teases.

"No, that makes me a hard worker," I retort.

For the next hour or so, she takes down my vital signs, gives me my medications, and asks me a bunch of questions.

"Did you do your back strengthening program?" she asks.

"Oh no!" I look down at my outfit. "Can we let it slide?"

"Absolutely not." She smiles. "Get changed, and we'll start with sit-ups."

I go back to my room and change in to a new set of sweats. Joanna sits on the couch and watches me go through the sit-ups, the back curls, and the special sit-up program developed for me.

"Your chest and back are showing real improvement." Her voice makes me pause for only a moment, but, then, I remind myself that her job is to watch for improvement. She isn't making a pass at me.

Although I have always looked forward in seeing Joanna, recently, she has been asking a lot of questions about my past, and, in many cases, I've not been keen on answering them. Maybe that is part of her job too, but I don't remember Ingrid asking such probing questions of patients.

"What is the weather like outside?" I ask. If the weather is nice, the two of us will take walks up and down Riverside Drive and spend some time sitting in a little park nearby my apartment.

"Nice enough to walk," she says, glancing at me quickly. Something in her look bothers me again. It is as though she is assessing me each time she looks at me. Sizing me up would be a more appropriate description.

"Let's get out of here," I say and smile. I hope she doesn't see anything in my look. I lead her to the door, and we go down the steps and out to our favorite bench. Lots of people walk by us, and, if someone was watching the two of us on the park bench, they might think we are lovers. I certainly don't want anyone to think those thoughts.

"I have noticed your memory is slowly returning," she says.

"Yes." I think about my next sentence. "I am remembering many details of my life I hadn't been able to recall until recently."

"Such as?" She turns and smiles at me. I had seen so many smiles like hers during my years on the stage. Something twists inside me.

"Primarily, I think about Ingrid." I look away, as if even her name is a betrayal in Joanna's eyes. "I miss her and want to find her."

"It isn't the time in your recovery to introduce her back into your life." Her words are sharp and final, as if it were her decision to make. I draw on my acting and face her with a small smile.

"If you don't think I'm ready…"

"No," she pauses and looks at me as if trying to read something deep inside. "But when the time is right, I'll help you find her."

"Okay." I look back at the people walking in front of us.

"For now, you should spend all of your quality time with me, working on getting stronger and continuing towards the goal of full recovery."

Her reply doesn't seem to have a thing to do with medicine, but it is also possible that I have more ego than I should, and she knows more about rehab than I do.

I have never really been the obedient sort, so, the following day, I end my early morning exercises sooner than usual, shower, dress, and place a call to the *Regal Fantasy's* corporate office in Miami. The woman who answers the phone in the personnel department is kind, but not particularly helpful.

"Ingrid Jameson, RN, disembarked in New York at the end of her contract in September."

"What was the date?" I ask.

"I'm sorry. I cannot tell you that." She pauses. "Security reasons. You understand."

I did, but it didn't calm my irritation. This was my best lead on finding her, and, now, I wasn't sure what to do next.

"Thank you," I say, hanging up.

"Who were you talking to?" Joanna demands.

I turn and see her standing not more than five feet from me, anger flaring in her eyes, her jaw stiff and tight.

"None of your business," I answer, the anger churning inside me now equal to the fury on her face.

For a moment, we simply stare at each other, and, then, her face softens a bit. "I heard you asking about finding Ingrid." Her tone is calm now. "I am only trying to help you—you must let me."

I am still angry, but I soften to her, as well. She has done so much to help me recover, and she only wants what is best. "I am just asking a few questions."

"It is not a good idea for you to be looking for Ingrid at this time." She steps forward, only compassion remaining. "She will take you away from me and the recovery effort we both are working so hard to accomplish."

The change in Joanna makes something deep inside of me tense, but I have to push those ideas away for now. I think it is best if I don't mention Ingrid for the rest of the day. The two of us get back to the daily routine of rehabilitation.

We workout, and Joanna does her normal routine, but I cannot fight the tension in the room. Maybe I am the only one who feels it. Joanna, for her part, is chatting along and smiling, like she always does. *Maybe it takes an actor to recognize a liar?* I'm not sure, but I don't like pretending. And, today, I don't like Joanna.

In the evening, after Joanna has left, I sit quietly in the living room, thinking about Joanna's outburst during the day. Try as I may, I cannot get the exchange with Joanna out of my mind. The nagging question is why my nurse is trying to stop me from finding Ingrid. For the first time since I have come out of my coma, I am really yearning to find and hold Ingrid in my arms once more. But I haven't the first clue about how to go about looking for her. A city like New York is a great place to hide, and all the airports and ships mean it is also a great place to leave.

The phone rings, breaking my ponderings for a moment. I walk to it, but, just before answering, I wonder if it is Joanna again. It rings a third time, and I decide to pick it up.

"George. How are you?" Franco's voice immediately relaxes me. It isn't Ingrid, but at least it is someone I feel I can trust.

"It's good to hear your voice, Franco. I have so much to tell you."

"Me, too," he says.

"You first," I respond, enjoying this distraction from my current worries.

Franco goes on to tell me how he had tried for months to call me, but didn't know where I was. He then told me how he saw my story and picture in the newspaper. "I am so glad your many months of struggle at Mt. Sinai are now over, John."

"John?" I ask, confused.

"Or should it be Mr. Doe?" He laughs, and it is a good-natured belly laugh. It is so good to feel connected again. I fill him in on the last several years on the cruise ships, my love of Ingrid, and assure him I am doing well.

"Your timing is wonderful," I say. "Because I'm trying to find Ingrid, and I have no leads."

"I will be happy to help. Love is a wonderful healer." His voice is teasing. He is an excellent agent, but his ability to make a person laugh is part of what makes him a great person and friend.

"How are you doing?" I think of Gina and how it must feel to lose so much and know that it will be impossible to ever have it back.

"It took a long time to get past, but the hurt goes away eventually," he says in a voice that reassures me that happiness after hurt *is*, indeed, possible. "True love can make anything possible. I had that with Gina, and I'll move heaven and earth to bring Ingrid to you."

"You should talk to my nurse," I say, not trying to hide my frustration.

"Why's that?"

I tell him about Joanna and her handling of my rehab. I tell him about her recent outbursts and strange behavior.

"And you haven't slept with her?" He laughs.

"No. I have no interest."

"Even with her throwing herself at you?"

"I love Ingrid," I say simply, and the sentence burns my chest.

"I would say you do." I think I hear a smile in his voice. He might just be proud of my growth. The idea makes me smile a little. We end the call, exchanging good wishes, and he reiterates his promise to do his best to help me start a new life in New York.

Although it had some bumps, the day was a good one. I go to bed and rest peacefully.

Rehab begins all over again the next morning. When Joanna arrives, she welcomes me with a big smile, as if nothing at all unusual had happened the previous day. She does her assessment and gives me my medicine.

"I am very sorry about my outburst yesterday," she apologizes. Her eyes are focused on the paper in front of her, as if it takes great effort to write the dosage and time she gave me my medicine. "You are doing exceptionally well, and I have an idea to break up our daily routine."

I feel my heart start to speed up. I don't want to hurt her feelings, but I sense she is about to try to move forward with her feelings, and I cannot reciprocate.

"Tomorrow is my day off," she continues before I have a chance to speak. "I will rent a car, pick you up, and drive into the country for a picnic lunch and walk in the woods." She pauses only long enough to take a breath. "I heard about a place from another nurse at work, the Croton Dam Reserve. It is filled with trails, beautiful views of the sky, and, some say it is quite a romantic spot. The ride will take approximately forty-five minutes, and I know it will do you a world of good. You will love the Reserve."

"That could be fun." I say, trying to keep my voice light, but my mind is stuck on the words *romantic spot*. I cannot allow her to believe I share her feelings.

"It will be good for least a day to get out of your apartment to new surroundings, and to an area much larger than the small local park we have spent so much time in recently." She puts the paper in the bag she brings for each rehab session and looks up at me. "The day after our picnic at the Croton Dam, I will start helping you find Ingrid."

I look up at her, stunned. The fear inside of me melts away, and I feel a bit silly.

"I realized yesterday that I haven't told you anything about me, and I would like to now," Joanna offers, leaning back in her chair.

"I would love to know more about you." And I mean it sincerely. Now that I know it is safe to talk to her, I suddenly feel happier and eager to know about the woman who brought me back from the brink.

"I was born in England. I am an only child, and both of my parents have passed away," she starts. "For many years, I worked in the critical care department of a large and well-respected hospital in mid-London. I was quite happy, but, then, my fiancé broke off our engagement, and realized I needed a change."

"I am so sorry to hear that." Suddenly, I realize why she was so negative about me finding Ingrid. After her own painful breakup, she was only trying to protect me. I feel awful for the things I'd thought about her. I am really quite lucky to have such a caring nurse.

"Quite honestly, I was very deeply depressed and couldn't concentrate on my work at the hospital. Someone told me of an opening at Mt. Sinai, and I jumped at the chance," she continues, completely unaware that my thoughts have drifted elsewhere. I turn my attention back to her. When she finishes, we both have an early lunch and talk a little more about the plans for tomorrow's trip out of the City to the countryside.

The rest of the day went by slowly. Joanna spent time filling out reports on my progress and introducing me to the new set of exercises from the physical therapists at the hospital.

"I will pack a meal and have it in the car when I come pick you up tomorrow."

"Is there anything we need from here?" I ask, walking to the kitchen to see what I have.

"No, just rest," she says. "In fact, let me make you dinner before I leave."

She goes to the kitchen, and I sit in the living room. Joanna seems completely different today than yesterday. On the one hand, it is good. She is helping me find Ingrid. On the other hand, she seems more like she is trying to be my friend than my nurse.

"It is ready." She calls from the other room, and I walk out to the small table in my kitchen.

"Thank you," I say as I look at the plate of food. "This is simply wonderful."

"I really enjoy cooking." She smiles. "And I finally feel like I'm settling in to America and my job."

"Well, that is a good thing to tell me *now*," I joke, "after you have taken care of me for months."

She laughs. "I know how to do my job." Then, she pauses and looks around the kitchen. "I just feel that I'm becoming me again." She bends down while I am sitting and kisses me directly and squarely on my mouth. "Goodbye, George, I can't wait to see you tomorrow."

I sit stunned as I watch her walk out of the apartment. "Goodbye," I manage to say as the door clicks shut behind her.

I am startled by the kiss and my reaction. In every one of my past relationships, if a young lady—or, for that matter, an older woman—kissed me on the mouth, I would have taken her to bed before they knew what had hit them.

Now, I realize even more how much I miss and want Ingrid. I am sure, beyond any reasonable doubt, that my feelings for Ingrid are not, and never were, purely sexual. I love her more deeply than I ever have anyone. I will need to make that clear to Joanna tomorrow at Croton Dam.

It was nice to trust her and to see where she was coming from, but all of the confidence I had vanished with that kiss. That kiss did not say for a moment that she understood my love for Ingrid. That kiss said she wanted to change my mind.

Tonight will be an early night for me. I'm going to bed immediately after dinner. Tomorrow will be tiring, and I will need extra stamina for the trip, the extra walking, the exercise, and the conversation at the Croton Dam. Not only that, but, the sooner I get to sleep, the sooner I get to tomorrow…and the next day. That is the day I'm most excited about—the day after tomorrow. The day I really get to start searching for Ingrid again.

Chapter 23

THE CROTON DAM

It was a beautiful Indian summer day in late September in New York City. I was standing outside when Joanna arrived.

"You *are* ready, aren't you?" she asks me, her voice light and friendly.

"I certainly am," I respond. "It is a perfect day for this outing, and the outing is a perfect transition to part two of my recovery."

"Yes, it really is," she agrees, and we walk to the car.

"It is a pretty long drive, around forty-five minutes. Maybe you should put your head back and take a short nap."

"No way," I say. "I am thrilled to leave the neighborhood and see something other than so many buildings. I'm not missing a moment of the scenery."

"Okay. Enjoy the trip," she says.

And I look out the window and think about Ingrid.

***

Franco was up early this Saturday morning. His apartment in New York City needed some cleaning, so he fought the urge to join all the other people outside enjoying one of the last warm fall days. He also had a few reports his boss had requested that he finish. He made a large breakfast and sat at the table. As always, he piled papers and books in front of Gina's chair. It made it seem less empty, as if she weren't sitting there, because there was no room, rather than no Gina.

The phone rang just as he sat down to eat. He looked at it. He had to answer. It would just keep ringing.

He walks slowly and lifts the receiver. The voice on the other end is urgent.

"Would you repeat that?" Franco yells into the phone. The caller says the same thing. Dread melts every muscle in him.

"Are you sure?"

The other agent is.

"I can't believe this." He hurries back to his bedroom to change from lounge pants to blue jeans. "I can't believe this."

He asks if the other agent can offer any help, and, being told that he cannot, he responds, "No, I know who to call. Thank you." And he hangs up. He pulls the phone behind him, the long cord installed before Gina died, so that she could wander their apartment when she was talking.

He punches in the first phone number. "It's Franco," he says. "Hurry up. Get your car and your partner, and meet me now. Go through red lights. We will take care of any tickets with the NYPD." He attaches his gun to his shoulder holster, finishes dressing, and runs down the stairs. There is no time to wait for the elevator. He paces outside his apartment building for about three minutes before he hears a siren. The car pulls up, and Franco jumps in.

"Go as fast as you can to the West Side Highway, and go north, heading for Westchester."

"What the hell is going on?" The agent in the back asks.

Franco spins sideways in his seat, so he can face both men. He looks to the driver, "Keep driving. Fast." Then he turns to the back. "I just received a call from England, from the handler of my CIA mole in the KGB. You know the nurse I told you about, who is almost living with George, helping with his rehab?"

"Joanna," The guy in the back says.

"Yes. She is a goddamn KGB agent sent by Kapersky to make sure George is killed this time."

"No shit!" the driver exclaims, and the car lurches forward.

"Yeah. She was supposed to earn his trust and, then, get him out of the City to kill him and dispose of his body."

"And you just found out?" The driver asks, and the man in the back simply shakes his head.

"Yeah, there was chatter last night, and it finally filtered through," Franco responds, dread snaking through him again. "Yesterday, I spoke with George. He told me more about this nurse. She is spending every day with him. I teased him about her wanting to sleep with him."

"Guess he's still got it." The driver laughs, and Franco stifles a small chuckle.

"I am sure he doesn't mind his ego getting shattered," Franco continues. "But he told me yesterday that she planned a quiet trip out of the City today to the Croton Dam Reserve. This early in the morning, and at this time of the year, no one will be around there. SHE IS GOING TO KILL HIM THIS MORNING," Franco exclaims, looking at the clock. "Step on it, or we are going to be too late."

***

"Not too much longer," Joanna announces. "Up ahead is a large sign, directing one to the right for the Croton Dam and Reserve."

"It is beautiful out there," I observe. "I cannot imagine why I never came here before."

"It will be very quiet. It is early, and it is the off season," she continues. Her face is calm and peaceful.

Joanna parks the car and rolls down her window. "Listen to that quiet."

"It is wonderful," I confirm, and it truly is. If I find Ingrid soon enough, I'm going to bring her here.

"Well, shall we get out?" She rolls up her window and opens the door.

"Yes." I get out and open the back door. "Let me help you carry all of this."

"I guess I *did* over-pack, a little."

"Well, not if you plan to move here," I joke, and I lift up the picnic basket and two bottles of wine. Joanna takes the blanket.

We walk for a few minutes to a beautiful spot far from the parking lot, just inside the woods near the water. It is simply perfect. She spreads the blanket out on the grass.

"I'm going to walk around for a minute," she says.

"I will join you after I put all this down," I tell her and start setting things around. There isn't a person here, and, unlike in the City, I'm not the least bit worried someone will steal our things.

"I'll come back for you. I just want to have a few minutes alone."

I set down the basket and wine and stand to stretch. The air is starting to have the damp coolness of fall, but there is still some lingering warmth. The only sounds are water cascading over the dam and the chirping of birds, and a damp breeze reminds me of nights on the ship.

"Come on, George. Let's take a walk?"

I open my eyes, and Joanna is holding out her hand. She isn't beautiful, but the softness and peace on her face makes her attractive.

I take her hand, and we walk along the first trail.

We walk for about five minutes down trails winding through trees.

"Can we sit down for a minute?" I ask when I see a small bench down the path.

"Not quite as strong as you thought you were, are you?" She smiles, and the teasing in her voice is pleasant. I hope she is being friendly and not flirtatious.

"I guess not," I say. We walk ahead and sit quietly.

We sit side-by-side for a few minutes, only listening to the birds and the scurry of animals going about their fall preparations.

"Did you have a place like this near London?" I ask.

"Not *exactly* like this, but I had quiet spots I went to when I needed to escape the city."

She sounds so happy, and I am very glad I decided to come out here with her. My leg muscles are aching, though, and I think I'm going to need to go back to the blanket soon.

"You look tired," she observes. "Do you need me to go back and get you something?"

"No, I will be okay. It's nice to just sit here."

She nods, but she seems anxious about something. It is probably Ingrid. For all her talk of helping me, that kiss last night tells me that she still hopes I'll change my mind. I don't doubt for a minute that with the wine and the picnic, she hopes to convince me to not search.

"Maybe I should go back and get some water for you," she says, her voice slightly agitated. "I'm a little worried we overdid it."

"Really, I'm fine," I assure her. "I'm enjoying myself."

She nods and leans back. For a few minutes, neither of us says much of anything, except to comment on a sound or something we see.

"George, I'm really worried," she says. "We have been sitting here for nearly twenty minutes, and you're not looking much better."

"But I feel fine," I say. "Do you want me to walk back with you?"

"No. I will go back to the basket and get some water and bring it back to you."

"But what if I need you when you're gone?" I tease, and she looks at me with a flash of irritation, followed by a smile. "I'm sure you'll be just fine. I can be there and back in about five minutes. You'll survive that long." She smiles again.

I nod, and she stands up, giving my shoulder a platonic squeeze before walking away.

Joanna's behavior has me worried. If she thought that she could convince me to love her, and I reject her, what will she do? My legs are still tired, but not weak. I could walk back to the blanket, meet her on the path, and tell her I changed my mind. If I look as bad as she says, which I'm sure I do not, she wouldn't object to a raincheck on our date. I look down at my watch and decide it would be best to leave.

I start down the path, soaking up the quiet and the beauty of the day. I really hate to leave, but Joanna's erratic behavior is really starting to concern me. I think it might be best if they assign me to a new nurse, too. She is *too* involved. The idea is at once freeing and upsetting. My legs ache. I shouldn't have walked so far out, but I also expected to have someone with me.

Three loud gunshots ring out and echo through the trees, and, for a moment, everything is silent. The birds no longer sing. Even the wind has stilled. Only the splashing of the water over the dam defies the order for silence the gun demands. I begin running down the path, dread threatening to overtake me. I recognized that sound from the days in the U.S.S.R. My steps crunch over twigs and dried leaves. My lungs burn, and I taste metal, but, still, I run. The clearing is closer, and I suddenly consider something. What if the shooters are still there? I slow and, then, stop. I'm alone. I'm wheezing.

"George!" I hear someone yell. "George, are you in there?"

I hear men. I move to the side of the path and behind a tree.

"George!"

A voice I recognize.

"Franco?" I call back, relief nearly causing me to collapse.

"Yeah, hurry."

I start walking quickly and, soon, I break through the tree line. Joanna, covered in blood, is sprawled on the picnic blanket.

I start yelling, but don't even understand the words coming out of my mouth. Franco walks to me slowly, his hands up as if to remind me he is a friend.

"Look at her hand," Franco instructs me, calmly.

"What?" I ask, no longer yelling.

"Her hand," he repeats. "The gun."

My legs give out, and I drop to my knees. Franco walks up beside me and puts his hand on my shoulder. "Joanna was sent to New York by Alexander Kapersky of the KGB to kill you."

"The KGB? How?"

"KGB agents in New York had seen your story and picture in the newspapers as an unidentified John Doe patient at Mt. Sinai Hospital. They sent the information back to Kapersky in Moscow."

"It makes no sense," I stutter, dumbly. "If she was going to kill me, she could have killed me anytime—in the hospital bed or any time in my apartment."

"Alexander had tried and failed to kill you in Russia and at Cape Cod. He didn't want any more failures, so his instructions were to take time to get into your confidence and carry out the killing away from any familiar surroundings."

"You mean to tell me she was nursing me back to health, just to kill me?" I look over at her body. The gun. I remember how weird she was acting today.

"Yes, she didn't care about your life, only about killing you at the right time."

"How did you know to be here today?"

"I received a call…" Franco starts to tell me about the call, the high speed drive. Arriving as she got back to the basket and shooting her just before she returned.

"And all while I was sitting in the woods trying to figure out how to let her down easy." I laugh. The irony makes me laugh, because I have no other emotions left.

"You always were a cocky S.O.B.," Franco chuckles.

"Guess I have to say thank you," I say, laughing at his jab.

"You bet your ass."

The two agents have joined Franco at the blanket. "No staff or visitors are at the Dam yet," one says.

"We must move quickly," Franco says. "Take the body and all of the remnants of the picnic, and dispose of everything over the top of the Dam wall, into the water below." He indicates the area, while one agent starts for the picnic. "Then, take her keys to the car, drive it to the top of the Dam, and send it down into the deeper water."

"Got it," the second agent confirms.

Franco looks at me. "Let's move. We want to make sure no one will ever know what has taken place here and that no traces of a Joanna Lee will ever be able to be linked to you."

I follow him to his car and get inside. I sit in stunned silence, watching the same scenery I'd passed an hour ago pass me in reverse. Franco spends some of time explaining what he learned about Joanna.

"She was a trained assassin. She and her parents had defected to Russia from England, but, then, she went back to London and got her nursing degree. She was working at The University Hospital in London when Kapersky found out you were in a hospital in New York. She lied to you about everything."

"Isn't that what spies do?" I joke, trying to liven up the mood. Then, I correct myself. "I mean… assassins." Franco is a true friend.

"If I wasn't so in love with Ingrid, I would have fallen into her romantic trap." I think about her weird behavior, and, suddenly, all the things that bothered me make complete sense, although I would have never guessed she'd been hired to kill me.

"Good thing you're honorable now." Franco glances at me, then, back at the road.

"That I am, friend." I rub my legs. They're throbbing now, and I am certain that I have put my rehab behind by a few days with all I've done. "Would you be able to help me find Ingrid now?"

"I will see what I can do," Franco says.

It is at least something for me to look forward to. We arrive at my apartment.

"Take the rest of the afternoon off and get some sleep," Franco instructs me. "I will call you tomorrow, to see how you are doing." I get out and watch Franco wind down the street. When will my life ever be normal? When will I be able to stop running?

CHAPTER 24

A KNOCK AND A RING

I wish I could tell you the plan for a good night sleep worked out, but it simply didn't happen. I was up most of the night tossing and turning. The thought of Joanna in my apartment—where at any moment she could have ended my life—had me shaken. Then, knowing Kapersky was still trying to kill me, after all these years, kept me awake, listening for the slightest sound. Every voice outside became a potential threat. The safety I thought was there is now gone. How could a man still harbor a grudge for so long?

For the next few days, I worked to keep my mind occupied with my daily exercise routines, but my mind was just not on them. Each exercise reminded me of the time I'd spent with an assassin. Who could I trust, if even the hospital hadn't been able to figure out who she was?

Franco was great. He called me the first day to check in and see how I was doing. I was still staring out the window, lost in my thoughts most of the time.

"I don't want the murder to come back to me, Franco," I say, watching the people milling about on the sidewalk below. "Someone will notice she is missing."

"Don't worry. Nothing is going to come back to you."

"Who else would they question?" Heat rises up my neck when I see a man stop and scan my building. "They knew she spent a great deal of her time with me." The man moves slowly down the road, turning once more to look at my building.

"It's a big city, George."

"It's a small world," I retort.

For a moment, the line was silent. "Franco?" I say.

"I'm still here," he replies. "I was just letting you get the paranoia out of your system."

"I hardly think what I have is paranoia." His voice does little to reassure me. "People will be suspicious."

"We have it covered," Franco reminds me. "We've fixed this problem a time or two."

The easy way he talked about covering up a murder gave me pause briefly, but I decided to leave it alone for now. Franco was here to help me. He had proven himself trustworthy many times.

"I will call the hospital then," I say, still feeling a bit awkward about the whole thing. Actually, I felt much more than awkward, but, since I couldn't fully define what I felt about all that had happened since saying goodbye to Ingrid on the ship, I decided to stick with that word. "It seems like what I'd naturally do if she hadn't shown up and I knew nothing about her."

"That is fine," Franco says. "Do what you'd normally do. No one knows anything, so don't feel paranoid."

We talk about nothing in particular for a few more minutes, and, then, I hang up the phone. My life has turned out so much differently than I had thought it would when I started in theater, or started in the spy game, or even started dating Ingrid. It seemed nothing about anything I did anymore ended up as I expected. I chuckle at that thought, considering the fact that I am now calling the hospital to throw any suspicion off of me. I dial the hospital and speak to an operator, who connects me to the ICU, where I'd been a patient.

"Hi. My name is George," I begin, my throat dry. I clear it and continue. "Joanna is my nurse and has been coming to my home to do rehab with me." I pause to allow them to reply, but they say nothing.

"I haven't seen or heard from her today, and I wondered if she was off or if I had a day written wrong."

"Just a moment." The person is short and thoroughly unpleasant. "I will get the nurse manager for you."

I wait a few moments, the sound of my pulse so loud that I worry I won't understand the nurse manager when she comes on the line.

"Hello, I'm Sheryl, the nurse manager." The woman's voice has a fake kindness that is generally reserved for administrators or those quite accustomed to working with the public.

"Hi, I'm George," I begin.

"Yes," her voice carries a smile, and this one sounds a touch more genuine. "You were our John Doe."

"Yes. I was," I reply—relieved that she is sounding even friendlier.

She launches into an explanation of how they will be sending over a new nurse. They apologize for any inconvenience. The response from the hospital staff is vague, at best. Nothing much is said about Joanna's whereabouts.

"We were already working on an emergency substitute," she says. "And you will get a call from our office before they come over."

I listen and answer where I know I am expected to speak, but I find it a bit odd that no one asks if I know anything about where Joanna could be, nor when I'd last seen her. I finish talking to them and go about my workout.

The next few days did nothing to make me feel any better. I guess I was struggling with some depression. It simply felt like I'd never have my life back. If I did anything I loved, a hit man might find me. Even taking a cab and having an accident put me at risk—well, beyond the risk of being in an accident. Everything about life is beginning to feel hopeless, and I continue to lose precious time that could be spent looking for Ingrid.

The hospital sent over a physical therapist, Evan Bennet, to take over the rehab role Joanna had previously filled. Evan worked me hard at my exercise routines and made sure, until a new nurse was assigned to the case, I took all my medications. The daily visits were purely professional. No talk about personal areas in both our lives. More importantly, nothing was ever said about Joanna, her life, nor her disappearance. I slowly put more effort into my exercise program, but didn't welcome the visit from Evan as much as I had from Joanna.

At the end of the week, Evan had just left when I received a phone call.

"Hello, I am Detective Michael Stuart, from the New York City Police Department. I am investigating a missing person report of a Miss Joanna Lee."

His words make my skin go cold. "Certainly," I say. "How can I help?"

"I have been told she was a nurse assigned for your rehabilitation program?"

"Yes, that is correct." I respond.

"I was wondering if I may come over to your apartment to talk."

"Certainly," I say and, then, I realize that repeating my words might tip him off that I feel uncomfortable. "That is to say, now is a good time. My physical therapist just left, and I have the rest of the day free." *What am I doing?* I sound terrified. Everything about my voice and words scream guilt or fear. I take a deep breath and draw on my acting to play the role of George.

"I will be over in just a few hours, depending on traffic."

"Okay," I reply, already feeling the calm of playing a role. "I will be happy to give you any information I can. I called the hospital to find out why she hadn't been over. I'm sorry to hear they've had to call in the police."

"Many times, these are simply a case of someone leaving town and forgetting to tell someone, but we have to look into everything. I will see you soon," he says, his voice friendly.

"I will see you then."

I hang up the phone and try to prepare for his visit. I went through the same practice I always did before taking the stage all those decades ago. I would be ready to talk to him. I place a coffee cake I'd bought the day before in the oven to warm slightly and set up a pot of coffee.

Detective Stuart arrives later in the afternoon. He is as tall as me, slightly balding, and carrying a bit of middle-age weight in his midsection.

"Detective Stuart, come in," I greet him. "Let's sit at the table."

I turn on the coffee, remove the warm cake, and take it to the table. Preparing everything gives me time to steady my nerves before I sit down to talk with Detective Stuart.

"I spoke to the hospital." His voice is deep, but not the least bit hostile. "I know all about your horrific car crash this past June."

"Then you know more than I do," I say, laughing slightly and setting the coffee pot on a hot pad and placing a mug in front of him. "Because I know very little about it."

He smiles warmly and thanks me for the coffee. Next, the conversation turns to a more social discourse. "George, when I was in college twenty years ago, I went to see you in a musical on Broadway."

"Really?" I respond.

"My girlfriend at the time, now my wife, had a crush on you. I can't wait to tell her I met you today." I relax a bit. We talk a bit about the theatre and my career, each of us pausing from time to time to warm up our coffee or take a bite of cake. I hadn't fully realized how lonely I'd been this last week, but I am also careful not to forget myself and slip out of character.

"Joanna Lee has been reported missing" Detective Stuart says. His voice has an edge of an apology in it, as if he is sorry that he had to stop our conversation to discuss the reason for his visit. "I have a few questions to ask you."

"I'm happy to help in whatever way I can."

"Was Miss Lee at your apartment last week?"

"Yes, a few different times, for my therapy."

"Was she here the day before her day off at the end of the week?"

"Yes."

"Did she come after her day off?"

"No," I reply.

The detective shifts in his seat a bit and flips through his notebook. "George, I am sorry to ask you this, but it is important that I know everything."

I try to control my expression, but I feel beads of sweat collect on my chest and back that roll down inside my shirt. The nerves are terrible, and I brace myself for whatever question was coming next.

"Did you have an affair with her?"

"No," I say, relieved that it was such a simple question. "Ours was strictly a professional nurse/patient relationship. In fact, I am in love with someone I worked with on a cruise ship in the Caribbean."

Detective Stuart smiles and asks a few more questions. Each moves further and further away from accusations and are much more general. "Sorry to take so much of your time," he apologizes, standing abruptly. "I will leave you to rest now."

"Thank you. I'm getting stronger all the time, but my physical therapist worked me pretty hard today," I say with a smile.

"George, I hope if I need to talk to you again, you will be available?"

"Of course, call me any time." I walk him to the door and we exchange goodbyes, but, as the door closes, I feel immense relief. Franco had been right. There was no real suspicion directed at me. The questions were routine, and it was time for me to forget Joanna, just as I had forgotten so many other people and events in my life.

Another week went past with physical therapy and my watching out my window. The police didn't contact me again, nor had the hospital mentioned anything more about Joanna. This morning, I sat down for breakfast, thankful that Evan wasn't coming today. My muscles are sore from yesterday, when we had tried a couple of new exercises. There is a knock on my front door. My breath catches in my chest for a moment. I'm not expecting anyone. I walk to the window to look down at the street. People walk back and forth. No one seems to be keeping watching or sitting in a get-away car.

There is a second knock, this one a bit louder. More urgent. I walk to the door and look through the peephole. The person stands to the side slightly, their face turned away, as though they are looking down the hall. It is a woman, but my peephole is distorting the image. I hadn't really had need of it before and hadn't noticed how scratched it truly is.

I open the door slowly and look in to the hallway. The woman immediately turns to face me, sending my heart racing. If I was in a show, rather than in my apartment, the orchestra would be playing, and maybe a cymbal would have crashed in a dramatic crescendo. Ingrid was like a dream that had come to life.

The two of us stand frozen, staring at each other for a long moment. Not a word is spoken; instead, we study each other, letting every detail confirm that our beloved is now within arm's reach. I open the door a bit wider and reach my right hand forward. Ingrid responds by swiftly coming in to my embrace.

"I love you," we say, almost simultaneously. I kiss the top of her head, her forehead, her cheeks. Her lips. In between kisses, I repeat, "I love you. I've missed you."

Ingrid holds on to me, her mantra "I missed you, I tried to find you," and, then, "I love you," again and again. I step backwards into the apartment, Ingrid staying in step with me. We are no longer fifty-year-olds; now, we are two young people brought together after a long, unfair separation. I take her face in my hands and kiss her deeply, at once silencing her declarations of love to me. I reach behind her and wordlessly slide the chain and engage the deadbolt, then kiss her, leading her back to my bedroom. We make love, and it is even more passionate, more intense, than it had been in all the daydreams and fantasies I'd had since waking in the hospital.

When the lovemaking is finished, we lay in my bed, her head on my chest, me stroking her hair.

"I tried calling the CIA," she begins, and tells me the story of her hunt to find me and the other dead ends she encountered. "I went up and down Park Avenue, too." Then, she told me about her unsuccessful trip to Riverside Drive. As I listen to her talk, I am overwhelmed by all she'd done to find me. In all past relationships—and even in my marriage—I'd never felt that I was important enough to be pursued. She'd physically walked the streets looking for me. I am overwhelmed by her devotion and love for me. I had known the ache in my chest, wondering where she was, thinking I'd never see her again, but, to realize that she loves me as intensely as I love her is a gift second only to feeling her in my arms again.

Now, it is my turn to tell her about trying calling the cruise line to find her. My story isn't nearly as impressive as hers, mainly because I was limited by Joanna, but I am glad I have a story to tell her, as well. I want her to feel the feelings I have right now. The feelings of being loved so much that there is no sacrifice too great in order to be together again.

As I begin to tell the story of my accident, I am interrupted. "I know all about the accident and the newspaper article about the John Doe at Mt. Sinai hospital. My girlfriend works at Mt. Sinai, and after I read the story in the newspaper; she obtained your address for me."

"So that's how you found me," I laugh and pull her tight against me again.

"I guess what bothered me the most," she says, her voice suddenly serious and quiet, "is that I didn't understand why you never came to the ship the entire summer." She runs her fingertips back and forth across my chest. Her fingertip traces my collar bone. "Now, I know why." She kisses my chest, my chin, my lips. "My contract was up in September—and, after looking for you, I went home to Norway for a week's vacation. It was horrible."

"I'm so sorry, Ingrid," I apologize, tracing her face with my finger. I can't believe she is here with me now. She is in my arms. Her eyes, however, are distant, sad.

"Every day, I yearned to be back in New York, looking for you."

I lift her chin and kiss her lips. "Well, you found me, and I will never let you out of my sight again."

What a glorious day, and it is only the beginning.

The next few weeks were terrific, the two of us spending almost every moment together, not all of them clothed, and we worked to make up for all the time we'd lost. Although I opened up about my entire past life to Ingrid, I made the decision not to discuss nor mention Joanna, nor anything about the circumstances of her disappearance. I trust Ingrid, but I don't want to lay that heavy burden on her. She knows all that she needs to of my nurse, and I'm happy to let her remain ignorant of how close I came to death a second time.

"I think I'm ready to get back in to theatre," I tell Ingrid one day during lunch. She sets down her sandwich and dusts her fingers lightly. Her face is unreadable, as if she is considering something or judging her response. Her pause is making me a bit nervous.

"I think it is good for us to both to start looking for some permanent work," she says, before picking her sandwich up again. "I want to find work in a hospital, and it would seem the only way that will happen is if I pound the pavement."

I begin to make plans to start looking for employment in the theatre by initiating the purchasing of every trade paper at the newsstands. After a week of searching, Ingrid is lucky enough to secure several interviews.

"Good luck." I say to Ingrid as she goes off for day one of her interviews. She's spent more and more time at my apartment, and it is wonderful to see her every day.

"Thank you. Hopefully, I'll have good news when I get home." She smiles and walks out the door.

Home. The power of that one word strikes me as I consider what it means. I've lived many places. I've had many apartments, rooms, and even a house, but I have only ever felt truly at home when I am with Ingrid. The thought made me a bit self-conscious, and I was glad she couldn't read my thoughts—or could she? I smile and put my coffee cup in the sink.

The phone rings, and I hope it is another interviewer calling to make an appointment with Ingrid. She comes alive with each call. She has seven different interviews lined up over the next two weeks, and I am very confident she will have a job soon.

"George?" The woman says when I answer the phone.

"Yes, can I help you?" I ask. The voice seems vaguely familiar, but that isn't necessarily a good thing.

"It is Maryanne Michaels," the woman says.

"*Maryanne!* How wonderful to hear from you!"

"I have a couple of things I'd like to talk to you about," she says. "Do you have a moment?"

Of course I have time, so I tell her so. She begins describing how she has acquired the rights to a theatrical property, being turning into a Broadway musical, with her producing. I am very excited for her. She was always a very wonderful woman, but I would be lying if I didn't confess that I had hoped that this conversation would hold some good news for me, as well.

"And this is where *you* come in." Maryanne's voice is nearly winded from excitement, and her comment sends my heart thundering, too. "The leading character in the musical is a fifty-nine-year-old actor, down on his luck, who is reborn as a star."

"Talk about art imitating life," I respond.

"George, you would be perfect for the role."

I have to sit down. This is more wonderful than I could have hoped. I look at the pile of newspapers with random casting calls circled. Now, she is handing me my dream on a platter. Something

THE ACTOR? 243

slides down my cheek. It could be sweat, or maybe a tear, but I don't swipe either away. I try to think of an appropriate response.

"George," she says, her voice still bubbling, "this show will make you a star again."

When I first sought stardom, I was after all the wrong things. I was after everything it would let me have, but I never considered the responsibility that went with it. The opportunity it offered. It had always been about my ego. Now, I thought about what it would mean to Ingrid and me. What this opportunity could mean to...my thoughts ran wild.

"Of course, I'd love to do it," I say, trying my best to sound excited and mature.

"I will call you next week, darling." I knew when she said darling that I was back in the Theatre.

That was that. I was, again, a star. I cleaned up the newspapers and threw them down the trash chute, then started cleaning the apartment to pass the time. It was an eternity until Ingrid returned home. After I finished cleaning, something that took under an hour, I spent my time pacing up and down and looking at the clock on the wall. The moment Ingrid came through the door, I started recreating every word of my conversation with Maryanne. We hugged, and I sat Ingrid down. When you get a second chance, you don't want to take a moment for granted. "Do you know what would make this day even more perfect?" I ask her, nerves and excitement coiling around in me.

"No," Ingrid says, smiling.

"Would you marry me?" Being an emotional actor, tears start rolling down my checks as I wait for Ingrid's response. I didn't have to wait long.

"Yes!" She wraps her arms around me. I'm not entirely sure why I am being given so much again. I certainly don't deserve it, but, just the same, I hold her tight, and, for a moment, I just let the joy—true joy, not fleeting happiness—cascade over me.

I knew the first person I wanted to call the next morning was Franco. For a moment, I consider calling him today, but it is after five in the evening, and I would rather have him fresh. The evening continued with Ingrid and me eating dinner and talking about the future. The weather joined us in the celebration with an unusually pleasant evening.

The next morning, I manage to wait until 8:15 before dialing Franco. I share the news of my phone call with Maryanne Michaels and my engagement. Franco just listens.

"That all sounds like things are working out," Franco says. If I didn't know any better, I would have assumed he didn't know anything about my being offered a Broadway Show.

"They are, Franco, and I'm sure you're the man to thank."

"I'm as shocked about all of this as you are," Franco responds. "And I certainly had no hand in getting Ingrid to marry you." He laughs. It is a light laugh. The kind reserved for people who have been through horrible times together and who now are happy to share the pleasant ones.

I end the conversation with, "Well, thank you anyway, Franco".

During the next couple weeks, Maryanne sent over the show's script and tapes of the musical score to me. It was like walking into my best memories when I opened those boxes. There were meetings to set up to discuss show production. I thrived on the long phone conversations about casting, costumes, scenery, and other technical aspects of the show.

"I think that is all we have to cover for today," Maryanne concludes after one of our longer calls. "Remember that we're meeting for lunch tomorrow with the team and, then, only with costume after that to get final measurements."

"Of course," I say, looking at my stomach and wondering if I should be in better shape for the role.

"And I need your thoughts on the changes to Scene Two, Act Two."

"You'll have them first thing tomorrow," I promise. "I will call before I leave for our first meeting."

"Great. We will talk then."

It is very gratifying to be consulted on decisions about the show.

"I don't know if I've ever seen you so happy," observes Ingrid. "I saw you enjoy getting ready for shows on the ship, but this is different."

"I *am* happy," I respond, walking over to the couch and sitting next to her. "I really never thought I'd do this again. I missed it."

She takes my hand and kisses it.

"My happiness may be short-lived, because a Broadway show's rehearsals and out-of-town tryouts can be pure hell," I say, only partially joking. "No one ever would ever wish the pressure, the fights, and the constant changes of a Broadway musical preparing to open on Broadway on one's worst enemy."

"I don't want to even imagine it," Ingrid says. "I'll stick to dealing with my sick patients."

"No matter the success or lack of success of the show, I will still have you."

Soon after, Franco comes to visit. He had seemed a touch coy after my last bit of good news I shared. I wasn't sure if I was ready to tell him anything else, but I was excited to introduce him to Ingrid.

"I've heard so much about you," Franco says, shaking her hand. "I am happy to finally meet you."

"You, too," Ingrid says.

Franco continues to smile, looking between Ingrid and me, and, for a moment, an uncomfortable silence seems to settle over the room.

"I have some good news for you, George," Franco interrupts the silence. He claps his hands together and rubs them for emphasis.

"I don't think I can stand any more good news," I say, wondering if Franco will now confess his involvement in my professional resurrection.

"I am sure you can handle this, George." Franco looks between Ingrid and me before continuing, as if debating whether or not to talk openly.

"She is fine," I say, indicating Ingrid, hoping this will prod his lips loose.

"My contacts in Russia have informed me that Alexander Kapersky has committed suicide," Franco begins.

The words smash against me and then release. I take a deep breath, as if suddenly emerging from a claustrophobic cave I've been hiding in for decades.

"He lost everything," Franco continues. "His career, his wife, and all respect from the Russian government. With the Cuban affair well over with, the KGB now has no interest in finding or eliminating you. You were Kapersky's personal vendetta, not the KGB's."

The full impact of what he is saying begins to melt over me.

"You do not have to worry ever again about Kapersky and the KGB."

I turn to Ingrid and, then, back to Franco. How is it possible that things just kept getting better? I couldn't put into words all I feel at this moment.

"Franco, I am so happy you've had a chance to meet the love of my life," I say, taking Ingrid's hand.

Franco stays and visits for about thirty minutes, and I am thrilled to see how well Ingrid and Franco get along. I am happy to listen to them talk while I sit and think about all that is happening to me.

"I should be leaving," Franco says. "It was lovely meeting you, Ingrid."

"You, too," she replies.

Franco begins to move to the door. "I will see you opening night of the show," I say. "And, then, possibly, at the film premiere." I think I can see a small hint of a smile forming on Franco's mouth, but I keep it to myself.

"He is nice," Ingrid says after Franco was gone.

"He grows on you." I smile. "Let's figure out when we can start moving your things over."

"I think we need to start getting you in shape for this rehearsal schedule. You don't get enough sleep, your diet could use some tweaking, and your rehab exercises really are not enough exercise."

"I guess it's a good thing I have a live-in nurse," I tease and kiss her on the neck.

I go back to the table and look over the script again. With auditions rapidly approaching, I am studying all the characters in the show and reading recommendations of various potential actors and actresses sent to me from the show's casting director.

Only three short weeks later, the first day of auditions arrives. I am up early, trying on different outfits in front of the mirror. What color pants would look best? Which tie would match? Do I stick with a white shirt, or should I add color? Exasperated, I toss one outfit after another on my bed. Twenty years ago, I would never go to an audition, nor, for that matter, a rehearsal, without wearing a matching tie, shirt, and a sport coat. For the past weeks, everyone I met has dressed like a slob. No time spent trying to look professional. I pick out a comfortable tie and carry the jacket over my arm to give a more casual air.

"I have breakfast," Ingrid calls from the other room.

I groan inwardly. My nerves would never tolerate food right now, but I cannot tell Ingrid that. She's worked so hard to help me get ready, all while starting her new job.

"Thank you," I say, looking at the plate. "This all looks delicious." I am able to sit down and force myself to consume a small breakfast.

"This is all great," I say, "but I'm just…"

Ingrid looks down at my plate and smirks. "Nerves?"

"Always," I say, pushing my chair in.

"I have something for you." She walks to the pantry and pulls out a goody bag. "Have a good day. I love you"

"I love you, too." I kiss her and walk out the door. In the past few weeks, I've said that phrase more than I did in all the years I was married. The funny thing is, I mean it so much more than even my words can articulate. I step outside our building and look in the bag she gave me. Ingrid has thrown my carefully executed diet to the winds. In the bag, she has included my favorite candies: red licorice, M&M's, and Hershey kisses.

I wait nervously to hail a cab in front of my building. A few go by, but none have their available sign lit. I look at my watch and fidget a bit more. I don't want to be late today. In fact, I want to be early enough to be by myself for a few minutes before work begins. I look down the road again and am frustrated to see only personal vehicles. Then, a cab stops in front of me and lets the person out and flips on their *vacant* sign.

I hold onto the door as the person steps out, and I immediately slide in. "St. James Theatre on West Forty-Fourth Street, between Broadway and Eighth Avenue," I start to give directions.

"I know how to go," he replies. He never turns around, but his voice is friendly. "I know the exact spot. Just sit back and relax. I will take care of everything." He isn't snarky, nor condescending. He must clearly recognize that I'm nervous. Surely, he has taken many a fare to the lights of Broadway.

I sit back for a moment, but, suddenly, I remember something urgent. "Please don't take the West Side Highway."

CHAPTER 25

THE AUDITIONS

As my cab arrives at the St James Theatre, I see dancers and singers milling about. Most of the people, while still the nomads and gypsies that make a Broadway cast, have come from hit shows, like *Chorus Line, Sweeney Todd, Evita,* or *Sugar Babies.* Everyone was hugging and kissing. While they were competing for a limited number of spots, they didn't forget the good times they'd had on other productions together. On Broadway, it is always a matter of moving onto the next and biggest potential hit of the season. I couldn't help but think of my early years of auditions, and, the very first time, I stood in line at one of these open call auditions. It had been a lifetime ago, when I was another man.

I moved past the throng of hopefuls waiting to go into the theatre. Their eyes held that unique combination of hope and desire that held the dreams of every performer. These people had fire in their bellies that allowed them to face rejection after rejection. I was grateful that I didn't have to stand in this line, but felt a twinge of hurt that not one person standing in line was at all familiar. I guess not having appeared on Broadway for more than twenty years, I shouldn't have expected anything else.

I go through the stage door and make my way to the stage. The three stage managers Mike, John, and Lee are waiting.

"George. Good to see you." Mike greets me. I walk down the line, shaking one hand and, then, another.

"We have a copy of the agenda here for you," John says, handing me a paper and a folder. I look at it a moment before taking my seat with the other three.

"Singers and dancers sent by their agents will be the first to be on stage," Lee says, using his pen to follow down his own page. "The next two weeks will be the auditions for all of the principals and supporting cast in the show. Then, the callbacks, and, finally, the open call."

"Okay," I say, looking at my copy of the agendas. I thought about the open call—which is called "the cattle call" in the industry, because hundreds are moved in and out of the theatre like cattle—that I first participated in. Chances of someone from open call making it on-stage are slim to none, but people still try.

"The first thing," John says, "Is the production staff meeting."

For the next hour, the production staff and the creative staff go over the names of those auditioning today. It is grueling work for everyone, not just those auditioning. Many of the people are good, some are even great, but there is a special, indescribable something that you look for in people. The entire audition focused on finding the unique something necessary for each show. This varied, based on character, cast, chemistry, and script. You are always very aware that people are going to pay to see an amazing show, so you have to be sure you found the right cast.

I steadied myself, and all of us took our seats halfway back in the orchestra section. The theatre is mostly dark, except a single spotlight shining on the stage. The auditions begin with the first group of dancers arriving on stage and getting various dance combinations from the assistant chorographer. For the rest of the day and into the next, dancers go through their routines. After seeing more than four hundred dancers, the show's choreographer chose thirty dancers for the final callback list. The next couple of days are for the singers who make up the chorus. They arrive with a ballad and an up-tempo song to perform for the musical director.

I sit through day after day, hour after hour of performers. Each day, I give my feedback on the various people auditioning, and, every day, I come home exhausted. I tell Ingrid how things are moving along and when I expected to be done with casting. I look forward to Ingrid's home-cooked meal and a long shower to make me forget how tired I really am.

"Franco called," Ingrid says, after I get out of the shower.

I look at the clock. It is almost eight, probably not too late to call. "Did he say what he needed?"

"Yes, he left a message," Ingrid says. "The U.S. government has just declassified the files of the Cuban Missile Crisis."

Finally, I am completely free. I am free to walk the streets, without fearing an assassin's bullet. I am free to work on Broadway without backlash. Now, I am even free to use my real name on Broadway.

"That is so great," I say, wishing I had another way to say it. The emotions threaten to overwhelm me. I have everything back to the way it was before—only now, I have a woman who truly loves me. I have a greater appreciation for what I am able to do for a living, and I am able to enjoy it more fully.

Ingrid has prepared a dinner for the two of us. I think about my previous life on Broadway. Eating at the restaurants. Meeting with the leading ladies at the hotel after rehearsal. I rarely came home and when I did, it was never to a home-cooked meal.

"This all looks so great," I say. She still has me eating healthier, but, now, she has added in a few treats for me each night.

"Eat and get to bed," she says. I know she understands: tomorrow starts the ordeal of the open call.

"If you think I was tired for the past several weeks, just wait until this cattle call is completed."

Arriving the next morning at the St James, the line of actors winds down Forty-Fourth Street and around to Eighth Avenue. I enter the stage door and meet on stage with the director and the choreographer to discuss the plans for the open call. In the wings are several actors who are allowed in the theatre to wait for the start of the auditions. Dancers, singers, and actors, in various stages of warming up, are being checked in by the stage managers. In the wings, I notice a young couple warming up. The girl is blonde and pretty, and she is singing with a handsome young actor. I would guess them to be in their early twenties. Physically, the two could be right for the two young lovers we need to cast for the show.

"Are you ready for this?" John asks, breaking into my thoughts momentarily.

"If I'm not, it's too late now." Something about these two seems eerily familiar to me, but I just can't put my finger on it. I look back a few times. The young man looks up, nods his chin in greeting, and points me out to the woman with him.

I start to leave the stage to take my place out front in the orchestra seats, when the young actor rehearsing with the blonde girl approaches. I look at him, still wondering who he must be related to. Nothing comes to mind.

The man's body language appears to say he doesn't want to intrude, but he does anyway. "Do you remember me, Mr. Toomey?" That he knows my name isn't remarkable. I'm more recognized now that I'm at the theatre often helping with pre-production.

"You look familiar," I say, honestly, "but I'm having a hard time placing you."

"I am Tom Willingham. You taught me acting at Barnstable High School on Cape Cod. Of course, then I knew you as Mr. Thompson."

"Tom," I say, remembering him instantly. "It is so great to see you." I give him a big hug. I think again about the high school and the fun times teaching. I remember Tom and his incredible talent. After all these years, he remembered what I said and actually listened to me.

"It is good to see you," I say. "How are you doing?"

"I graduated high school and was accepted in the theatre program at Northwestern in Chicago," he says, "just like you told me to do."

I smile, remembering. "Smart boy."

"I graduated several years ago, and have been acting in various companies in Chicago."

I listen and marvel at what he's saying. I'm so incredibly proud of what he is accomplished. More than that, I'm so happy that he took my advice to continue his education at Northwestern.

"You had real potential" I say. "I'm so happy to hear that you decided to pursue a career in theatre."

"Me, too," he replies. "I have been in quite a few productions, and I absolutely love it."

"Tom, who is the young actress with you today?"

His expression wavers for just a moment, and I wonder what it is about her that he doesn't want to share with me. I look from her to him. His eyes seem to be following the same trail, because, by the time I look at him, he is looking at me. A smile spreads across his face. "She is a Chicago girl, graduated a couple of years behind me at Northwestern, and, now, is my steady, live-in girlfriend.

"I would like to meet her," I say, not voicing my questions. She is, likewise, so familiar, a fact that is bothering me more and more. I haven't been around the Chicago acting scene in a long time; I can only assume that a friend of mine moved to the area, because I am certain I've met her parents or a family member.

Tom leads his girlfriend to me. Before any introduction, I turn to her "You look so familiar to me." I extend my hand. "My name is George Toomey."

I am pulled in her stare, and a strange feeling comes over me. I am not sure why, and I certainly can't explain it, but I am pulled to her.

"My name is Ellen Miller. I lived in Chicago with my mother and sister until we moved here." She motions back to Tom. She continues to look at me, as if that should clarify everything, but still I look at her, wondering what I'm missing.

"George, you don't remember me?"

I am stunned. I do remember her, from a long time ago, but, somehow, I cannot lock that recognition into place. I stare harder, as if the force of my thoughts will finally bring revelation.

"I am your daughter, Jody."

My whole life, I always felt I had complete control of my feelings and their responses, but, just like when Ingrid walked into my life again, seeing my daughter here at an open call, after twenty years, has me completely undone. I am frozen. I am in shock. Finally, my arms loosen, and I wrap them around Jody, I mean Ellen—I must get used to calling Jody by her stage name. Then, I cautiously utter the words, "I missed you."

She responds by wrapping her arms around me.

Not completely sure of what my next words would be, I ask; "How are your mother and sister?" This would be a good time to have my writers feeding me lines. I'm blank. My tongue feels huge in my mouth, and every thought seems confused and muddled.

"Lee, I'm going to be over here for a few minutes," I call over to the stage manager, and I step to the side with Tom and Jody. After some catching up, the conversation turns to acting, theatre, and the show.

"Today's auditions are for individuals, but I will request that both you and Tom audition together."

"Okay," Jody answers. I see a bit of her mom in her smile, but her eyes are mine. She is happy and talks freely with me. I reflect again upon the layer after layer of good I've received this last month, and I'm so grateful.

I see people starting to move into position. "It's almost time for the auditions to start. I need to get out to my spot."

"It was good to see you again," Tom says.

"Yes, you too." I stand. "We have a lot of catching up to do." Tom nods.

"I can't wait to see your audition. Let's have lunch at Sardis after your audition," I suggest and, then, move quickly to my seat. Remarkable. My daughter. My protégé. Here on my show.

I sit, waiting. I look back at them and see they've resumed their warm-ups.

Ten actors and ten singers filed on and off the stage, but I really didn't hear much of the morning auditions. My mind and thoughts were drawn completely to my daughter. What wonderful karma, fate, or kismet that they are dating and that I saw them today.

Tom and Ellen walk out on the stage. They give their names, and the audition begins. The director gives them some sides from the script of the show to read. They are told the parts are of two young actors, falling in love and choosing a life in the theatre. They read, and I can feel their chemistry. The way Tom looks down at my daughter makes me wish Ingrid were beside me, so I could hold her hand.

The choreographer is next, giving them some steps. They pick them up quickly and seem to flow together as a single unit. I am so proud. It was what I'd known that Tom could do when we first met at his high school.

Finally, the musical director and the rehearsal pianist have them sing a slow and an upbeat song to finish the audition. They do great. They don't have perfection in every move, but they have that something that we look for—that single spark—that can ignite a fire in the audience.

"Tom and Ellen." I stop to look at the director. I haven't given him any feedback on this audition yet. I hope he isn't dismissing them already. "I would like to work with you for the next hour on your audition. Can you stay?"

I look at him, nearly as shocked as they must be.

"Of course," they both reply, and I look from them to the director.

They go through two musical numbers from the score of the show, then, they read more from the script. They perform more dance steps and transition from lines to a song with basic choreography. Throughout the hour, I sit stunned as I watch my daughter being put through her paces.

"When have you ever seen a director do this?" I ask.

"Never," Lee replies. "But they're keeping pace, and they're really good."

I continue to watch and feel a lifetime of pride inside of me.

"Go in the wings, please," the director says to Tom and Ellen, and, then, he turns to all of us in our seats.

"What chemistry these two actors have," the director says, gesturing back to them with his thumb. "They are perfect for the two young leads in our show. I want them."

Each member of the creative team is polled for their reaction to hiring Tom and Ellen. All agree with the director. When they reach me for my opinion, tears are flowing down my cheeks.

"George, are you alright? Why are you crying?"

"They are perfect," I blurt out. "They are exactly who I would want."

I wipe the tears off of my cheeks quickly, and I tell them about mentoring Tom, losing Ellen, and, then, meeting them here today for the first time in a long time.

"I didn't want any claims of nepotism, so I didn't say anything, but I think they really have the right skills," I say, looking to where they must be waiting.

"I do, too," the choreographer agrees. "I don't care who they are or are not related to. They have what we want."

The director walks to the stage and calls into the wings, asking Tom and Ellen to join the staff in the seats out front.

"We'd like to have you as our two young lovers," the director says. I can't hear anything beyond that, because of the chatter. There are hugs all around, with the biggest coming from me.

"Remember my invitation for lunch down the street at Sardis," I say, between hugs.

For me, eating at Sardis had never been as happy an occasion as it was that day. I looked at Ellen. She had many lunches with me there when she was little girl. I doubt she remembers many of them, but, now, she has been hired for her first Broadway musical. If my show is a hit, she may, one day, have the opportunity of having her caricature hanging on the walls of Sardis, like mine in the past, and so many other Broadway stars.

The hour-and-a-half lunch flew by quickly, as we covered twenty years. I ask her about her mother and her sister back in Chicago.

"Ellen, do you think you can arrange a meeting between me and your younger sister?"

"I will do my best," she says, but her smile gives me hope that it won't be too hard.

"It looks like we all will be together for a long time because of this show," I say, pulling money out of my wallet for the bill. "I truly want to spend the entire time making amends for the past twenty years of our lives." We all kiss goodbye. I leave for the theatre, and Tom and Ellen will go back to their apartment. They certainly have a number of phone calls to make. They will be in a Broadway musical with a major cast. George Toomey, Tom Willingham, Ellen Miller. They started out big, that is for sure.

Chapter 26

OPENING NIGHT

We had five weeks of great rehearsals. Some on the creative team felt they were going a little too well. "Today is the test," I say to Ingrid. "It is the gypsy run-through." It was the final go before going to Boston to open. The casts of every show on Broadway are invited to watch this final rehearsal.

I step onto the stage, feeling the energy of the audience again. I was no longer the father of two adults. I was no longer, what some considered, aged out of Broadway. For this number, I was a young man again. Doing the numbers and saying the lines.

The first song ended, and the audience yelled, screamed, applauded, and jumped up and down yelling, "Bravo." Then, they did it after the next. And, then, the next. All the way to the final curtain call, the audience loves us.

Backstage, I look in the mirror. Normally, I'd be taking off my stage makeup, but the gypsy run-through has no frills. No lights. No curtains. No makeup. Just acting. I run my hand over my face, just the same, considering everywhere I'd been and what led me to this moment.

"The show looks too good," someone says in the hallway.

"The real test will be Boston," the other replies.

The words turn my sweat to ice, but only because I know it is true. Boston is the true test. It doesn't matter what everyone said here today.

What matters is the Boston reception. I am worried about how good the show looked.

It had been a struggle for me to get the producer to put the money for a pre-Broadway tryout in Boston and Philadelphia in the original budget. Almost every show I have ever starred in opened in Boston, except for the couple that opened in New Haven. I remember like yesterday my conversation with Maryanne.

"It's been a while since you were in the theater," Maryanne had said to me.

"We can't open cold in New York," I said. "We need an out-of-town tryout to work everything out."

"But we have a good show," she'd insisted. I understood her reasoning. It was expensive to go there, but there was precedent. There was reputation. There was even superstition.

"I'm not having a thing to do with this current trend," I'd told her. "Richard Rodgers said, 'I wouldn't open a can of sardines without taking it first to Boston.' And who am I to argue with him?"

She relented, it was put back in the initial budget, and we are taking the entire theatrical company to Boston.

In Boston, I make sure the creative staff and some principal cast members will be staying at the Ritz Carlton. I have stayed there many times before with the creative and principals of other Broadway shows. I arranged to have Tom and Ellen stay here, too, and paid for their room. The short walk to the Colonial Theatre overlooking the beautiful Boston Commons would make the two-week stay very enjoyable for everyone. Already, it is bringing back so many pleasant memories for me.

"Before everything starts tomorrow, you should take some time looking around and enjoying the moment," I say to Tom in the lobby of our hotel. "You will only have your first Broadway show once, and you are building your life each moment."

He smiles at me with the arrogance of youth. It was the same invincible smile I'd had at his age, I'm sure. It is the one that doesn't fully realize the full value of time, until it has been squandered or mostly used.

"I'm walking over to the theatre to watch all the scenery, costumes, and props being loaded into the theatre." I say. "I could sit for hours in the back row of the theatre, watching the entire load in crew setting up the stage," I pause a moment, and he faces me. "You're welcome to join me."

"I might," Tom answers. "But, first, I'm going to walk around and enjoy the moment. I'll only have my first Broadway show once." He smiles at me. He is a good kid, and I enjoy his sense of humor.

The first day is a blur, and, before I know it, we have already had rehearsals and the first two previews. They all went very well. I call Ingrid from my hotel.

"The third performance is the official opening. That is when we will hear the critic's responses to the show for the first time."

"I'm sure they'll love it," she says, always my champion. I had missed out on so much in my earlier career by not experiencing a love like this. Not being a man like I am now. Not having the support of a woman I care for so deeply.

"I hope you're right," I finally say, realizing I hadn't responded to her. "I want this show to go well for all of us."

She was right. All the critics in Boston loved the show. There was some constructive criticism for tightening up the show by cutting ten minutes from the running time, but the creative staff had already planned to cut ten minutes from the show. Night after night, we performed. The critics said good things about me. Tom and Ellen were singled out as future Broadway stars.

After the first run of shows, I sat in my hotel room alone. So much had changed inside of me. I don't know that I had ever really been comfortable with who I was. I had always needed someone with me to help me avoid thinking. Now, I loved the quietness of the room. I longed for conversations with Ingrid or reading a good book. The adventure from Broadway star, to spy, to fugitive, to star again had somehow transformed me. I hadn't really noticed it fully as it was happening, but I could tell now that it had. I had grown as a person. In many ways, I was sorry about the man I had been. There were certainly things I would change if I could, but, in changing those things, I would no longer be who I am now. I like who I am now.

There were voices in the hallway. People walking to their room, laughing together. I took a sip of my drink and set it back down, thinking about how many drinks I'd had, how many women, how many adventures. How many roles had I played in my life, as well as on the stage?

Again, I was nervous about everything going so well with the show. That much hasn't changed in me. I will always be a bit superstitious; it is part of the industry.

The two remaining weeks brought very enthusiastic audiences, but everyone was cautious not to become overconfident.

"Let's not get overconfident." John called when the previous night's reviews came in. "We've done good work," he continued. "We've worked hard, and that's why people love it. That means we need to keep working hard to keep them loving it."

"Let's go over Act 1, Scene 2's choreography again. I want that song *perfect*." Lee said. That wasn't my scene, so I stepped off stage and thought about Ingrid. She was coming to Boston again to see me, and I couldn't wait. She loved staying at the Ritz, walking the Boston Commons, and eating at the famous restaurants in town. She was staying for these last three nights and would go back to New York when I headed to Philadelphia. The time passes so quickly during productions. You're in a constant cycle of rehearsal and performances, reworking lines and blocking. Each day, however, I look forward to going back to the hotel and to Ingrid. Each morning, I look forward to going to rehearsal and seeing the entire cast—particularly my daughter and my protégé—doing what we all love.

We continued through the rehearsals and those performances, and, already, it was time to leave Boston for Philly. Leaving Boston was a letdown for Ingrid, but also for everyone else in the cast who loved the experience of Boston.

Just as in we did in Boston, in Philadelphia, we rehearsed while the show was being loaded into the Shubert Theatre. The place to stay in Philadelphia was the Bellevue Stratford Hotel, just up the street and a short walk to the theatre. I had looked forward to being there again. It had always been such a beautiful place, and I had so many wonderful memories of the principals and me from past productions sharing great times there. Unfortunately, the hotel's reputation was ruined a year ago, when a bacteria that came to be known as the Legionnaire's disease infected hundreds. From that outbreak, 34 guests died, and 200 more were sickened. With such bad press, no one was willing to stay there, so all of us—the principals, the creative staff, and Tom and Ellen—decided to check into other hotels in the city.

Despite that disappointment, everything else about Philadelphia was better than I could have even hoped. The reviews, once again, were raves. The Philadelphia critics loved the show even more than their counterparts in Boston. Ingrid visited me again in Philadelphia. I loved seeing her for her visits, which, just like in Boston, brought welcomed relief from the long days of rehearsals and performances at night and on matinee days. Since the show was in such good shape, the cast was able to have extra time off. Ingrid and I used the time to spend quality time with Tom and Ellen. We all enjoyed being together, and I couldn't have been more pleased and thankful this new relationship was going so well.

The stay in Philadelphia flew by fast with few changes and a less-grueling-than-usual rehearsal schedule.

"Okay, everyone. I'll see you in New York," John concludes.

I look around at the cast and realize how truly lucky I am.

"George," Tom says after we dismiss. "Is it always like this?"

"Like what?" I ask.

"So much work, but so exciting." Tom leans against the doorway, and I consider his question for a moment. He looks tired, but his eyes sparkle.

"When you're lucky, it is," I say. "I've had some shows that were much more grueling. I've had rewrites that exhausted me from one show to the next."

"I understand that," Tom says. "This is so much more work than I'd ever expected it to be, but I look forward to it every single day."

"Me too," I say, my insides swelling with pride that he has captured this truth at his young age. I had so little to do with it, but I like to think that my encouragement at a crucial time had helped lead him to this moment in time.

"I still look forward to it," I say, truthfully. "I put my head on my pillow each night feeling like I've poured every ounce of myself out there and given the audience all that I have."

"That is why people love your acting."

"You have been very lucky on this first show," I say, deflecting the compliment. "This wasn't your typical pre-Broadway tour. Usually, it is pure hell."

"I've heard that from a couple of people," Tom replies, looking around at the flurry of activity around us. The production is loaded out for the five-day trek from the Shubert Theatre to load-in at the St. James. We'll be live on Broadway soon.

"What do you plan to do with your days off?" I ask him.

"I'm not sure." He looks around. "Probably sleep."

I laugh and pick up my things to start for the exit. Ingrid is waiting for me, and we have a full few days. Not much time for me to sleep. "We will be looking for a larger place that is closer to the theater and the hospital where Ingrid works," I say.

"How much bigger?" Tom asks.

"Well, I guess that depends on the success of the show."

We are both quiet again. I wonder what he is thinking about, but I don't ask. We have gotten closer since working together, but I don't want to force the relationship. I remember that I am the lead, and he isn't. He is also dating Ellen, and I don't want to risk pushing too hard to rebuild that relationship.

Instead, we say our goodbyes, and I don't see him or talk to him again until rehearsals resume four days later.

When the cast comes back from their short time off, Maryanne calls us all together. "Do not become complacent!" she immediately bellows. "The New York critics and audiences are not the Boston and Philadelphia ones."

That was completely true. While a few newer cast members seemed taken aback, all of us veterans were familiar with these speeches. We also understood how necessary they were. For all the posturing, the fact was that New York had a different crowd, and Boston and Philadelphia were to get us ready for the true test in New York.

"I have been with shows that received raves out-of-town and were roundly panned by the New York critics," she continues.

John takes over the tirade, his face looking as grim as if we'd been eviscerated by the critics, "We will rehearse almost right up to opening night, and the show will not be frozen until the day before opening."

There are nods around the group. "I want everyone giving their full effort. Do you all understand me?"

"Yes."

"You've got it."

Various other affirmations echo around the room. I certainly agree with the director. I have seen many times before that raves from the New York critics could not be counted on, just because the out-of-town critics love a show.

After the dressing down, Ellen comes over to me. "George, I have some good news for you."

"I'd love to hear it."

"I spoke to Missy, and she will be coming to see the show."

I'm not sure how to respond. It is as if I can no longer speak. I had hoped my other daughter would decide to come, and she has. Whether it is to support her sister, to see me, or both didn't matter a bit. I was going to see my other daughter. I could start the process of earning forgiveness. I know all the gifts and cards I'd sent over the years couldn't replace the father I hadn't been, but I wanted them to know the new George. The one who wanted a relationship with them.

"Thank you for telling me," I say, finally. "And thank you for asking her to come."

Ellen simply smiles and walks away. Despite my faults, and those of her mother, Ellen has grown to be a wonderful woman. I am immensely proud of her. Knowing Missy is coming makes it even more difficult to wait for opening night, but the work keeps me busy enough that it flies past me.

After the opening night performance in New York, my dressing room is filled with family and friends: Ingrid, Franco, Tom, Ellen, and my daughter, Missy. The place is simply electric.

"I need some time to get ready for the opening night party, so why don't all of you head over to Sardis, and I'll meet you there." Everyone starts to file out of the room. I finish dressing, and, as I leave my dressing room, I continue the tradition that has followed me my whole career. I take my fingers to my mouth and kiss the star on the door. I hurry to join everyone for what I hope will be a very upbeat opening night party.

Chapter 27

Second Opening Night

Will this total euphoria ever end? The show was great. Every fiber of my being is worn out. I know that at any time, this can all go away. I am always looking behind me. I have nightmares when I enter any cab; driving for more than two blocks is a struggle for me to endure. Then, there is the darkness in the back of the theatre during performances that keeps me wondering whether there is someone out there who still plans to kill me. *Will I lose my family again? Will I slip into a mistake causing me to ruin the perfect relationship I've built with Ingrid?* So, now you know why I feel paranoid all the time. So much has gone wrong, but, now, so much is going *right*. I told you I am a superstitious fellow. What else could possibly go wrong with my life?

The night after opening can't be a letdown. I pushed harder tonight than last night. The second-night audience is filled with critics from magazines, television, and radio to write their reviews. I have invited all my friends and family back to bask in the excitement of this night's show.

I know that tonight's performance was as good as last night, and I look forward in seeing everyone afterwards in my dressing room and a special dinner I have planned at Sardis. The dressing room fills up quickly, and, once again, I receive rave comments from my friends and family present.

THE ACTOR?

The press agent for the show, Susan, got the remaining reviews from last night. All were raves. "Listen to these," I say, the papers shaking in my hands. "'Run, don't walk to the box office,' 'Will be the biggest hit of the decade,' 'Pure perfection,' 'Broadway welcomes back George Toomey with bravos' and 'Tom Willingham and Ellen Miller have so much chemistry on stage, it will assure them of future star status on Broadway.'" I pause to look around the room, hoping to see the same excitement on their faces as I feel inside me. "I don't think we could have hoped for better in New York." I say.

"I don't either." Tom chimes in.

Ellen throws her arms around Tom, and I am so happy for them. To hit it this big, this early, is truly amazing. They'd worked hard and earned every single accolade, but I also noted in them that unique something that always separates the good from the great. When that was combined with a strong work ethic, it is only a matter of time before they were noticed.

"Look, everyone; I need to shower and change for dinner." I say. "Why don't you all meet me at Sardis." There is a slow exodus from my private domain and down the street, but Tom and Ellen linger a bit. They seem nervous and don't look directly at me.

"Can we speak with you?" Tom finally asks. Ellen still isn't looking at me.

For a moment, my breath catches, but I nod and move to sit next to Ingrid. Everyone is gone now, except the four of us. Ellen closes my door and takes Tom's hand.

"What did you need to speak with me about?" I ask, trying not to think too much of their averted glances and sudden quiet.

"George," Tom begins, nervously. "Ellen and I have spoken and, well, I need to ask you something."

"Yes," I say, not willing to utter another word. My throat is too dry and their manner so odd that I am growing concerned by what they might say.

"I would like your permission to marry Ellen."

Both Ingrid and I jump up off the couch, "Yes, yes, you have my permission."

I look at Ellen, who is looking at Tom. She is nodding *yes*, but I know she had already agreed before they came to me.

All of us hug and kiss. "Maybe we could have a double wedding," I say to Ingrid. I hug her again. *How is it possible to have so much good in my life?*

"All three of you meet me at Sardis in thirty minutes." I hug Ellen, shake Tom's hand, and kiss Ingrid goodbye before closing the door behind them.

I am all alone in my dressing room—looking into the full wall-to-wall makeup mirror. Mirrors have played such an important role in my life. In my teens, I would perform in front of a mirror. I sang songs from every Rodgers and Hart musical of the 1930s in front of a mirror. There wasn't a show I was ever in that didn't have me in front of a mirror developing my character. Every night before I went on, I sat in front of a mirror, putting on my makeup and thinking about the performance I was going to be giving that night.

Likewise, the end of every performance is held in front of a mirror. So, as I have done so many times before, I start taking off my makeup, and begin talking into the mirror. "The theatre broke up my family, and it took the theatre to return my family." I swipe makeup from my cheeks. "I am back. I am a star on Broadway again, but the only thing that is really important to me now is my family." I apply cold cream to the other cheek and wipe the makeup off. "I will be able to give them all my love, full-time," I promise the mirror. Then, I swipe my entire face with a warm, damp rag and dry it again with a towel. My makeup is fully removed. I jump into the shower and dress for the party.

As I begin to exit my dressing room, the phone on the table rings. I pick up the phone.

"Hello?" I ask, wondering who would call me tonight, here.

"Hello," the voice on the other end of the phone greets me. "This is Ted Ashley, from Warner Brothers."

I can't believe the famous studio head is calling me. I put my coat down and lean against the wall. "How can I help you?" I ask, trying to sound calm.

"I would like to buy the rights to your show."

I'm not entirely sure how to respond to his proposal, so I say nothing.

"And I'd like you to star in the film version," he continues.

Film. The thought at once excites and overwhelms me. It is a much different kind of acting than Broadway. Here, you get one take, and, then, you perform it night after night. Not so in film, where the order is based on lighting and production schedules more than story flow. Just the same, it is something I've always wanted.

I take a deep breath before answering. I start speaking slowly into the receiver. "Mr. Ashley, it is a great honor to speak with you, and, more importantly, a great offer you have given to me."

Taking another deep breath and not believing what I'm about to say, I continue, my voice cordial. "Let me think about it." I say with a confident smile on my face. "Goodbye."

I put on my jacket, turn the lights off in my dressing room, and head for the dinner party at Sardis—but not before taking my hand and placing a big kiss on the star on my dressing room door. Tonight, something extra happens: for a brief moment in time, my whole career surges through my fingertips, and I seem to relive everything in a fleeting glance.

Then, as I touch the star on my dressing room door, I say with complete confidence, "You're never too old to start all over again." My paranoia has slipped away into the night.

Acknowledgements

To the editors who read my first draft, thank you for telling me; "It is one hell of a ride" and informing me of changes needed to make it a better ride.

To Andy Baldwin and the staff of Bookstand Publishing for taking the manuscript to the next level.

To my publicist and editor, Brittany Bearden, of At Large PR, thank you for making sure everyone learned about the novel.

Last, but not least, to Tiffany Colter, of Writing Career Coach, my writing coach and editor, who was with me in every step of the journey.

Look for *THE ACTOR? PART TWO, THE PREQUEL* in 2017.

CPSIA information can be obtained at www.ICGtesting.com
Printed in the USA
BVOW01s0443160816

458511BV00010B/44/P